Watching him, Katlyn's heart beat faster and harder

She didn't know whether it was from nerves or from a growing sense of annoyance with the arrogance radiating from the man.

He made his way to her in a few long-legged strides, offering her a curt nod of his head and a cool handshake in welcome. "I'm Case Durham. I own the St. Martin. We've corresponded several times."

Katlyn nodded in reply. This close to him, she could see he wasn't as dark as the shadows had painted him, with the exception of his expression. His hair was more the color of polished oak, his eyes a deep, mesmerizing green, sharp and hard as gemstones.

As hard as Case Durham seemed to be.

Get caught reading Harlequin.

D1018771

Praise for author Nicole Foster's first book
JAKE'S ANGEL

"An endearing tale…the characters shine."
—*Rendezvous*

"…a classic romance…
any reader devoted to this genre will love this book."
—*Romance Communications*

"*Jake's Angel* will charm you
from the first page and hold you until the last…
you won't be able to put it down."
—*The Road to Romance*

CIMARRON ROSE
Harlequin Historical #560 May 2001

CIMARRON ROSE

NICOLE FOSTER

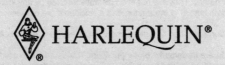

HARLEQUIN®

TORONTO • NEW YORK • LONDON
AMSTERDAM • PARIS • SYDNEY • HAMBURG
STOCKHOLM • ATHENS • TOKYO • MILAN • MADRID
PRAGUE • WARSAW • BUDAPEST • AUCKLAND

ISBN 0-373-29160-4

CIMARRON ROSE

Copyright © 2001 by Danette Fertig-Thompson and
Annette Chartier-Warren

Printed in U.S.A.

Available from Harlequin Historicals and
NICOLE FOSTER

Jake's Angel #522
Cimarron Rose #560

Please address questions and book requests to:
Harlequin Reader Service
U.S.: 3010 Walden Ave., P.O. Box 1325, Buffalo, NY 14269
Canadian: P.O. Box 609, Fort Erie, Ont. L2A 5X3

To Nicole and Foster, kindred spirits like their mothers.

Chapter One

Cimarron, New Mexico territory, 1875

A gust of wind rattled the window of the small room, its cool draft sliding inside to brush against Katlyn McLain's neck. She shivered, drawing her thin woolen shawl a little more tightly around her as she bent over the bed to look again at the woman lying there.

In the wavering lamplight, stripped of her glitter and paint, Penelope Rose seemed small and faded. Katlyn touched her mother's face, then tucked the blanket more snugly around her. Even without the doctor's grim news, she had known her mother was ill. Her pale thinness, the dullness of her penny-bright hair, the droop of her shoulders all betrayed Penelope's sparkling facade.

Katlyn dropped back down onto the wooden chair she'd pulled close to the bed, feeling a little pale herself.

She hadn't slept since she'd arrived hours ago in Cimarron, cold, wet, aching, and half carrying Penelope, with nothing between them but the clothes on their backs.

A tap at the door brought Katlyn to her feet again. Before she could move to answer it, the owner of the boardinghouse, Mrs. Donaldson, pushed open the door and came inside. She put the tray she carried on the dresser top and then looked sternly at Katlyn.

That expression made Katlyn want to laugh. A thin little sparrow of a woman, Elspeth Donaldson appeared meek—until she spoke and a rich Scottish burr rolled out. "Now, lass, I've brought you some tea, and a wee bit of that stew I had left from supper. You won't be doin' your ma any good by starvin' yourself."

"Thank you," Katlyn said, smiling a little at Mrs. Donaldson's fussing. "I am hungry. But I—"

"I won't be hearin' any more about you payin' me," Mrs. Donaldson said, giving Katlyn one of her daunting stares. "You just eat that. I know you're hungry, walkin' all that way after such a terrible experience. You're a brave lass, and there's no one can say different."

Katlyn wanted to say she felt anything but brave. But she only smiled her thanks and went to pick up the steaming cup of tea.

"A nice sleep will do your ma good, you'll see," Mrs. Donaldson added, eyeing Penelope with a shrewdness that made Katlyn feel the other woman knew everything about her mother. "She might feel differently about stayin' though. I don't suppose she thought it would be like this.''

No, of course she didn't, Katlyn silently agreed as she shut the door behind Mrs. Donaldson.

Her mother should never have come here. Penelope belonged back on the Mississippi riverboats, where she was flattered and pampered, not in the New Mexico high country.

But Penelope had insisted on coming to Cimarron to sing at the St. Martin Hotel. And when her mother made up her mind, no one could convince her otherwise.

Katlyn hadn't believed her when Penelope said she needed a rest, a change of scenery to revive herself. Then, when she'd added that it would be lovely, being so near her only daughter, Katlyn knew something was very wrong.

Nothing would have caused her mother to leave St. Louis except failure.

Now Katlyn worried she would also fail. Fail her mother when she most needed her.

The doctor made it clear Penelope couldn't be moved, perhaps for several weeks, and then only to a hospital that offered a special treatment for her condition. Expensive treatment Katlyn had no idea how she would afford.

The trip here had been cursed from the start. First, by storms. The stage sat mired in mud after the sheeting rains, vulnerable to the three outlaws who had robbed the passengers, leaving them stranded miles from Cimarron. The long walk into town across the rugged terrain had caused Penelope's collapse. Katlyn felt lucky they had at least been able to find shelter at one of the town's two boardinghouses, knowing her mother would rather have died than have been carried into the St. Martin, sick and bedraggled.

"Honey, you look fierce enough to scare away a ghost." Penelope smiled when Katlyn, startled out of her dark thoughts, jumped out of her chair to her mother's side.

"How are you feeling? Is there something I can get you?"

"Yes, Katie, my dear, you can stop looking at me as if the undertaker is waiting outside the door."

Katlyn breathed deep. "Mama…"

"Oh, please—" Penelope waved a limp, shaky hand at her daughter. "Don't go repeating all those dreadful things that doctor tried to tell me. I've told you, I just need a little rest. A few weeks and I'll be ready to sing again."

"You're going to be in bed a few weeks, at least. And then…then we're going to Las Vegas. It's west of here, in the territory. There's a hospital there and—"

"And I will not go anywhere! I can't lose this job, Katie. I can't." Penelope's voice dropped, and she looked away from Katlyn.

But not in time for Katlyn to miss the sheen of tears in her mother's lovely eyes. "I'm sorry, Mama," she said softly, taking Penelope's hand. "I know how much you wanted this job. But the doctor says you need to be at that hospital."

Katlyn struggled to sound confident, optimistic, to say something to assure her mother she would be taken care of, even though Katlyn had no idea how she would do that. Robbed by the outlaws of the money they'd carried with them, alone in Cimarron, without even the promise now of work—Katlyn forced away the worries threatening to overwhelm her.

"I'll find work here, until the doctor says you can travel. Then I'll find something in Las Vegas. I'll take care of you, I promise."

"I do believe that's supposed to be my promise, honey. And I've done it, haven't I? All those years, by myself, after your daddy decided to leave me with nothing but a kiss and a baby. I had my singing and that was all I needed to keep us, and keep us well. You aren't going to be able to do the same washing dishes or teaching school."

"Maybe Isabel could help," Katlyn said doubtfully. She'd stayed with her half sister for a little more than a year, elated to find her after growing up apart. But Isabel was now recently married, with two boys, a baby on the way, and her ailing grandmother living with them. Every cent and every inch of space in the household were spoken for, and then some. Katlyn knew even as she said the words that apart from offering a sympathetic ear and a recipe for a soothing balm, there was nothing Isabel could do.

"I'm sure your sister is a fine woman, but she's not my daughter." Penelope echoed her thoughts. "No, Katie, I'm not the kind to take charity. You ought to know that about me by now. And we don't need to. Why, it'll be so simple.''

"Simple?" Rain slashed the window, the rhythm of it pounding in Katlyn's head. She was tired, worried, afraid if she dared to admit it. What could her mother be thinking?

"Of course. I already have a job here."

"Mama, you can't—"

"No, darling, but *you* can."

Katlyn stared. Triumph had put a delicate flush into Penelope's pale cheeks. Katlyn wondered if fever had made her mother delirious.

"That's ridiculous," she said, her spirit reviving at the mere idea of taking her mother's place. "I'm not a singer. All I've ever done besides follow you is a little teaching. No one would ever believe I was you, even if I was crazy enough to agree to do it. Tomorrow, I'll go to the hotel and tell them the truth. Then they can look for someone else to—"

Katlyn suddenly stopped, appalled as the tears started spilling down her mother's ashen face. Her mother, who always laughed her way through hardship and pain.

"Katie, *please.* You can't tell them I'm—like this. If anyone knew, if anyone would *see* me now... Katie, I would rather die."

Penelope grabbed at her hand when Katlyn opened her mouth to try to comfort her. "Don't say no. I'll be well again soon and then it won't matter. Just don't let them *know*. Please, do this for me. Promise me you will. And think of the money. It's more than you could ever make in some little teaching job or worse, cleaning or cooking. Why, what do you know about that, anyway? We need the money, and you can get it for us. I know you can sing and that's all that matters. I'll teach you anything else you need to learn.''

Katlyn sat back down and tried to think of an argument that would persuade her mother of the impossibility of what she was asking. Katlyn McLain, become the St. Louis Songbird? She nearly laughed out loud.

And yet… She thought of the money she could make to help her mother. Penelope was right—the salary the owner of the St. Martin had promised was far more than any money she could make at a menial job even if she worked day and night.

And, though it chafed to admit it, Penelope was also right about her skills. What work could she do? She had grown up on riverboats and in hotels, watching her beautiful mother charm with her golden voice. Penelope had never taught her anything about cooking or sewing or keeping a house. Knowing how to dress for a performance, paint her face and arrange her hair, Katlyn was sure, were skills not in great demand in Cimarron.

But far more compelling was the fact that her mother needed her—desperately. No one had ever actually needed Katlyn McLain before. All her life, until this very moment, Katlyn had felt that fate had misplaced her. Growing up she was a burden of responsibility to her mother. And when she'd gone to live with her sister, she was an extra mouth to feed.

If by some miracle she succeeded as a singer, she could take care of Penelope without having to depend on charity from anyone. She could finally be of some true value to someone she loved and cared for. And she could carry on her mother's tradition of independence with pride.

"You have my hair, that won't be a problem," Penelope was saying, her voice trembling. "Those blue eyes are your daddy's but no one will take notice of that. If you use a little paint they'll believe you're older. I'll dress you, tell you how it should be done. Thank goodness you've inherited my curves! You'll do fine, Katie, I just know it."

"It would be a lie," Katlyn said more to herself than to her mother.

"We're not hurting anyone."

"Aren't we? They're expecting the St. Louis Songbird."

"Well, I'm giving you my name. That's what they're paying for. They'll have their singer and I'll have my reputation. We're not cheating anyone of anything. They need me and I need you. It's that simple."

Katlyn couldn't help but laugh. "It won't be simple at all. I'm not you, Mama. I'm just plain Katlyn."

"Not anymore," her mother said firmly. "Now you're the St. Louis Songbird."

Case Durham paced the wide length of the St. Martin's lobby, looking over the four people who made up most of his modest staff at the hotel. Stern appraisal marked his sharp emerald gaze. He lifted one dark brow and looked down his nose at his employees. "I trust everything is in order for her arrival?"

"Oh, yessir, Mr. Durham, sir," the young girl he'd paused in front of blurted out nervously. "Spit and polished everything top to bottom." The girl motioned to the left of the lobby. "And our town's band—what there is of it—they're all tuned up and ready to play."

Case took in the ragtag-looking group of makeshift musicians greeting him with jagged toothy grins and what looked like from the faded wear and ill-fit of them, second- or third-hand uniforms.

What they lacked in skill, at least they might make up for in enthusiasm, he told himself.

A gangly boy, with a stray piece of straw lodged in his mussed hair, anxiously twisted a worn cap in his hands as he nodded toward the balcony. "And I painted the banner up there on the railing, just so she knows fer sure she's welcome here."

Case turned toward the bright red letters splashed across a huge white banner that read Welcome To The St. Martin Hotel St. Louis Songbyrd.

Suppressing a smile at the misspelling, Case turned back to the young man. "Bucky, I'm sure she'll appreciate that very much. I didn't know you could read and write. Who taught you?"

Bucky stopped twisting the cap in his hands and straightened. "My ma did, 'fore she passed on."

"Well, I'm glad to know that. In time, there may be a place for you under this roof." Case flicked the straw out of the lad's hair. "Unless you're particularly partial to sleeping in straw, that is."

Bucky seemed to search Case's unsmiling face, then returned his employer's serious look. "Thank you, sir. I'd be honored to sleep in a real bed here in the hotel."

Again, it was all Case could do to hold back a grin, but better he intimidate them a little. Employees were more productive if they harbored a little uncertainty as to their boss's satisfaction with them. Hard work and respect went hand in hand when it came to making a venture successful.

And, damned if he wasn't going to see this disaster through until it was precisely that.

He'd sunk his last dime into this gamble. Taking a calculated risk, Case relied on his keen business sense, which told him that the gamble would eventually pay off in spades. But this place was fast impressing upon him that he would finally be forced to learn what had always gone against his grain: the fine art of patience.

And right now, the key to that success was giving him his first lesson. For the dozenth time, he flicked open the silver pocket watch in his palm. She was over an hour late. And nothing irked him like tardiness. Especially when he thought of the salary he'd had to promise the famed St. Louis Songbird to lure her out West to his godforsaken hotel. She was probably some pampered prima donna, used to making her hosts wait just so she could make an entrance. He'd have to bite his tongue, he was sure, and he would, as long as she pulled in the customers the way everyone swore she would.

He'd never tell her as much, but the truth was the renowned singer was his last hope in saving his hotel. Unlike his other ventures, nothing had seemed to work when it came to trying to clean up this place and draw decent folks in.

It had seemed a reasonable gamble at the time he'd chosen to buy the hotel, but of late he'd begun to question whether his instincts for investing had abandoned him. Cimarron, positioned advantageously on the Santa Fe Trail, had begun to thrive with the profits of ranching, mining and trading. There was plenty of money being made to be spent, and few places to spend it.

But after six months in business, Case saw that his best customers were still renegades, gamblers and assorted desperados on the run from the law. Not only did that kind scare other customers away, but more importantly, they made the hotel unsafe for his six-year-old daughter Emily.

After all it had cost him to clear the debts Emily's mother had left him to face, if this hotel failed, he'd lose everything. Everything but what mattered most, that was. He would not risk losing his little girl. Not after the fight it had taken to keep her with him.

He kept telling himself leaving Emily in Colorado would have been far worse for her. But in truth, he had to accept the fact that he couldn't keep her here with him safely much longer if the St. Martin continued to draw trouble like flies to honey. He guarded

Emily with his life, but this was no way for a child to live.

If the St. Louis Songbird didn't turn his luck and do it quickly, he'd have to swallow his pride and his pocketbook and give the whole thing up.

Case clicked his silver watch open and closed, his polished boots slapping hard and fast across the glistening pine floors. His small staff waited in a line, barely daring to breathe as he strode past.

"She'd better be worth the wait," he muttered to no one in particular.

"Oh, Mr. Durham, she's supposed to be the best! Just the best!" the girl declared. "I ain't never heard her sing, mind you, but some of the folks who come through here from out East say her voice puts a hold on you like a magic spell."

"We'll see, Becky," he murmured impatiently. "But if she doesn't get here soon, we may never find out if she can even carry a tune."

Or rescue a hotel, Case added silently, wondering with growing cynicism just how impressive a woman this St. Louis Songbird really was.

Katlyn smoothed sweaty palms down her mother's yellow satin skirts as she stood in front of the St. Martin Hotel.

The plain two-story beige frame building didn't look like much, even compared with the more ruggedly built storefronts and saloons. In fact, rather dusty and neglected-looking, it would be easy to ignore.

Katlyn wished she felt the same. Instead, she felt ridiculous. All this face paint and these fancy frilled clothes felt as foreign to her as her sister's Mexican food had tasted when she'd first come out West.

All this pretense was her mother, not her.

Catching a glimpse of herself in the hotel window, she adjusted her hat with its jaunty yellow plume and scolded herself. "Well, Katie, my girl, like it or not, it had better be you if you're going to pull this off. You've promised her and you can't turn back now."

Straightening her shoulders, she hitched up her flagging courage along with her petticoats and shoved open the hotel door.

The door barely had time to close when Katlyn froze in utter surprise. Nothing her mother had told her had prepared her for this!

"She's here!" someone shouted, and the room swelled with sudden applause and cheers of welcome. A little brass band launched into playing some festive tune she couldn't quite make out, nearly unnerving her. At one boy's prompting she gazed up to a balcony and saw a sweeping banner painted especially for her mother. Loud clapping and smiling faces filled the lobby with welcome. She didn't know whether to laugh or cry at the sad irony of it all. Everyone there seemed truly delighted *she'd* come.

Everyone except for *him*.

Off to the side of the little gathering, a dark imposing figure of a man towered above the others. He stood still and in silence, as though merely an observer, not part of the celebration.

Katlyn's eyes met his razor-sharp green gaze, and the look he gave her made her nervous heart skip a beat.

This she hadn't counted on. The patrician nose, the arrogant lift of his chin, the expensive cheroot at his lips, the tailored cut of his clothes told her he must be Case Durham, the hotel owner.

He might be just a little demanding, darling, her mother had said.

But one look told Katlyn he was far more than that. Impossibly tall, his angled face and stern glare stripped her of her remaining bravado. She instinctively wanted to run.

In the same instant an image of her mother, desperately pale and weak, intruded. And Katlyn heard her own voice, vowing she would do anything to help Penelope. Anything. Even face Case Durham.

The object of her fear quieted the fanfare with a single sweep of his palm. His staff took a step back and waited while, in a leisurely ritual, he doused his cheroot and buried it in a tray.

Watching him, Katlyn's heart beat faster and harder, whether purely from nerves or from a growing sense of annoyance with the arrogance radiating from the man, she wasn't sure.

He made his way to her in a few long-legged strides, offering her a curt nod of his head and a cool handshake in welcome. "I'm Case Durham. I own the St. Martin. We've corresponded several times."

Katlyn nodded in reply. This close to him, she could see he wasn't as dark as the shadows had painted him, with the exception of his expression. His hair was more the color of polished oak, his eyes a deep, mesmerizing green, sharp and hard as gemstones.

As hard as Case Durham seemed to be. An image of the many dashing gamblers and fancy gentlemen who, upon first meeting her mother, had swept Penelope's hand in theirs, bowing deeply into it with gentle kisses, made this first introduction sorely lacking by comparison.

Mister Durham, it seemed, wasn't impressed by reputation.

"We're glad you've finally arrived. It's so late, I was beginning to worry for your safety."

Katlyn bristled, but bit back her temper. How dare he make a comment about being late after all she and her mother had gone through to come to his wretched hotel?

"I'm late, Mr. Durham, because my stagecoach was attacked and robbed before I reached Cimarron. I suppose you could have found that out if you had bothered to inquire."

A wry smile almost teased at one corner of his mouth, but in the next instant it vanished. His eyes riveted on her and he laid the palm of his large hand on her arm, commanding her full attention. "Tell me. Were you hurt in any way?"

Surprised, Katlyn shied back. "Thank you for your concern," she said, not quite sure whether to believe in his sincerity or not. "I was shaken, naturally. And many of my belongings—and all of my money—were stolen or destroyed. But, I feel lucky. From what I've heard, it could have been far worse.''

Katlyn glanced past Case to the openmouthed stares from several of those in the welcome party that told her her fears were justified.

Case released her arm. "I'm sorry. This can be dangerous country.''

"So I gather.''

"Well, then,'' he said, resuming his cool distance, "we'll have to see to a new wardrobe, won't we?'' He turned to Becky, hovering close by. "You help her get what she needs right away. She'll have to look her best.'' With that he turned back to Katlyn, appraising her from the feather on her hat down to her kid boots.

She looked much different than he expected. He'd imagined a red-haired siren, brassy and bold. She had the red hair, an abundance of it, defying her attempt to bunch it into a tame roll. Case couldn't see any signs of a siren in her, though. The paint stood out boldly on skin as pale as milk, and blue eyes so dark they were nearly violet, looked back at him with an odd mixture of defiance and apprehension he didn't understand.

"Do I pass inspection, Mr. Durham?''

Case snapped his thoughts back to the job at hand and focused on her face. "You're every bit as lovely as I've heard, Miss Rose. Though, I have to say, you're younger than I'd expected. You've accomplished quite a lot for your age.''

As she felt heat rise to her cheeks, Katlyn was glad

for all the makeup to hide it. "I started singing as a child, Mr. Durham." That part was true at least. "And I've never stopped."

Something unnerving—was it disbelief?—flashed across his face, settling in a single arched brow. "We're all extremely anxious to hear you. I know you won't disappoint us."

Katlyn resisted the urge to fidget with something. "Of course, I'll need to rehearse before I perform."

Case looked at her speculatively. "Naturally. Take the entire weekend to rehearse, if you'd like. I've scheduled your first performance for Monday night."

"Monday?" This time Katlyn couldn't hide the panic. That was only three days away!

"Is there a problem?"

"I—of course not."

"You must realize, Miss Rose—is that your name by the way?"

"No!" Katlyn blurted before she could stop the word. She forced herself to meet Case's intimidating gaze. "Penelope Rose is the name I use as a singer. My name is Katlyn. Katlyn McLain."

"I see," Case said, sounding as if he didn't. "Well, as I said when I wrote to you, Miss—McLain, the salary we finally agreed on is based on your ability to draw in new customers. I was completely honest with you in my letters regarding the status of my hotel." He stepped inches closer. His deep bass voice seemed to resonate through the whole room. "All I ask of you is that you give me the same honesty. Then, Miss McLain, we'll get along fine."

Honesty! Katlyn nearly let go a hysterical laugh.

She struggled over a murmured reply, at the same time thinking that of course she could manage to get along just fine with Case Durham. It wouldn't be difficult at all.

If she stayed as far away from him as possible.

Chapter Two

Case broke the awkward silence between them, summoning Becky with a sharp gesture.

"Show Miss McLain to her rooms, please." He turned back to Katlyn. "I'm sure you're exhausted from your ordeal. Becky can bring dinner to your suite tonight, if you'd like."

"M-my suite?"

"Of course." Case narrowed his probing gaze. "It *was* one of your requirements for taking the job."

Katlyn avoided his eyes and busied herself pulling off her white kid gloves. She waved them in a little flirtatious gesture she'd seen her mother use hundreds of times to avoid awkward situations. "Yes. Indeed it was. I must be comfortable if I'm to survive this wild country any length of time at all, mustn't I?" she said, managing an uncomfortable laugh.

"By all means. We want you to feel at home here."

The edge of sarcasm in his voice told her he didn't appreciate her weak attempt at levity.

Glad to escape his unnerving presence, Katlyn eagerly fell in behind Becky as the girl motioned toward the stairs. Katlyn lifted her heavy skirts and petticoats and began the ascent, but halfway up the staircase she stopped cold.

What was she doing! She couldn't possibly stay here and leave her mother at the boardinghouse. Couldn't and wouldn't. That's where she'd draw the line in this farce.

She turned back around to find Case standing at the foot of the stairs like a centurion looking up after her, back straight, feet shoulder-width apart, arms crossed over his broad chest. He stood watching her, staring actually, his expression offering nothing but a handsome mask of cool politeness.

Only his eyes, deep and searching, held any hint of emotion. Annoyance, Katlyn thought.

Case waited impatiently, wondering how a woman who seemed so lacking in poise had managed to become so successful before an audience. He supposed she must be a better actress than she seemed. Perhaps the trip here had unnerved her more than she admitted.

"Is there something else, Miss McLain?" he prompted when she stayed frozen on the staircase, looking down at him as if she expected him to pounce at any moment.

"Actually...there is."

"Do you intend to tell me, or should I guess?"

Katlyn ran the tip of her tongue over dry lips. "It's my—traveling companion. She helps me dress and do my hair and makeup. But the robbery and the walk to town had a terribly ill effect on her. Her health has been fragile since the start of our journey and now…well, I've secured a room for her elsewhere, but I can't leave her at the boardinghouse alone.''

Case said nothing, taking his time pondering the situation, much to Katlyn's irritation.

''She can stay with me,'' she said finally, more sharply than she intended. ''I wouldn't ask for another room.'' Still he held back, the silence of waiting growing like thunder in her head. ''Mr. Durham—''

''Bring the woman here at once,'' he answered, his tone an abrupt contrast to his words. ''Becky, I'll have Sally see to the laundry for a time so you'll be free to help Miss McLain and her companion.''

Becky practically burst with joy. ''Yes, Mr. Durham!'' The girl leaned close to Katlyn and said, ''I'd be right proud to help you and your friend, ma'am.''

Smiling back at Becky in thanks, Katlyn breathed a heavy sigh of relief. She could watch over her mother day and night now. Having Penelope close would make the whole ruse livable.

The doctor would be discreet, she thought. He called her mother Mrs. McLain and neither Katlyn nor Penelope had corrected him. But Penelope had insisted no one else learn of her and Katlyn's relationship. Lending Katlyn her title was one thing, playing the role of the St. Louis Songbird's ailing mother was quite another. Katlyn was certain, once the doctor understood her mother's delicate and volatile tempera-

ment, he would agree it was in Penelope's best interest to keep their secret.

"That's very kind of you, Mr. Durham," she told
Case. "I'll see to having her moved here this evening."

"I'll send Bucky along to help."

"Thank you," Katlyn nodded, then turned back to
climb the stairs to the landing.

"Miss McLain—"

Case didn't know what impulse prompted him to
call her back. Maybe it was the way she kept surprising him. He didn't like surprises. Or mysteries.
And Penelope Rose, Katlyn McLain, or whatever she
chose to call herself, was both.

She looked back at him, clearly startled.

"If you're not too tired, perhaps you'll join me this
evening in the saloon for a brandy," Case said. "I'm
sure you'd like to see the stage."

Choking back the lump that rose in her throat at
the mention of the word stage, Katlyn nodded down
to him and hurried after Becky.

They turned the corner out of Case's view at the
top of the stairs and, away from his disturbing scrutiny, Katlyn's tension ebbed a little.

A dimly lit landing separated one door from the
rest of the rooms that lined the other hallway. As
Becky motioned her to the landing, Katlyn caught
sight of a little flash of white moving behind the railing.

She squinted and looked harder, making out the
image of a child's face pressed through the spindles

of railing. The apparition looked like a little dark-haired girl, crouching down, who appeared for an instant then vanished behind a velvet curtain.

"Hello?" Katlyn ventured. When no one answered, she turned to Becky. "Who was that?"

"Oh, just Mr. Durham's little girl."

So he was married. Her mother hadn't told her that. In a way, it was a relief to know he had a wife and child. There must be some trace of warmth in him after all.

"Could you ask her to come out so I can meet her?"

"I can try. But she don't like strangers. She's real shy. Don't say much to no one." Becky turned toward the curtain. "Emily, this pretty lady wants to meet you. She's the new singer your daddy told you about."

After several minutes of coaxing from Becky, at last the heavy drapes swayed and a pair of beautiful, wide-set eyes and pink cheeks peeked out from between the crimson folds.

In that quick glimpse, Katlyn saw the biggest evergreen eyes and the sweetest little peaches and cream face she had ever laid eyes on. She was struck at once by the child's remarkable beauty—and by the joyless expression that marred it.

"Hello, Emily," she said, speaking softly and bending to eye level with the little girl.

But in the next instant, the precious face vanished once more behind the curtain.

Bewildered, Katlyn looked to Becky. "Where did she go?"

"She ain't supposed to talk to guests. Mr. Durham has a playroom fixed up for her in that nook behind the curtain. Only the real fancy guests stay in the suite here. Her room is away from the others, so it's safer over here for Emily when her daddy's busy.

"Doesn't his wife watch over her?"

"Wife?" Becky shook her head. "Mr. Durham ain't got a wife. Don't know if he ever did. Never said a word about her if he did and I ain't gonna be the one to ask. He don't cotton to no questions about himself or his little girl. Guards her like gold. No one dares so much as talks to her without his sayin' so. 'Cept me and Bucky, that is. We're twins," she added proudly. "Did you know that?"

"Why no, you with your blond curls and he with that brownish mop of hair, you two don't look much alike. But—" Katlyn appraised Becky more closely "—there is something in your mouth that is similar to his."

Becky nodded and smiled. "Mr. Durham hired us right away after our ma died and our pa sent us out to find work."

Judging the girl to be only about thirteen, Katlyn frowned. "You seem a little young to be working in a hotel."

Becky shrugged. "I'll be fifteen next spring. And Pa needs the money fer his whiskey. Besides, me and Bucky, we'd sure rather be here with Mr. Durham than at home with Pa when he's had a bottle or two.

Mr. Durham might not be real friendly sometimes, but he'd never lay a hand to us. He treats us mighty fine.''

Katlyn thought of herself at fourteen. Although Penelope had hardly been an attentive mother, Katlyn never feared a beating or wanted for anything. Her image of Case Durham shifted slightly as she considered his willingness to take on Becky and her brother.

''So, Mr. Durham only lets you two talk to his daughter?''

''Mostly. 'Cause we're like kids, too, I guess. He knows us real good. Knows we'd never lie to him or cheat him or hurt Emily.''

''I'm sure he can count on you both.'' Katlyn looked away from Becky, her heart suddenly racing with guilt she feared would show in her eyes.

''Mr. Durham's a real fine man. But he don't abide no liars or cheats. And Lord help anyone who gets too close to his little girl! He loves Emily more than anythin'. Anyone with eyes can see that.''

Imagining the child's angelic face behind the curtain, Katlyn's eyes turned there, wondering if Emily were listening. Betting she was, she said clearly and with surety, ''Well, I think Emily and I might become better acquainted.''

Katlyn anticipated Becky's protest and waved it aside. ''Don't worry. I just think maybe Emily could use another friend.

''And I know what it is to be lonely,'' she added softly, thinking of Emily's sad eyes and another little girl who'd also grown up in hotels and on riverboats, a lonely little girl who'd also hidden in the shadows, waiting and listening, hoping for a place to belong.

"I won't discuss it any further." Penelope clenched her thin fingers together atop the quilt. "My mind is made up."

"But, Mama, the suite is beautiful, wait until you see it! Much of the hotel still needs work, but Mr. Durham had the suite redone completely for you, and it's lovely. I don't know how he knew, but it's all in pinks and greens. And roses. The colors and the flowers you love most. Bucky is waiting outside with the buggy to help move you there."

"It sounds perfect," Penelope said, a trace of regret in her voice. "Perfect for you."

Sick or not, Katlyn decided it was time to be firm with her mother. "Mama, I will not live there without you."

Penelope straightened in her bed. "Oh, yes, you will."

Exasperated, Katlyn started to insist when a light tap sounded at the door and Mrs. Donaldson pushed into the room, her thin arms laden with a tray. "I was thinkin' you ladies might like some tea and cookies."

Penelope flashed one of her brilliant smiles. "Do come in, Elspeth, and tell my daughter what a nice arrangement we've come to."

Katlyn bristled. What had her mother done now?

"Why, your ma told me all about your troubles," Mrs. Donaldson said. "And pleased I'll be to have rent from a regular boarder. Besides, it'll do me old soul good to have another woman 'round the house to talk with now and again. And you'll be just a wee walk away, so you won't have to be worryin' about her.''

Bestowing a beaming smile on Katlyn, Mrs. Donaldson bustled out of the room, leaving Katlyn to confront her mother.

''Don't say it. It's settled.''

''Mama, I need you with me. It'll be so much easier, don't you see?''

''No, I do not. And I won't hear any more about it. I've told you, I won't have anyone pitying your poor, ailing companion, and you certainly won't tell anyone I am your mother. You promised me, Katlyn. Remember that.''

Penelope's voice betrayed her exhaustion, fading to a near whisper. Katlyn decided it best not to argue further with her. ''Whatever you want, Mama,'' she said, patting Penelope's hand to calm her, ''for the time being.''

''There won't be a time when I agree to go to that hotel. Now—'' Penelope stubbornly forced her weakened body up a little farther against her pillow and leveled a sharp glance at Katlyn. ''We've got work to do, Katie, my dear.''

Katlyn stood in the middle of the saloon and stared at the stage. Small but elegant with its dark gold velvet hangings, mahogany-cased piano, and polished pinewood floor, it was the most terrifying thing she had ever seen. On Monday, she would have to stand there, pretend to know everything about pleasing an audience with her voice and her smile, and pray that no one saw Katlyn McLain behind the borrowed glitter.

Sitting at one of the round tables pushed close to the stage, Katlyn drew a long shaky breath and let it slowly go. She had made her decision, there was no going back.

If she broke her promise, it could cost her mother her life. She had to earn enough to take Penelope to the hospital in Las Vegas as soon as she was well enough to travel. Her mother depended on her and Katlyn vowed to not let her down.

She distracted herself wondering where Mr. Durham was and if he remembered his invitation to meet her here this evening. He didn't seem the kind of man to forget—or forgive—anything. The thought jerked Katlyn to her feet and set her pacing the room.

If he ever discovered her charade...

She was on the verge of leaving Case Durham to drink alone when a sudden commotion of raised voices sounded just outside the saloon doors. Before she could react, the crack of a gunshot resounded off the walls, followed by a grunt of pain and a string of cursing.

Instinct sent Katlyn bolting for the doors. She flung them open—just as a second shot whizzed over her head, hitting the wall behind her.

"Get down!" Case shouted at her.

Katlyn dropped to her knees, more in surprise than in response to his command.

A few feet in front of her, Case confronted a hulk of a man waving a six-shooter in one hand and a whiskey bottle in the other. The man swung the Colt in Case's direction. But before he could fire another shot, Case knocked his arm up and at the same time slammed a fist into the man's jaw.

Case's motion was so quick and supple, Katlyn scarcely believed she'd seen it until the man crumpled and fell face-first to the floor.

Case kicked the Colt across the foyer. Then he grabbed the man by the collar, hauling him up.

"I told you, you're not welcome here, Charlie. I'm tired of you shooting up the place after you've had a few too many." Yanking the befuddled man to the front door, Case shoved him outside. "Next time, I call in the sheriff. Now get home before you hurt someone."

He jerked the doors closed behind the unfortunate Charlie and swung his glare to Katlyn.

"Are you trying to get yourself killed or do you make a habit of running toward bullets?" He didn't give her time to answer but strode over and took her hand, pulling her to her feet. "Are you hurt?"

A strange breathlessness attacked Katlyn, though from anger at Case's rough tone or his sudden nearness, she didn't know. He had shed his jacket and, in his shirtsleeves, his smoothness ruffled by the scuffle with Charlie, he looked a different man.

At first, he had unnerved her because she feared he would see through her pretense. Now, he disturbed her with this new image of a man as adept at protecting his property as he was at operating it. Her initial impression had been of a polished and intimidating businessman.

Her impression of him now was something very different. He unsettled her on another level, somewhere deep and private. The aggressive anger in his eyes, his mussed hair, disheveled clothes, the power written in the taut muscles straining against his rolled-up sleeves revealed a strong, rugged and terribly masculine side she found herself completely unprepared to face.

"Well?"

"Well what?" she asked, baffled.

"I asked you if you are all right."

"Oh. Of course. Yes, I'm fine," she said, realizing he still held her hand and looked at her as if he worried the close encounter with the bullet might make her turn and run. Instead, she banished the flash of fear at the idea she might have been shot, pulled her hand and her eyes away, and stepped back. "Interesting customers, you have. Does this happen often?"

Case shrugged. "Fourth one this week," he said, taking a closer scowling look at the bullet hole. "There are so many holes in this place it's a wonder it didn't start leaking long ago." He laughed shortly at Katlyn's dubious expression. "This isn't St. Louis, Miss McLain. Did you think it would be?"

"I didn't think I would be dodging bullets," Katlyn snapped back. "Are these the kind of people you expect me to entertain?"

"Charlie is relatively harmless. He dips a little too

far into the bottle and decides to come here and fire a few shots at the woodwork. That's all.''

''He nearly took a shot at you.''

''He would have missed. And to answer your question, the kind of people I want you to entertain won't set foot in here because they're afraid of the guests that have been here in the past. I need you to change that.''

Katlyn looked away and Case frowned a little. For a woman who earned her way and her reputation catering to audiences, she seemed oddly inhibited when he made any reference to her singing. From her letters he'd expected a pretty, vivacious woman, decidedly vain, experienced at flattery and expecting her share of honeyed praise in return.

Katlyn McLain seemed someone else entirely.

''Sing for me,'' he said abruptly.

The color drained from her face, leaving two spots of rouge staining her pale cheeks. ''Now?''

''Why not?'' Case shoved open the door of the saloon. ''I'd like to hear what I'm paying for.'' Holding out a hand, he invited her inside.

Or ordered her, Katlyn thought, tempted to refuse him. But if she did, she would only give him another reason to suspect her.

Slowly she walked in, acutely aware of Case behind her, watching. Katlyn sat at the piano. She flexed her fingers a little, trying to keep them from shaking, and blessed her mother's insistence that she learn to play. At least this way she wouldn't have to look at

Case while she tried to convince him performing came as naturally to her as breathing.

She chose the first song that came to her, a sweet, sad Irish ballad she'd learned as a girl. At first the notes and words came tentatively. Then, gradually, without her being aware of it, the music flowed into her and out in her voice. For a few moments she closed her eyes and she was Katie again, sitting alone in her mother's hotel room, singing romantic ballads to herself and dreaming of true love.

Case stood at the bar, his hand arrested in the motion of reaching for glasses, and stared at her.

She sang like an angel, the sweet clarity of her voice weaving magic into the air like pure gold threads in a tapestry. There was nothing contrived or practiced about her singing. Nothing he ever expected to hear from a woman who had earned a reputation from entertaining on riverboats.

Instead, her song touched him, warm and true, and caught him in a moment of enchantment.

When she finished, Katlyn sat with her hands on the piano keys for a moment before she came out of her dream and slowly turned to face Case.

He looked almost stunned and her heart plunged. "I—I haven't practiced," she stammered. "I'm sure once I'm able to—"

"Practice, yes, I know," he said, his voice low and rough. "It doesn't matter. I'm sure your reputation alone will make you a success."

Katlyn opened her mouth, closed it, and finally

managed to find her voice. "I don't want to be a disappointment." To anyone, she added silently.

"Why should you be?" Case shifted as if throwing off some troublesome feeling, the edge back in his voice and demeanor. Moving behind the bar, he poured out two glasses, offering one to Katlyn.

"A toast," he said, raising his glass to hers when she stepped up to the bar to take the drink. "To Penelope Rose, my new songbird."

Katlyn acknowledged the toast with a forced smile. She took a sip of the brandy and tried not to cough. She had always hated spirits.

Case laughed at the slight grimace she couldn't quite curb. "I have no idea why you're here, and I can't picture you on a riverboat stage. What a puzzle you are, Miss McLain."

"Do you think so?" Katlyn walked away from the bar. She went around the room, idly touching a table here, a curtain there. "You're more the puzzle. You don't seem the kind to invest so much here, in Cimarron of all places. Why not Denver or Las Vegas or even Santa Fe? And why a hotel where bullets in the walls are as common as nails?"

Case walked around the bar and went through the ritual of cutting and lighting a cheroot and taking a long draw before answering her. He leaned back against the ornately carved oak bar, appraising her with that calculating glint in his eyes Katlyn found so disturbing. "Why not?"

"Your daughter. It's not exactly the place for a child."

"Touché, Miss McLain. Except my daughter is not your business. I'm here because of her and that's more than you need to know."

"And I'm here because I choose to be and that's more than you need to know," Katlyn snapped, stung by the brusqueness in his voice. "Now that we have that settled, I'm going to bed. I have a lot of practicing to do before Monday."

She stalked toward the doors, intending to leave with the last word. But before she could push her way out into the foyer, a long, low moaning sounded through the room. It might have been the wind, though it had a peculiarly human quality to it.

Katlyn's determined stride faltered.

"Is something wrong?" Case asked.

Katlyn whirled on him. "No, only I should have expected this place to be drafty considering you admit the walls are used for target practice on a regular basis."

"Oh, that's not the wind." Case saw the flash of uncertainty cross her face. He knew he shouldn't risk unnerving her any more tonight. But her bravado seemed forced, a part of the persona of the St. Louis Songbird, not the real Katlyn McLain.

That made it irresistibly tempting to tease her into revealing more of the woman hiding behind all of the theatrical trappings. The warm, passionate woman he had heard when she sang.

He gave her a wicked smile. "Don't worry," he said. "It's harmless. It's only one of my resident ghosts."

Chapter Three

One hour. The clock on the writing desk ticking off the seconds sounded unnaturally loud in the quiet room. Every tick grated at Katlyn's nerves until finally she snatched up the clock and jammed it under the bed pillows.

She hardly needed another reminder of what she had to do tonight.

Turning back to the full-length mirror, she fidgeted with the shoulder of her dress, wondering how her mother ever felt comfortable wearing so much flounced satin and lace. The emerald satin did compliment her coloring. But Penelope had painted her face and arranged her hair so elaborately, Katlyn felt like a stranger to herself.

A stranger she didn't particularly like.

Very soon, though, that stranger would have to stand onstage and pretend to enjoy singing to an audience. Katlyn, countless times over the last two days, had come close to confessing all to Case Durham and offering to wash dishes, or scrub floors, anything but pretend to be the St. Louis Songbird.

Then she would look at her mother, pale and fragile, and see the hope in Penelope's eyes, or the satisfaction when Katlyn successfully copied one of Penelope's mannerisms, or echoed her singing style.

So she stayed. In this blasted hotel, where the guests shot holes in the walls, the staff teased her about the ghosts of dead gunfighters haunting the halls, and Case Durham watched her as if he had known all along she was a fraud.

"Miss McLain?" the voice foremost in her mind called through the door.

Katlyn jumped. The man must be a devil, reading her thoughts.

"Miss McLain?" Case said again. "I'd like to speak with you a moment."

Wonderful, Katlyn thought, just what I need now. She could hardly refuse him, though.

Tweaking the shoulder of her dress one final time, she breathed deep and flung open the door. "Yes, Mr. Durham?"

Case, confronted with an image of emerald ruffles and a defiant blue glare, could only stare at her for a moment, struck by the picture she presented. Although the dress and the rouge and the piled-up curls fit the image he'd had of Penelope Rose, it all looked wrong on her.

Except for the defiance. Somehow, he had the feeling he wasn't the first man to see that fire flash in her eyes.

"I see you're ready," he said finally.

"Of course," Katlyn said. Her nervousness receded in a tide of indignation. He had assumed his polite mask, but not before she saw his obvious disapproval. "Now that you've satisfied yourself I'm not still in my petticoats, is there anything else?"

Case smiled a little at her flushed face and the mutinous cant of her chin. No meek little sparrow, his songbird. "I came to wish you luck."

"Don't worry, I won't embarrass you. I *can* sing."

"Yes, I've heard you." He had, many times over the past few days. She had spent numerous hours closeted in the saloon or her rooms, practicing song after song. Case appreciated her willingness to work, and he couldn't fault the quality of her voice. But her lack of polish puzzled him.

He didn't like it. Something about Penelope Rose rang false, and it was more than just the wrong clothes and the overdone curls.

"You can sing," he added, almost to himself. "I'm still waiting to see you perform."

"Oh, please, don't overwhelm me with your compliments," a combination of nerves and annoyance caused Katlyn to snap. She resisted the urge to fidget with her dress or her hair once again. "If you're done with your inspection, it's nearly time for me to go downstairs and *perform.*"

Case didn't seem inclined to move. "Not quite yet. Are you satisfied with the piano player I hired?"

To Case's surprise, Katlyn burst out laughing, the unrestrained, joyous sound filling the room. Suddenly she seemed to come alive, not his singer in fancy flounces, but the woman behind the carefully painted facade.

"Jack Dakota is no piano player," Katlyn said finally, breathless with laughter. "He's a gambler who happens to know how to play piano. If he hadn't bet his last dollar on a queen-high flush, he'd be sitting at one of your tables trying to fleece your customers instead of behind your piano trying to entertain them. But yes, I like him. And considering your clientele right now, he's perfect."

Her teasing words drew no answering smile from Case. "I'm expecting you to change the clientele."

"You make it sound so desperate, Mr. Durham," Katlyn said, forcing a lightness she didn't feel. "I'm not a miracle worker. All I can do is sing."

"Oh, I'm sure you'll do fine," Case said slowly. He looked her up and down, slowly appraising. "If you'll just be yourself."

They locked gazes. Katlyn felt the force of his aura of command in his steady, faintly sardonic focus on her. She wanted to shift away from it but held her ground, determined to not let him unnerve her any more than he already had.

"You hired the St. Louis Songbird. And that's who those people downstairs have come to see."

Something hard struck his expression and for a moment Katlyn had the wild notion he intended to expose her then and there. She didn't consider how he knew, only that he did.

Then the moment passed and Case stepped back with a wry smile, gesturing toward the stairs.

"Well, then, my songbird," he said. "Your audience awaits."

Katlyn swept past him, her flush of bravado carrying her down the long staircase and to the doors of the saloon.

Then, as Case opened the doors for her, a tremor of fear spiraled through her heart, settling as a lump in her stomach. She refused, though, to let Case know how terrified she really was, so she put her chin up and walked into the room as if she had done it a thousand times before.

Case touched a hand to her waist to escort her to the stage and felt her tremble. It surprised him, even as he admired her proud walk through the room, looking as if she expected nothing less than adoration from her audience.

As she stepped up onto the stage, Jack Dakota turned on his piano stool and grinned at her, then blew her a kiss. Katlyn's smile flashed out and Case felt a stab of irritation. He forced it back to introduce her, but it scratched at him as she barely seemed to acknowledge his announcement or the audience awaiting her.

Her eyes instead kept flitting to Jack until Case stopped talking and a few seconds of awkward silence filled the room.

"Well, is she gonna sing or ain't she?" a harsh voice called from the back of the room.

It jolted Katlyn and for the first time she looked fully at her audience.

She doubted these were the kinds of people Case expected her to entice to the St. Martin. Most of the men looked like the gamblers and roughriders she'd seen around the hotel, and the few women couldn't even charitably be called ladies. None of them looked particularly impressed.

Case stepped down from the stage and left Katlyn standing there, staring back at the audience. She might have stood there until Case pulled her offstage if Jack hadn't started playing a lively tune they'd practiced just that morning.

Almost automatically, Katlyn responded and took up the words, her mind racing to remember not only the lyrics, but all the little mannerisms her mother had insisted she use. Jack started up another song as soon as she'd finished, giving her no time to gather her wits.

After finishing the fourth tune, Katlyn sensed disaster looming.

Only half the audience paid her any attention and a few of the men jeered and snickered, not bothering to hide their contempt.

Jack tried to encourage her with a smile, but Katlyn stumbled through the next song, wishing all the while she could simply vanish into the woodwork.

She glanced toward the back of the room as she finished and saw Case. His gaze fixed on her and she caught her breath. The blackness of his expression should have stopped her cold.

Instead, inexplicably, it gave Katlyn a rush of courage. He expected her to fail. All at once she determined to prove him wrong.

With a quick word to Jack, she moved back to center stage and forced herself to ignore the restless audience, the smoky, close air, and to focus on the sweet, soulful music. It wasn't a song her mother would have chosen, but she decided at that moment, Penelope's choices weren't doing her much good.

Katlyn forgot all her carefully memorized lessons and gave herself to the music, all the while keeping her gaze on Case.

> "'I wander lonely, lost,
> searching for what's true
> afraid I'll never know it,
> and then I look, and there is you
> beckoning me home.
> But when I reach out,
> there's only longing,
> and truth I cannot doubt,
> for I am left alone again
> with only the dream of my heart.'"

Case found himself unable to look away.

With a song she had transformed herself. Minutes ago, watching her awkwardly stumble through her repertoire, he'd been certain he'd made one of the biggest mistakes of his life in gambling his future on the St. Louis Songbird.

Now, listening to her, he could almost believe Katlyn McLain was a miracle.

He had never been fanciful, but the magic she worked made him imagine she had opened her heart and let the feelings there pour out through her voice. It softened her, lent her a grace not even green satin and rouge could overshadow.

Katlyn scarcely noticed anyone but Case until she let go the last lingering notes of the ballad. Then she breathed deeply, breaking their locked gazes—and became suddenly aware of the almost awed silence.

Everyone stared at her. Katlyn had the feeling she wouldn't have shocked them more if she'd stripped to her petticoats and danced a jig.

Her eyes went almost involuntarily back to Case.

He looked back, his face expressionless.

Before Katlyn could try to decipher what that meant, a loud, raucous applause started, interspersed with whistling and demands she sing again.

Katlyn hesitated, then caught up in the warm flood of approval, complied with two more songs, not any of her mother's, but songs she loved and felt comfortable sharing. By the time she finished, she felt almost giddy with the appreciative response from the audience.

Moving off the stage she went over to Jack to thank him and he caught her hands, bringing them to his lips. "I'd say a celebration is in order. You were wonderful."

"Hardly that," Katlyn said, laughing. "It was very nearly the worst thing I've ever done."

"I'd gamble on your success, sweetheart. If I had anything left to bet." Jack winked at her, flashing that rogue's grin.

His smile was infectious and Katlyn found herself grinning back. "Maybe you'll get lucky tonight."

"Only if you agree to join me later for champagne."

"Oh, Jack, I—"

"Already have an engagement. With me," Case finished for her smoothly.

Katlyn jerked around to find Case standing beside them. He didn't look any more pleased than he had when she'd started singing and Katlyn's high spirits took a plunge. His stance seemed easy but she saw him fingering the cheroot he held as if he needed some outlet for his tension.

What if he asked her to leave? Her heart clenched. She couldn't lose this job, not now. It meant everything to her, and to Penelope.

But she wouldn't grovel for him, nor would she allow him to bully her.

"I don't recall us having any plans together," she said, facing Case squarely.

Case nearly smiled at her show of defiance. For a woman experienced in pleasing men with her voice, she didn't hesitate to challenge him, given the chance. "I want to talk to you," he said. "We can have a late supper in the dining room."

Jack made a move as if to object, but Katlyn touched his sleeve in warning. Neither of them could afford to be out of work now. She turned to him with

a smile, saying lightly, "I know you're anxious to
find a game. I'll collect my champagne tomorrow, if
your luck is good."

"Count on it," Jack said. He gave Case a sharp
nod before moving off toward one of the crowded
gaming tables.

Case watched him for a moment, frowning, and
Katlyn couldn't help contrasting the two men. Jack,
with his sun-gilded hair and carefree smile, was all
lightness, while Case, dark and imposing, seemed to
command her attention just by his presence.

Looking at him, she had a sick feeling he'd arranged this little supper to tell her nicely to leave his
hotel. When he turned back to her, Katlyn decided to
fling caution aside and confront him. "If you intend
to tell me to go, I'd rather you do it now."

Case raised a brow. "I intend to have supper."
Grinding out the cheroot on the tray at Jack's piano,
he told her shortly, "In two hours, in the dining room.
I'll be expecting you. Now, if you'll excuse me, I
need to have a word with one or two of my guests."

He left her before she could refuse and as Katlyn
watched him go, she wondered if her short career as
Penelope Rose was over before it had really ever begun.

Katlyn retreated to her rooms to strip off the emerald satin, yank the pins from her hair, and wash
away her heavy makeup. After a short rest, she hesitated, then put on the simple dark blue dress she'd
worn on the trip to Cimarron. It wasn't exactly ele-

gant, but it was hers, only one of two that had survived the stage robbery. If she had to wear her mother's frills to perform, at least she would be comfortable when she stepped offstage.

Downstairs, she glanced into the saloon on her way to meet Case in the dining room. A few stragglers stood at the bar, tossing back the last dregs from a whiskey bottle. Seeing her, Case snuffed out his cheroot then moved to ease the men out of the saloon. He draped his arms over their shoulders and led them toward the door. Amiably, they swayed out of the saloon, leaving Case and Katlyn alone to face each other in the hallway.

Case looked at her, momentarily caught off guard by her transformation. Dressed plainly, with her hair loose and her face scrubbed clean she looked so completely different he wondered if she were the same woman.

The change in her reminded him of her performance, affected and awkward at first, natural and engaging at the end. Except which image was the true Katlyn McLain?

"Are you hungry?" Case said suddenly, breaking the awkward silence between them.

Katlyn chose to ignore his scrutiny of her. It was obvious her change in appearance confused him, and she didn't want to encourage unwanted questions. "Starving. I was too nervous to eat all day."

"You? Nervous?" He cast her a doubtful glance. "I find that hard to believe. Though I suppose that would explain your testiness before your performance.''

"If I was testy, it was only because this was an important night," Katlyn retorted. "I wanted to do well."

"But this can't be new to you, you must have sung in places like this countless times."

"No, Mr. Durham, I can honestly say I've never sung in a place like this. And besides, believe it or not, some things just don't get any easier."

Case gave her a wry smile. "That much is true." He offered her his arm. "Dinner is ready. Let's go celebrate your first performance at my hotel."

"I'm not sure a celebration is in order," Katlyn muttered under her breath. But she laid her hand on his arm and let him lead her toward the dining room.

Katlyn tried to appear cool and poised as she walked alongside Case. Inside, she quaked. The flex of hard muscle under her fingers reminded her too forcibly of Case Durham's strength, both in body and will.

Beside him, she felt an unsettling combination of vulnerability and reassurance. With a word, he could leave her desperate. Without saying anything, he made her feel strangely secure, as if she could trust his strength to protect her.

It made no sense and Katlyn didn't try to figure it out. All she wanted now was to get through dinner with her job and her secret intact.

As they walked into the formal dining room, she saw only one table was still draped in crisp white linen, set with fine china and crystal champagne goblets. Three silvery roses blossomed out of a cut-glass vase that picked up glints of light from the lamps and chandeliers, completing the elegant setting.

Katlyn glanced from the table to Case. "This is lovely. Thank you."

"You're welcome," Case said as he pulled her chair out and seated her, then took his place across the small round table. "Except I'm afraid I'd be less than truthful if I said this was especially for you."

"I see... After my performance, I suppose I should consider myself lucky to be sitting here at all." As soon as the words left her lips, Katlyn inwardly groaned. She had to find some way of harnessing her tongue instead of impulsively blurting out the first thing that came into her head, or she'd soon find herself giving up all her secrets to Case Durham.

She looked at Case, half expecting to see his intimidating scowl directed fully at her. Instead a corner of his mouth twitched up in a half smile, and Katlyn had the distinct impression he was laughing at her.

"It's clear I'll never have to guess at what you're thinking," he said.

"I shouldn't have said that."

"Why not? You're direct, I like that. It's honest."

Honest... Katlyn felt hot color burn her face. She tried to laugh in return, acutely aware of how strained it sounded. But before she could think of any reply, Case, for the first time since she'd set foot in the St. Martin, smiled fully at her.

The gesture drove any thought from Katlyn's mind.

Warm, for once lacking that faint sardonic edge, his smile made her suddenly aware of how many facets there were to his attractiveness. It betrayed a certain kindness and understanding he hid well behind the impression he usually projected as a commanding employer and ambitious businessman.

"I should explain, about dinner," Case said. He leaned back in his chair. "This is something of a ritual with me, my peace after the saloon closes. After Emily is in bed and the hotel is quiet, I come here to relax." He laughed wryly. "Call it my one indulgence." He pulled a chilled bottle of champagne from a silver cooler. "But this is in honor of you. To congratulate you on your first performance at the St. Martin."

"It's very generous of you. But I hope you don't feel you're wasting it. I know tonight was less than impressive."

Case took his time filling their glasses, appraising Katlyn as he handed her one. She obviously expected his criticism, or worse. Sitting stiffly in her chair, her color bright and her chin high, she kindled a reluctant admiration in him.

She might be afraid of whatever he had to say, but she wouldn't cower or plead. If he knew anything for certain about her it was that Katlyn McLain was a fighter.

"At times, you were very impressive," Case said, remembering how she had sung that sweet, haunting ballad to him alone. He lifted his glass. "To the St. Louis Songbird."

"To the success of the St. Martin," Katlyn amended as she touched her glass to his.

She tried to feel relief at his words. Yet she hated accepting any praise as Penelope Rose or the St. Louis Songbird, no matter how slight. She wasn't Penelope.

And she wondered if she could ever successfully pretend to be. How she wished her mother had been here this evening. Penelope could have accurately judged the audience's reaction. Katlyn could have trusted her critique.

Instead, she had to trust her debut hadn't been a complete disaster by Case's reaction. At least he hadn't fired her.

Katlyn took a small sip of her champagne, just kept herself from wrinkling her nose at the taste, then put the glass back. As she did, a flash of white caught her eye.

Through the partly open door Katlyn guessed led to the kitchen, she glimpsed a small barefoot figure in a ruffled nightgown. Emily peeked inside, darting back when she saw Katlyn look her way.

"So, your daughter is tucked in for the night?" she said, turning innocent eyes to Case.

"She's been asleep for hours. With all the chaos around her, I insist she stick to a strict schedule."

Before Katlyn could respond the cook shoved into the dining room holding fast to Emily, who all but refused to put one foot in front of the other.

"I don't want to go, Tuck," Emily whispered fiercely to the burly man.

"Well, I think your daddy wants his supper before midnight. I had less trouble gettin' a meal done when I was feedin' twenty hungry cowhands," Tuck muttered, depositing Emily at Case's side. "Found her in my kitchen again, spyin' on you, Mr. Durham." Muttering about supper being late again, Tuck lumbered back to his domain.

Emily stared hard at the floor. Katlyn bit her lip to keep from smiling.

Case looked at Emily a full minute before pulling her into his lap. He lifted her chin with one finger to turn the little girl's eyes to his. "What are you doing down here this time of night? You know the rules."

"I wanted to hear her sing," Emily said so softly Katlyn barely heard the words. "Becky said she sounded like an angel. I've never heard an angel before."

"Well, this is not the time or the place," Case said firmly. "You should be in bed."

Emily sniffled loudly and scrubbed at her nose with the back of her sleeve. She ducked her head, her face hidden by a tangle of dark curls.

A rush of empathy flooded Katlyn. She remembered all the times she'd been scolded for sneaking out to hear her mother sing, all the times she'd been escorted back to bed by a convenient chambermaid or her mother's dresser.

Penelope made it clear work supported them and so work came first. Her mother scoffed at the idea of wasting time playing games or simply sitting and talking with her young daughter when there was always practicing and more practicing to be done.

Growing up, Katlyn recalled having everything she needed—except the one thing she wanted most, a sense she belonged in her mother's life.

"I would be happy to sing for her," Katlyn said softly, her eyes on the little girl. She felt Case's scowl turn on her but she refused to back down. "It's a special night. I'm sure Emily would like to share it with you."

For the first time Emily lifted her head and pushed the hair away from her big green eyes. She looked up to Case, blinking away tears. "Please, Daddy?"

The rigid lines softened in Case's face as he gently brushed a strand of hair from Emily's forehead. "It's hours past your bedtime, sweetheart."

"And?" Katlyn risked provoking him further. "She can sleep a little later tomorrow."

"Don't make this your business, Miss McLain," Case said sharply. "I understand my daughter's needs far better than you do."

"That may be true, but couldn't you make an exception just this once?"

They stared at each other in a silent standoff, Emily, eyes wide as saucers, glancing from one to the other.

Case's first instinct was to flatly refuse Emily's request and to make it clear to Katlyn McLain just how unwelcome her interference was in his decisions.

Except when he honestly looked at his reaction, he knew it was also because he didn't want to give the woman across from him any foothold in his daughter's affections.

"All right, Emily, one time," he said finally. "This one night you may stay up late. But if you ask again, I'm warning you now the answer will be no."

Katlyn looked at Emily, making no attempt to hide her smile. Emily stared back at her, unsmiling, but with a distinct sparkle in her beautiful eyes.

"Would you like to sit on my lap while I sing to you?" Katlyn asked her.

Emily responded by shoving closer to Case, laying her head against his chest so she could just peer at Katlyn from the corner of her eye.

Suppressing a smile, Katlyn began to sing a lullaby her mother's old dresser had taught her, a gentle, soothing melody about a brave princess's journey through a magical forest to find her prince.

With her attention focused on Emily, Case could watch Katlyn freely. His irritation with her ebbed as her voice spun out the lilting notes, bringing to vivid life knights in shining armor, fire-breathing dragons and tall castles. Case wasn't given to flights of imagination. But when she sang like this, it seemed to him she changed the very texture of the air with her song, making it warmer and softer.

He realized suddenly how beautiful she was. The lamplight favored her ivory skin and wove fire into the dark auburn mass mantling her shoulders. Even Emily seemed entranced by the picture his songbird made, and his daughter was rarely captivated by anything.

Emily obviously missed having a mother. Case had known from the beginning he could never fill that place in his daughter's life.

But he knew also he didn't want Katlyn McLain filling it, either.

Katlyn or Penelope or whatever she called herself had secrets, of that he was certain. Just like Emily's mother.

He'd been a fool then. But never again. He would never be so gullible as to allow either Emily or himself to be hurt by lies. Women were deceptive. That lesson he had only to learn once.

As Katlyn finished the last of her song, Case gathered Emily close and stood up.

"Thank you, Miss McLain," he said, steeling himself against responding to Katlyn's look of hurt confusion. "If you'll excuse me, I'm going to put Emily back to bed. Go ahead with your supper, I may be awhile."

Katlyn barely had time to nod before Case whisked his daughter out of the dining room. As they rounded the doorway out of the room, Emily peered at her once over Case's shoulder, her hand lifting in a small wave.

Returning the gesture, Katlyn forced a smile. Inside, though, a cold emptiness settled around her heart, quelling the warmth the three of them had shared when she sang. A familiar voice reminded her why.

You're an outsider, Katie, you don't belong here any more than anywhere else, and you never will.

Chapter Four

Case pounded the last wooden plug into the wall with enough force to rattle the globes of the lamps. He'd spent the past half hour patching the bullet holes in the foyer walls, figuring it was better to vent his frustration with the hammer rather than his fists.

Just before dawn, he'd been jerked out of bed by a loud and rowdy brawl between two miners. They'd broken two chairs and a mirror before he'd managed to separate them, rouse the sheriff to haul them off to the jail, and finally break up the guests that had gathered to watch the ruckus.

It was then he discovered his missing songbird.

She hadn't slept in her room last night, and no one seemed to know where she'd gone. Case had an idea and he didn't like it.

Jack Dakota had a room at one of the boarding-houses. Case remembered Jack's invitation to Katlyn after her performance and wondered if she'd accepted it after he'd left her alone.

It irritated him to imagine her with Jack and at the

same time, he was angry with himself for thinking it mattered. He had hired her to sing. How she spent her time otherwise, or whom she spent it with, had nothing to do with him.

The front door swung open a few inches and Case turned, the hammer still raised in his hand.

Katlyn slipped inside, her shawl pulled up around her and her hair loose and tumbled. She glanced over her shoulder before carefully closing the door, not seeing him until she started to head for the staircase.

"Oh!" Her hand flew to her mouth. She stopped, staring at him with wide eyes.

She looked the perfect picture of guilt. Case deliberately turned back to the wall and slammed the plug one more time for good measure before saying smoothly, "Have a pleasant night, Miss McLain?"

"And what is that supposed to mean, Mr. Durham?"

The bristle in her voice turned Case around again. She had thrown her shawl back and stood with her arms folded. Case already recognized that defiant cant of her chin that betrayed her lightning temper.

"It means, I hope you had a pleasant night," Case said, starting down the ladder. "You didn't sleep in your room."

"I didn't realize I was required to. It's not your business, but I spent the night at Mrs. Donaldson's boardinghouse with my—companion. I told you, she's ill, and I stayed so late last night, it seemed foolish to come back here. Especially considering I

never know who I'm going to run into in your foyer,''
Katlyn couldn't resist adding.

Case scowled. He strode over to the front desk,
jamming his hammer with unnecessary force into the
toolbox he'd laid there. ''None of the staff is required
to stay here, particularly you and Dakota.''

''Jack? What has Jack got to do—'' Katlyn stared
at him a moment, then burst out laughing. ''Oh, you
thought—you thought Jack and I—''

Her annoyance evaporated as if it had never been.
She'd been afraid Case had been baiting her in an
attempt to ferret out her secrets, when all along he
was irritated because he thought she'd been dallying
with Jack.

''You seem to find that amusing,'' Case said
coolly. He leaned back against the desk, lighting up
a cheroot and taking a long pull on it before returning
to a study of her.

''It's more than that, it's crazy.'' Katlyn tried to
not stare at him in return. Although he exuded that
familiar polished command, something had roughed
his armor this morning. Slightly rumpled, his shirtsleeves rolled up and his hair ruffled, as when he'd
dealt with the drunkard, he seemed more dangerous
to her than the astute businessman ever did.

Dangerous in a way she didn't want to consider too
closely.

''I like Jack, but that's as far as it goes,'' she said,
more to distract herself than to answer him. ''He's
too much like my father and every other gambler I've

ever met. Risk-taking infects them and they never recover. How could you ever trust a man like that?''

To Katlyn's surprise, Case's expression suddenly sobered. ''Trust is more important than anything, I agree.'' He looked at her a moment then added with a twist of a smile, ''Although, somehow, I can't picture you being satisfied with someone nice and tame.''

''Oh, well...'' Katlyn shrugged. She started moving around the foyer, touching a chair here, a curtain there. ''I thought I would be, once.''

She glanced up at him quickly, smiling at his raised brow. ''I was engaged to a rancher before I came here.''

''I suppose compared to the riverboats, ranch life hardly offered the same excitement,'' Case said.

The edge to his voice didn't escape Katlyn but she only shook her head, her expression thoughtful. ''No, it wasn't that. It was...the challenge.''

She stopped near him at the desk and leaned her back against it, like him. Case watched her impatiently push a few unruly curls behind her ear, her tongue darting over her lips as she struggled to put her feelings to words. This morning, the gestures seemed to him both young and endearing.

''Marriage should be about building a life together, sharing the adventure, good and bad. But he needed me to always be waiting, to help him build the life he wanted, not to share in deciding what that life might be. I just wanted more.''

She felt the weight of his perceptive gaze, piercing

the confidence and bravado she'd managed easily with her former fiancé. Case had a way of making her feel exposed, vulnerable to her emotions, her insecurities. Vulnerable to him.

"Didn't you have all of those things with your wife?" Katlyn said, turning to him impulsively. "It must be so difficult now, raising your daughter alone. My sister was widowed once and I know how hard it was for her, being alone with two sons to raise."

Case looked away from her, taking a hard draw on his cheroot. "I'm not a widower. I just don't have a wife anymore."

"You—" Katlyn stopped, not understanding his words or his abrupt coldness.

"She didn't die. But she might as well have," Case said, the words falling hard between them. He ground out the cheroot with a vicious twist of his hand. "I married her thinking she was what I needed. She wasn't. It was all a lie, from beginning to end. She deceived me into believing she was exactly what she appeared to be."

"I—I'm sorry. No one should be hurt like that."

"I survived. And it won't happen again. With anyone. I'll never take a chance on allowing my daughter to suffer hurt again."

Katlyn abruptly turned away. She knew if she didn't, he would see everything she felt mirrored on her face.

She hated this deception, hated being torn between living a lie for her mother's sake and wanting to be honest about herself. She searched for something, anything to distract him.

"Have you decided to redecorate?" she asked a bit too suddenly, to divert both herself and Case from the painful topic of truth.

Case eyed her questioningly. He didn't know what possessed him to confide in her like that except her willingness to entrust him with a little of her past had prompted him to equal honesty.

Now it appeared she regretted their shared confessions and attempted to ignore them. He didn't know whether to feel relieved or affronted.

"The stage is coming in this afternoon," he said at last, keeping his voice carefully neutral. "I'm expecting new guests who might not appreciate decor that includes bullet holes."

"They might not appreciate those curtains, either," Katlyn said.

Striding over to the window, she tugged at the heavy plum-colored velvet, wrinkling her nose when dust puffed up from the folds of the worn fabric. "These must be relics from some great-aunt's attic. They make the whole room look depressing."

"Miss McLain—"

She spun around to face him again. "Will you quit calling me that? The way you say it makes me feel like a great-aunt. My name is Katlyn."

"I think I've just been insulted," Case said. He looked straight into her eyes, watching a warm pink glow blush her face. He suspected the color came from temper rather than embarrassment at her impulsive words. "Are you insinuating I'm stuffy?"

"As these curtains," Katlyn returned smartly, spurred by the sardonic amusement in his eyes and voice. "Although the curtains I can remedy."

Without asking his permission, she flung off her shawl, dragged a chair over to the windows, stepped up on it and yanked off one side of the curtains.

Her energetic tug released a cloud of dust that set her coughing. Trying to cover her mouth, she lost her grip on the heavy velvet and the material fell, tangling at her feet.

"Is this your idea of an improvement?" Case asked, close behind her.

Katlyn jumped, hearing him so near. She lost her balance on the chair and teetered precariously. Before she could grasp a handhold, Case's hands came around her tiny waist, steadying her.

"Careful," he murmured close to her ear, "this redecorating can be dangerous business."

For a moment Katlyn froze. In all her life she couldn't remember being so aware of a man. His hands felt warm and strong against her, his breath made her skin tingle as it brushed her ear. And the scent of him, a mingling of tobacco and something clean and sharp and male, seemed to her as heady as any spirits she'd tasted.

If she made the slightest move backward, she would be in his arms. The impulse to do just that tempted her and at the same time frightened her with its intensity.

Case realized he'd made a mistake the moment he touched her. His body responded to her even as his common sense warned him to walk away. Except his mind didn't seem to be listening to sense any more than the rest of him.

Katlyn shifted, turning within his hold to look at him. Her eyes, like the violet blue of a sunset sky, searched his.

He waited, expecting someone like Penelope Rose to respond with enticement, boldness even.

Instead she did nothing except look uncertainly at him, as if she had no idea of how to respond. The color had fled her face, leaving her pale.

Katlyn floundered. No man had ever made her feel so foolish and shy. Why was her confidence abandoning her now?

Case reached up one hand and touched her tousled hair. The coppery curls slid like silken fire through his fingers. He felt her tremble. Something inside him jerked, as if prodded sharply.

"Maybe I underestimated your talent," he said softly. "This is an improvement."

"Yes... Well, I mean it's much warmer. The velvet kept out the sunlight and...and..." Katlyn stumbled over her words and finally stopped. She tried to draw a calming breath and instead it came out a shaky sigh.

What was she doing, letting Case Durham turn her inside out like this? She was supposed to be Penelope Rose, used to men and their attentions. Her mother never would have stood this close to a man like Case and alternated between gaping at him and babbling about curtains. Her mother would have smiled, let her fingers graze his shoulder, and made some coy remark.

But Katlyn couldn't take her charade that far. Not with Case Durham. Not even for her mother. Looking away from him, she turned in the chair again, deliberately staring up at the remaining curtains. "I'll get the rest of these down, then the windows and woodwork need to be washed and—"

"Come down from there before you break a leg." Without waiting for her to obey and ignoring the squeal of protest she made, Case lifted her off the chair to the floor. "I've invested too much money in you to have you laid up for weeks. I didn't hire you to climb chairs and scrub windows."

Case deliberately made his voice and manner brusque and was rewarded when the flush came back to her face and the fire to her eyes.

He hadn't been prepared for her pale and trembling at his touch. Looking at her like that, he had lowered his guard and for a moment she'd slipped under it. She'd shaken his defenses and he determined she would never do it again.

Katlyn recognized the wall Case put up and almost welcomed it. At least it was familiar. "You hired me to rescue your hotel," she said. "Consider this a bonus to my singing."

She made to get up on the chair again but Case stepped in front of it, stopping her. "If you're so determined to tear apart my foyer, I'll help you. Maybe

I can keep you from pulling down the entire window.''

"Be my guest, but you aren't going to talk me out of washing this glass.''

"Has anyone ever told you you're hardheaded?'' Case asked as he pulled the ladder over to the window and started to climb the rungs.

"Practically everyone I meet,'' Katlyn said, smiling sweetly up at him. "So you'd better get used to it.''

Three hours later Katlyn stood at Case's side and surveyed the work they'd finished with satisfaction.

He'd grumbled a good deal about her giving orders to him and his staff, and about her making good on her promise to scrub both the windows and woodwork. But even he couldn't argue with the results.

The wood and glass, from windows to walls, gleamed after Katlyn's attack with soap, vinegar and beeswax. Case had moved all the furniture so the rugs could be taken outside and beaten, and then after everything had been thoroughly cleaned, Katlyn guided where to place things, rearranging everything to better suit the space. She'd also insisted the curtains from her suite be hung in the foyer. The light fabric in shades of rose and ivory perfectly complimented the room and let enough sunlight in to gild everything in mellow tones of gold.

Katlyn shot Case a triumphant smile. "I knew this would be better.''

"I'm beginning to wonder who's in charge around

here," Case muttered. But he couldn't help smiling at her sudden scowl. With her hair escaping its rough braid, her face smudged with dirt, and her dress dusty, she looked more real to him than she ever had carefully primped and painted. Seeing her now, he marveled at how she could transform herself to be at home on a stage.

"All right, it's better," he said. "You win. This time."

Cocking a brow at him, Katlyn put a hand to her hip and leaned back a little to look fully at him. "Is that a challenge, Mr. Durham?"

"It's a warning, Miss McLain, not to make a habit of rearranging my life without my invitation."

"I wasn't aware that improving your foyer had such an impact on your life. Do you find redecorating and cleaning that disturbing?"

"Maybe it's you I find disturbing. You're never what I expect you to be."

Case said the words thoughtfully as he watched her, making Katlyn feel as if he were stripping away her secrets one by one. "You don't know me well enough to expect anything from me," she said lightly. "And I like the idea that I can surprise you."

"I don't like surprises. I've had enough to last a lifetime." His expression hardened. "I want to know what to expect up front."

As if deliberately flaunting his warning, she caught his attention again by smiling instead of retreating. "Where's the fun in that?" she said, the gleam in her eyes pure mischief.

Case fought a surge of irritation. She'd managed once more to slip under his skin with that way she had of doing what he least anticipated.

"I've annoyed you again," she said. "I'm sorry."

"Are you?"

"Not really."

Shaking his head, Case gave up. "Well, at least that's honest. And now—" He glanced quickly at his watch. "It's time for Emily's lunch and I always try to have it with her. If you'd like to join us—"

Katlyn didn't have time to decide whether to accept or not. The clamor of wheels and horses' hooves drew their attention to the window as the stage rumbled past, leaving a wake of red-brown dust.

"It looks like my guests have arrived early," Case observed.

"I'll finish cleaning this up. I suppose it's not good business to have your guests tripping over buckets." Glad for the distraction, Katlyn hurried off to retrieve the bucket and cloths that Becky hadn't yet taken away. She left Case to remove the ladder as she gave the furniture a final swipe with her rag.

She'd just finished stowing the last of it when Case strode over to pull the front doors open and welcome in two elderly couples, one of them accompanied by a young woman.

Katlyn scarcely heard Case's smooth greeting and the easy way he had of organizing his staff to collect luggage and escort the guests to their various rooms. Instead she tried to stay as far in the background as possible, waiting for a chance to ease away before anyone noticed her.

She could have cheerfully strangled Case when he turned from welcoming the guests and beckoned, fixing all eyes on her. "Miss Rose, come and meet our guests."

Just stopping herself from glaring at him, Katlyn pasted on a bright smile. As Case introduced her as Penelope Rose, she tried not to cringe at the name or to think about how she looked after a morning of bathing in dust.

"Oh, Miss Rose, it's such a pleasure," one of the gentlemen said as he took her hand. He peered at her through small, round spectacles, his withered hand pumping hers in pleasure. "I heard you sing once, oh, many years ago, when I was visiting a niece in St. Louis. I told my wife then, I had never heard such a beautiful voice. You're the reason we decided to stop here on our way down to Santa Fe. When I heard you were here at the St. Martin, I insisted we come."

"Thank you. Perhaps you'll come and hear me sing again tonight then," Katlyn said, fervently wishing he would do anything but.

Unfortunately, the man bobbed his head in enthusiasm. "I shall, we all shall. You know, my dear..." He took off his spectacles and polished them on a large handkerchief. Then, putting them back on, he squinted at her again. "You look as young and lovely as you did then. Why it seems you haven't changed a bit in all these years."

"Our songbird never ceases to amaze me," Case said.

Katlyn didn't dare look at him, but she clearly heard the dry note in his voice and could tell without seeing he had that cool, mocking look in his eyes.

"I'm sure you're too kind," she told the elderly man. "But I hope you will enjoy my singing now as much as you enjoyed the St. Louis Songbird then."

She managed to make her escape finally, after accepting several more effusive compliments from her admirer, and being introduced to his wife, daughter and friends. Pleading the need to freshen up and rest before her performance, she headed for the stairs and the sanctuary of her rooms.

She didn't realize Case followed her until his hand on hers stopped her on the first step.

"Is something wrong, Miss McLain?"

"Katlyn," she snapped. "And no, nothing is wrong. Why should there be? I'm just tired, and I'm not used to greeting people looking like this."

Case nearly came back with some caustic retort about her renewed testiness but something in her face stopped him. She was pale and tense, and the pulse under his hand beat frantically. It was then he realized she wasn't having a fit of temper over being seen with dirt on her nose.

Katlyn McLain was scared to death.

Chapter Five

Katlyn hated disturbing her mother, but a choking panic at the thought someone might expose her as a fraud drove her straight to Penelope's side.

"Mama?" Katlyn knelt by the bed and gently stroked her mother's fragile hand. "I'm sorry, Mama, but I have to talk to you."

Penelope's eyes fluttered open, their usual sparkle replaced by a dull haze. "Katie, you're back already? What time is it?"

"It's only afternoon. I'm sorry to wake you, but I had to come."

Struggling to pull herself up against the pillow, Penelope squinted a little at her daughter. "What is it? What's happened?"

"Something—maybe nothing. Someone came to the hotel today who's seen you sing before. He's elderly and his vision is poor, but he told Case I hadn't changed at all in years." Katlyn fussed with arranging her mother's quilt until Penelope swatted at her hand in exasperation. "What if he remembers how you sing? What if he figures out I'm not the St. Louis Songbird he remembers? What if—''

''What if you stop all this unnecessary fussing? You listen to me, Katie. If this gentleman insists on remarking on your looks again, you simply tell him in your most charming way that a lady does what she must to stay one step ahead of the competition.''

''But—''

Penelope's body drooped and she had to stop to catch her breath. ''Do as I say.''

Realizing she'd taxed her mother terribly with her outburst, Katlyn regretted it. ''I always have, Mama,'' she said softly as she helped her mother lie back down. ''Don't worry, I always will.''

To Katlyn's relief, the elderly couple didn't come to her performance that night or the next. She learned later from Becky that the wife pleaded exhaustion and her husband refused to leave her side.

When they did finally appear in the saloon with their friends one night, the audience was so raucous they'd ended up sitting far in back, near the doors. For the next few nights, knowing they'd be there, she'd used extra makeup and slipped out after her performances to retreat to her rooms before they could approach her.

But tonight Case had snagged her during her escape, demanding she speak with the couple.

Now Katlyn paced by the bar, fidgeting with the pale green lace at her sleeve, growing more irritated by the minute.

''Can I get you a drink, Miss McLain?''

"Will someone please call me Katlyn?" she snapped, immediately regretted it and gave Bat Pacheo a rueful smile. "I'm sorry. It's been a long evening."

The bartender smiled back, understanding in his eyes, and handed her a glass of apple cider. He took extra care with the simple motion, as if concentrating on each movement of the bent and twisted fingers of his right hand.

"Oh, you remembered, thank you," Katlyn said, grateful for the small kindness. "This is wonderful."

As she took another sip, Bat nodded behind her. "Looks like the boss is comin' your way."

Good for him, Katlyn thought. At that moment she imagined she could actually hate the man. She certainly detested his arrogance. By forcing this meeting, he could expose her and ruin everything. And maybe, she thought with a combination of fear and anger, that's what he intended.

The object of her thoughts strode up to her side, tall, handsome and confident, his guests following.

He swept Katlyn with an appraising look, his expression offering no hint of emotion. "Miss Rose, our visitors have been anxious to talk to you," he said coolly.

The elderly bespectacled gentleman made his way to her and offered greetings and a polite bow. "My wife and I and our friends are leaving tomorrow. But our stay here would not have been complete without a chance to see you again."

Katlyn gulped back the lump rising in her throat. "I—I'm sorry I've been unavailable," she stammered. Then an idea struck her. She shot Case a look of challenge. "But, you see, my singing schedule here is somewhat taxing, and I find I simply must retire early if I'm to be at my best for the next night's performance."

"Well, we can certainly believe that. You've performed every night since we've been here." The man pulled his spectacles from his wrinkled face and looked at Case. "Don't you believe in giving your employees a day of rest, Mr. Durham?"

Case's jaw went stiff and his sharp green eyes narrowed on Katlyn. So she wanted to duel with him, did she? "Miss Rose has tomorrow night off."

The surprised look on her face was almost comical. "I do?"

"Of course. You've done your job well enough."

"You're being overly generous," Katlyn said, her smile sweet but her eyes flashing fire.

Still, she couldn't help glancing around at the few people left in the saloon. It'd been a fair showing tonight, better than some other nights, but nothing to boast about.

The elderly gentleman patted her arm affectionately. "Nonsense. Just you wait and see. Once word gets around, you'll have people waiting outside to see you, just like in St. Louis."

"Oh, we're all certain of that," Case said.

Katlyn shot him a glance but she couldn't tell from his face whether he intended the remark to be sarcastic or not. How well he masks his emotions when it suits him, she thought with frustration.

"I still say it's remarkable," the man continued, squinting at Katlyn. "She hasn't changed at all."

The plump, pink-cheeked woman on his arm shook her head. "Yes, dear, as a matter of fact, she has."

Before Katlyn could draw breath to interrupt, the woman looked accusingly at Case and said, "She's much thinner. She must be working too hard."

Katlyn felt her heart start beating again.

"I'll have to remedy that," Case said. He looked at Katlyn. "Don't worry, I intend to take very good care of my songbird."

Morning poured into Katlyn's room in a bright golden flood, taking the edge off the chilly mountain air while she rekindled the fire. She'd spent the night with her mother again, but at least today, for the first time since her arrival in Cimarron, she'd slept in late.

Through the open doorway, Becky bustled about Katlyn's sitting room, dusting this, straightening that, while Katlyn sat on her unmade bed counting up the money she'd saved so far to use to take her mother to the hospital in Las Vegas. She'd hiked her night-dress up around her thighs and her coppery mane hung in a wild mass about her face. She hadn't both-ered to brush it yet or to dress.

"Twenty-three, twenty-four..." she whispered to herself, carefully laying aside each hard-earned dollar. When she'd finished, she tucked them all back into a pouch she hid in the drawer near her bed.

Becky danced into the bedroom then, whistling a catchy tune. She stopped when she saw the expression on Katlyn's face. "What's wrong, Miss McLain? Ain't you enjoyin' your first day off?"

"What?" Katlyn muttered, distracted.

Becky came closer, cocking her head at Katlyn in confusion. "You look plain miserable. Are you that ready to get back to practicin'?"

Katlyn brushed heavy waves of hair away from her face and moved to search for something from her wardrobe. "No, it's not that. It's just that I'm trying hard to save all I earn, but it seems I'm not making much progress."

Becky plopped down on Katlyn's bed and toyed with fluffing her pillow. "Why not? Ain't Mr. Durham been payin' you enough?"

"Oh, yes. But, with the robbery, I had to replace clothing for myself and my companion. Then there's the rent at the boardinghouse, the doctor's bills, medicines." She riffled through her scant selection of dresses and settled on a plain, pale blue striped cotton. "I just thought I'd saved more, that's all."

"Why does saving so much money matter? You got a room and a good job," Becky asked, shoving off the bed to begin straightening the sheets. "And Tuck makes sure we all eat every day. That's good enough for me."

"You're very young, but you'll soon realize it's important to plan for the future. I'm just beginning to realize how important."

Becky stopped and dropped the quilt she'd yanked up over the pillows. "That's the same thing Mr. Durham is always tellin' Bucky and me." She stood ramrod straight then, mimicking Case's stance, pretending to draw on an imaginary cheroot. "There are no guarantees in this life, Becky. You must learn to take care of yourself and be careful not to trust the wrong person."

Becky giggled and Katlyn forced herself to smile back. Though Becky's imitation was so accurate it was funny, her words seared Katlyn's conscience like fire.

Would she one day give Case reason to wish he'd heeded his own advice?

"I won't sit in my room all day like moss on a log!" Katlyn whirled away from Case to return to her scrutiny of the dining room walls.

Case stood behind her, arms folded. Becky and Bucky waited a safe distance away, exchanging half-smothered smiles. Sally Carver, the widow who came each day to clean the rooms, poked Bucky in the ribs with a disapproving frown. Beside her, Bat grumbled about wasting time when he needed to finish polishing bar glasses.

Tuck poked his head out of the kitchen, took one look at the scene, muttered something about more noise than a cattle drive, and retreated.

"The guests said you look tired," Case said to Katlyn's back. "I can't have that."

"Oh, please, you don't believe that any more than I do. Now, what you can't have is this—" Katlyn flung both hands out toward the wall "—this horrid wallpaper in the dining room. It ruins my appetite just looking at it!"

Case felt the blood pulse in his temples, but he

managed to keep his voice level. "I don't recall asking your opinion, this time or the last several."

Damn but the woman had a mouth on her. And it wasn't just for singing he was finding out.

They stood only inches apart, facing each other down, neither showing any sign of retreat.

"Mister Durham, sir, excuse us," Bucky piped up nervously. "It ain't any of our business, I guess, sir, but we're all wantin' to see yer hotel get lots of new folks in. And, well, we was talkin' here and I don't know about the color and them flowers and all, but that paper does look mighty worn in spots."

"She does have a point about the color," Sally said. "It looks like the red mud my boys grind into their pants with smudges of gray here and there."

Sally prodded Bat and he shrugged. "Don't like them flowers myself," he said shortly.

"It looks as if you've incited a mutiny, Miss McLain," Case said, never taking his eyes off Katlyn.

Katlyn nearly backed down under his intimidating glare. He seemed so large, so overpowering as he towered over her, his broad shoulders enveloping her in shadow.

She supposed that look of his should inspire fear in her. It seemed to in everyone else. But she only felt an odd, heady excitement.

Katlyn ran her tongue slowly over dry lips and the look in Case's eyes immediately changed. Instead of ice, she saw a flare of heat.

Case found his gaze drawn to her mouth, scarcely aware she was speaking.

"May I at least find out what new paper would cost?"

"Paper," he heard himself saying. "Yes. Bring me an estimate."

She smiled at him, fully and freely, her eyes shining, and Case felt it as powerfully as a force. She stepped closer and laid her hand on his arm. Her fingers pressed quickly. He could smell the lilac scent of her, warm and sweet, and it went straight to his head.

"Thank you," she murmured. "You won't be disappointed, I promise."

In that moment Case couldn't have refused her anything, would have trusted her with his life.

But she turned away, sweeping his staff into her plans, and he realized with a sharp return to his senses it was only a moment, nothing more.

And that moment had passed.

Katlyn sat at her dressing table and pulled a brush through her hair, trying to use the soothing rhythm to make herself drowsy. A midnight stillness had settled over the hotel and, alone with her thoughts in the quiet twilight of her room, she felt restless, unable to relax.

She didn't want to think about the day, about Case, about anything. Right now, all she wanted was to close her eyes and forget about everything for a few hours.

The hotel creaked and Katlyn jumped, dropping her brush. Katie, my dear, you're turning into a mouse, she told herself. You never used to be afraid of anything.

Of course, she never used to live in a disreputable hotel pretending to be her mother, either. With a rueful smile at her own foolishness, Katlyn bent to pick up the brush.

A low, deep groan stopped her in midmotion.

She stayed perfectly still, her hand poised over the brush, and listened intently. For several moments she only heard the thudding of her own heart.

Then it came again.

Katlyn fleetingly remembered all the teasing she'd endured about Case's resident ghosts. But the pained note in the sound convinced her that this time someone needed help—or wanted to play a not-so-amusing trick.

Determined to find the source, Katlyn hurried outside to the stair landing. She waited and listened but heard nothing. No one seemed to be awake but her.

And she was starting to feel a bit ridiculous, traipsing about the darkened hotel in her nightclothes. At the same time, she refused to quit without an answer.

Maybe it had come from downstairs. Katlyn cautiously maneuvered down the staircase, keeping her ears perked.

A soft diffused glow lit the foyer, and she stepped into it before she realized what she had done.

Case, sitting behind the desk, studying an open ledger while fingering a cheroot, looked up in surprise at the slight hiss of her sudden intake of breath.

He'd obviously been working for a while. His jacket and vest carelessly tossed on a chair near the desk, his shirtsleeves rolled to the elbows, he looked as if he'd been running his hand through his hair in frustration over the numbers in front of him. A brandy bottle and half-filled glass stood to the side of the ledger, and the remains of several cheroots were crushed in the tray next to them.

"Miss McLain..." Case slowly ground out the cheroot then looked fully at her. "Is something wrong?"

"Wrong?" Katlyn threw up her hands. "You had to hear it!"

Before he could answer, the moaning came again, shuddering through the foyer.

"That! You had to hear *that!*"

Case resisted a smile. "Oh, that. It sounds like Rattlesnake Cooper, up to his tricks again."

"Not your ghost stories again. Do you truly expect to believe that nonsense?"

"Who says it's nonsense?"

Pushing back his chair, Case stood and walked around the desk. He picked up his brandy glass and offered it to her. "Here, you look as if you could use this."

She looked at first as if she would refuse. Then she reached out and took the glass, her fingers just brushing his. Watching him over the rim, she took a small sip. She made a little breathy sound at the taste.

Case found his eyes drawn to her mouth. His gut tightened when her tongue darted over her full, pink lips. All at once he noticed how the thin white cotton she wore lay like a caress against her skin, how her hair mantled her shoulders in a tumble of copper and gold.

"Come and sit by the fire," he heard himself saying, hardly recognizing his own voice.

Katlyn nodded, handing the glass back to him. The intent look in his eyes confused her. Or maybe it was her own chaotic feelings that were confusing.

A little unsteadily, she moved to one of the armchairs and sat, tucking her bare feet underneath the hem of her nightgown. "So, you're sticking to this ghost story?" she asked, trying to regain her confidence if not her dignity.

"Why not?" Case said, leaning back in his own chair, his previous tension seemingly vanished. "With your bent for the dramatic, I would think you'd agree it gives character to the hotel. Besides, Cooper is harmless enough, even though Becky swears he likes to scare the guests by slamming doors behind them."

Katlyn rolled her eyes. "And just who is—was— this Rattlesnake Cooper? Or did you make the name up, too?"

"No, he used to live here at the hotel. By all accounts he was an ornery old cuss who liked to tell tales about his wicked past as a gunslinger."

"I suppose he wasn't."

"He was a wanderer who tried gold mining once in a while. But he liked pretending, and one day he apparently boasted to the wrong man. The man really was a gunslinger and challenged him." Case smiled at Katlyn's wide-eyed expression. "Lucky for Cooper the man was drunk. Cooper accidentally killed him, and instantly became a legend in Cimarron.''

Katlyn wriggled a little, feeling acutely uncomfortable with Case's story. ''So what happened to him? I suppose his charade eventually got him killed.''

''You could say that. He died in bed after a romp with a saloon girl who wanted to be with the legendary gunman.''

Case laughed with her, infected by her delight in the tale.

''Now, I suppose he won't leave,'' Katlyn said, wiping at her eyes.

''Supposedly. The hotel is drafty, but I prefer to think of the groans as Cooper, grumbling about the food or the whiskey.''

''It seems even your ghosts are disreputable. Why did you ever take on a place like this?''

The question caught him off guard. Case thought a moment before saying, ''For the challenge. Anything easy is probably not worth winning. Isn't that how you feel?''

''I—well it's certainly more satisfying when you do finally win.'' *If* you finally win, she thought, thinking of the risk she took for Penelope.

Would a man like Case ever understand her decision? Katlyn nearly laughed out loud. If he ever discovered her deceit, she'd be out on her ear in seconds flat.

Case watched her expression shift from a relaxed enjoyment to a frowning distraction. He wondered what she was thinking to bring about the change. He wondered more what she was hiding, what frightened

Katlyn McLain so that she felt the need to hide the natural exuberance he'd seen in her time and again.

Lost in her thoughts, Katlyn didn't hear Case move until she felt his hand touch her shoulder. She started, looking up at him.

"You had better get to bed before you fall asleep here," he said gently.

"Yes…of course." Katlyn put a hand to her hair, all at once feeling self-conscious about having spent the past half hour sitting in her nightdress, talking with Case as if they were comfortable with one another.

Turning her face away, she got to her feet and started in the direction of the staircase. Case stood in front of her, blocking her path. Katlyn swallowed hard.

"Mr. Durham—Case…"

They stared at one another and Katlyn sensed a draw between them as powerful as a physical touch. She knew he felt it too, and for a moment from the glint in his eyes and the tensing of muscle she thought he would kiss her.

Case found himself starting to make the motion to pull her into his arms when he stopped. What the hell was he doing? He had no business getting involved with this woman.

But he couldn't look at her without being tempted.

She stood still, as if waiting for him to decide. As if she'd already made up her mind and knew he wanted the same. Yet there was nothing coy in her. Only an honest need.

And that tempted him more than anything.

Except he couldn't be sure if it was real.

Katlyn knew the moment he conquered his impulse and shut himself away from her again. She drew in a long breath and looked away. "I'll go back to my room now."

"I'll walk with you," Case said, every word sounding forced. "I'll bring the lamp."

Not wanting to argue with him, Katlyn accepted his escort without saying anything. When they reached her door, she turned only to thank him.

Case nodded with stiff politeness. "Good night, Miss McLain."

A small moan whimpered through the landing.

Katlyn gave a little half smile. "I told you I hate it when you call me Miss McLain. I don't think Cooper approves, either."

"Good night then—Katlyn."

He said her name in a low rough voice that was so different from his usual cool sardonic tone that Katlyn stared at him.

Case sensed she wondered what he was thinking. If she asked, he would have to tell her she didn't want to know.

Because what he was thinking would only mean trouble for them both.

Chapter Six

Some nights she almost enjoyed this. Standing close to the piano, Katlyn finished the last bars of the sentimental love ballad with a flourish. The audience broke into enthusiastic applause and Katlyn grinned when Jack winked at her. He then started up one of the more lively tunes he liked about a roving miner, a lucky strike, and a gal named Sal.

Katlyn joined in with confidence, buoyed by Jack's encouragement and the audience's appreciation. She turned with a flip of her skirts to walk back to center stage—and found herself confronted by her mother's doctor.

It was immediately obvious he hadn't come for a night's entertainment. The expression on his face told Katlyn something was terribly wrong.

She faltered over a line of the song, recovered, and managed to finish the tune, glad Case had left the saloon a few minutes earlier. Forcing a smile, she excused herself to the audience, quickly whispered a few words of explanation to Jack, and then hurried to draw the doctor to a corner of the saloon, praying all the while Case stayed away a little while longer.

The unexpected absence of Katlyn's singing drew Case back to the saloon. Seeing the empty stage, he searched the room for his songbird. He'd just promised the new guests he'd been greeting in the foyer that Penelope Rose wouldn't disappoint.

But it seemed she'd suddenly taken flight.

He'd made it a habit each night she sang to listen to at least part of her performance. At first, he stayed because he doubted her talent. Now, he admitted to himself, he stayed because he enjoyed hearing her when she forgot to perform and sang from her heart.

It was then that she worked her magic, captivating him and anyone listening with her sweet, pure voice.

Case started over to Jack to ask why Katlyn had left in the middle of her performance when he saw her in close conversation with Frank Garrett.

Without stopping to examine his reasons, Case strode up to them in time to hear Katlyn's last words.

"You never told me she might go blind! I've got to get her to Las Vegas now."

The doctor shook his head. "No, she can't possibly travel now, not for weeks, maybe months. It would kill her."

"Is there a problem, Miss McLain?" Case interjected smoothly, startling both the doctor and Katlyn with his sudden presence.

Katlyn flushed and tried to look anywhere but at him. "Yes—no...I mean, yes, Dr. Garrett just gave my…my companion some upsetting news. I must go to her.''

She looked at the doctor, appealing. He frowned before slowly nodding.

The exchange roused Case's suspicions anew. Katlyn was concerned, that was plain. But he thought he also detected an underlying guilt in her. She appeared unreasonably rattled with him there, anxious to escape.

''I'll walk with you to the boardinghouse,'' Case said. Katlyn stared at him, her eyes wide. ''It's dark. You shouldn't go alone and I can easily escort you. There's no reason to keep Dr. Garrett any longer.''

''Th-that's not necessary,'' Katlyn protested. She fought against a rising panic. ''It's a short walk and I may be there a long time. I'll just tell Jack I'm leaving and I'll go—''

''Not alone.''

Katlyn's heart plummeted as she recognized the hard note of authority in Case's voice. In this mood, he wouldn't take no for an answer.

But she had to keep Case away from her mother. If he saw Penelope he would know without a doubt they were related and he would be quick to figure out their charade.

She tried to think of an argument that would convince him but Case was already steering Dr. Garrett toward the door. Glancing toward the piano, she wondered if she could quickly convince Jack to follow her and persuade Case he needed to stay and tend his hotel.

"Jack can keep the company entertained while we're gone," Case said, squelching her fleeting hope. He took her arm when she opened her mouth to protest again and guided her out of the saloon and out the doors to the street.

"This isn't necessary, Mr. Durham."

Case set a brisk pace in the direction of the boardinghouse. "I think it is."

"Why? You don't know my companion."

"No, but it's obvious you care a great deal about her. Whatever Dr. Garrett said upset you, too. I care about that."

Katlyn stiffened and fixed her eyes straight ahead. "You needn't worry this will interfere with my singing. The doctor said it was urgent or I wouldn't have gone tonight."

"Katlyn—" Case stepped in front of her and put both his hands on her shoulders, stopping her. "I wasn't talking about your job. I meant what I said, I care that this upsets you."

He slipped his hand under her chin and lifted her face to his. Even in the pale moonlight, he could see the sheen of tears in her eyes, though the stubborn set of her mouth was mute testimony she refused to give in to them. The look was so like her, a curious mix of vulnerability and determination.

"I'm not so hard-hearted I would turn you out just because you left early one night to comfort a sick friend."

"I—I know that," Katlyn said. And she did. For all his rigid, no-nonsense approach to life, she trusted him to treat her fairly and honestly. Which was more than he could trust her to do. "I'm just...I'm worried about her, and the treatment she needs doesn't come cheaply."

Case let her pull free from his hold, walking beside her as she started for the boardinghouse again. He realized from her words she was paying for her companion's medical care, as well as her room and board. It made his earlier suspicions of her seem small and unfair.

Obviously her nervousness had been because she was worried he would be angry with her for leaving early and she couldn't afford to lose her job. Only she had been too proud—or too afraid of his reaction—to confide in him.

They reached the boardinghouse and inside the door Katlyn turned to him. "Thank you for walking me, I'll be back as soon as I can."

"I'll wait."

"That's not necessary. Dr. Garrett said she was very upset, it may take me a while to calm her. I'm sure you're anxious to get back to the hotel."

"I'll wait," Case said firmly. "Would you like me to go up with you?"

"No!" Katlyn drew a deep breath at his raised eyebrow. "I mean, no thank you. My companion is very ill, and she won't want to meet strangers now. I'll go alone."

She spun away from him, intending to rush up the stairs before he could protest. In her haste, she nearly collided with Mrs. Donaldson who was hurrying down.

"Oh, I'm glad you're here, lass. Your poor—"

"Yes, the doctor said she was upset. My friend has been so ill, I know this latest news must be especially hard for her."

Mrs. Donaldson looked confused. "But I thought—"

"Why don't you tell me about it on the way up?" Katlyn said, taking Mrs. Donaldson's arm to hustle her back up the stairs.

Case watched until the two women disappeared into one of the upstairs rooms. Minutes ago he'd nearly convinced himself he could trust Katlyn.

Now he wasn't so certain.

"You can't let this happen to me. Katie, you just can't!"

Katlyn held tightly to her mother and rocked her gently. She had never felt more helpless in her life, never more afraid of failing.

"Dr. Garrett said you can't travel now, Mama. It could kill you."

"I would rather be dead than lose everything like this! He said I was going blind. Blind! Oh, Katie, how could this happen?"

"I'll get you to Las Vegas soon, I promise. As soon as the doctor says it's safe for you to go."

Penelope clung to Katlyn, her tears soaking the shoulder of Katlyn's dress, staining the gaudy yellow satin. "I'm afraid, Katie," she said, the words muffled. Even without seeing her face, Katlyn could tell by the rigidness of her mother's body, her tightly clinging fingers how much the admission had cost Penelope.

"I've never been afraid of anything, never. But now, all I am is frightened."

Katlyn tried to think of words to comfort her mother. But with the truth of the doctor's grim prognosis between them, she could think of nothing that wasn't a meaningless lie.

An hour later Katlyn slowly walked back down the stairs, feeling drained of everything but a numbing tiredness.

She'd cajoled Penelope into drinking some of the draught Dr. Garrett had left, and her mother had finally fallen into an exhausted sleep. After talking with Mrs. Donaldson and being reassured the older woman would check on Penelope, Katlyn decided she might as well go back to the hotel for an hour or two.

It was nearly ten o'clock, but some of Case's guests might still be lingering in the saloon, and she could at least promise them better entertainment tomorrow night.

Katlyn put a hand to open the front door when she heard a familiar step behind her. She turned, unable to hide her surprise at seeing Case. "You're still here."

"Yes, I told you I would be. How is your friend?"

"Dr. Garrett gave her something to help her sleep, I don't think she'll wake until morning. Then..." Katlyn shook her head and half raised her hand in a motion of helplessness.

She looked so utterly defeated Case instinctively reached out and laid his hand against the softness of her cheek. Very gently, he rubbed his fingertips against her skin, feeling the wet kiss of the single tear she couldn't hold back.

Katlyn turned her face a little so her mouth just brushed his palm. How comforting it would be to confide in him, to lean on his strength and, for just a little while, to let someone share her troubles.

But that was impossible, it would always be impossible. She could never forget that.

"I was going to go back to the hotel, but on second thought, I'd better stay the night here," she whispered, closing her eyes so he wouldn't see her need for him there. "I'll be back at the hotel in the morning."

"Come back with me, at least for a little while." When she looked at him as if to protest, Case said quickly, "You said she would sleep, probably for the night. Have dinner with me. It will do you good. You may decide a good night's sleep in your own bed would be more helpful for both of you."

"Case, I—" Katlyn began, then stopped. Tears welled in her eyes. She wiped at them angrily, hating her own weakness.

That sudden gesture, both vulnerable and defiant, broke Case's restraint. He gathered her into his arms and held her close against him, feeling a fierce and completely unexpected sense of possession as she held tightly to him as if she would never let go.

As he looked across the candlelit table in the hotel dining room, the deep violet circles beneath Katlyn's eyes aroused a disturbing combination of protectiveness, admiration and compassion in Case.

And it aroused something else. Guilt. For doubting her. For suspecting her motives.

At the same time he couldn't rid himself of images of the times he'd seen fear in her eyes, her reluctance to talk about the past. He wanted to trust her; he didn't know if he could.

It irritated him he couldn't make up his mind about her, even more so because it shouldn't have mattered. He paid her to sing and she gave him his money's worth. Her secrets, if she had any, had nothing to do with business.

Yet watching her now, staring at nothing as her fingers twisted the napkin in her lap, Case found it impossible to view her as simply a business investment.

"You aren't eating," he said. He used his fork to pierce a morsel of spiced peach and offered it to her.

"What?" She looked up, taking in his gesture. "Oh, thank you, but I don't have much appetite tonight."

She tried to smile and Case's chest tightened. His eyes followed the sweep of her lashes against the delicate rise of her cheeks.

"You wouldn't have me break my promise to your

admirers, would you? I told them I would see you fed, remember?'' He moved the fork gently toward her mouth. ''Even Emily eats more easily than this. Don't tell me I have to sink to playing 'time to fill the berry basket' to get you to eat.''

Katlyn couldn't help but smile, genuinely this time. His tender concern touched her. Since the day they'd met, she'd only seen him reveal glimpses of this side of himself with Emily and she found it irresistibly appealing tonight.

Finally she parted her lips to his urging, her eyes locking with his.

Case slid the tip of the fork over her tongue, his hand almost shaking with the strength of the feelings she aroused in him. She looked so alone, so needy. How easy it would be to take her in his arms and give her the comfort she wanted.

Except somewhere in the back of his mind the fear that he'd felt this way before haunted him. And the consequences of caring too much for the wrong woman had seared his memory permanently. Even so, that thought tormenting him now, he could not pry his eyes from her face. She looked at him with wide, beautiful blue eyes, trusting, wanting, needing something he instinctively ached to give.

His mind warning him furiously away, her gaze burned through him, kindling a fire. Slowly he finished what he'd started and pulled the fork back. She touched her tongue to her lips as if savoring the taste he'd given her.

A small sheen of fruit syrup at the corner of her

mouth caught his eye and before he could check the impulse, Case slid the pad of his thumb across it. Her lips parted slightly in response to his touch, her quickened breath kissing his skin.

Case pulled his hand back. The strong, sudden desire to taste where he'd touched jolted him.

Instead he offered her another bite of fruit, their eyes never leaving each other. The room around them seemed to fall away into darkness save for the small golden flame of the single candle glowing between them.

Katlyn longed to suspend the moment, to let the warmth in his touch, in his eyes, shelter her from the cold storm of worry and fear, so she could forget how alone she was.

She took her own fork and speared a piece of peach. ''You've forgotten yourself,'' she murmured. ''Here, let me give back what you've given me.''

Case sensed she meant something far beyond the sweet taste she offered. Her bold yet innocent attempt to return his kindness found him suddenly awkward and unable to accept. For the first time since they'd sat down, he dragged his eyes from her face.

As gently as he could, he held up a hand in pause. ''I— That is, thank you, I—can't. I confess, I don't have much appetite, either.''

Katlyn stopped midmotion, utterly confused and embarrassed. ''Oh...I see.'' She flushed, looking everywhere but at him.

What a fool she was! She'd imagined something more behind his gestures than compassion borne out of decency or his determined sense of honor and duty. But that's all it had been, the gentle touches, the kind words, the morsels of food. Compassion, just as he'd shown toward Becky and Bucky, Sally, Tuck and Bat. All of his orphans.

To him, she was simply another lost and lonely soul looking for a place to call home, in need of someone to care. Perhaps that's why the ghosts stayed in this hotel, she mused. For despite his almost fierce bravado, the truth was Case Durham didn't have the heart to send any needy spirit away.

Case finished his wine in one drink and shoved his plate away. He drew a gold case from his vest and took out a cheroot. Cutting the tip and lighting it, he took one long draw before facing her again. "I'm concerned about your companion. I didn't realize she was so ill."

"Thank you," Katlyn murmured, unable to meet his eyes. She tried to push the last few minutes from her mind. What he'd felt, what he'd shared with her, was nothing more than empathy or something she wanted far less: pity.

"What's her name?"

Katlyn's eyes snapped to his at that. "Her— name?"

"I presume she has one. But you never call her anything but your companion."

"Her name is—Beatrice, Beatrice Riley," Katlyn blurted, using the name of her mother's former dresser. Beatrice was nearly eighty now and hadn't dressed anyone in over fifteen years, but Case didn't know that. And at least if he mentioned the name again, she would recognize the new persona she'd just given Penelope.

"We've known each other a long time, we're very—attached. I owe her a great deal."

Case leaned back in his chair, his long legs stretching well to the side. "I see that. I only wish I could be of more service."

"That's very kind of you. But there's nothing anyone can do right now." She stumbled over the last words and blinked back the tears burning her eyes.

Case saw her lose her struggle for restraint as several tears slipped down her face. His heart twisted. "You can quit singing for a time, with pay, if need be, to take care of her," he offered.

That did it. His arrogance and his cold distance Katlyn had defenses against. His tenderness and generosity, she didn't. Unable to hold back another moment, she broke down and began to sob openly, feeling humiliated by her outburst. But, tired and worried beyond reason, she couldn't stop the flood tides of emotion.

Immediately, Case doused his cheroot and moved to her side. He bent close to her, dabbing at her eyes with his napkin. How could it be that the moisture on her flawless skin brought a beguiling glow to her cheeks? He yearned to kiss away the drops, one by one, but willed himself to give her only comfort.

"I promise I'll do whatever I can to help," he murmured, gently lifting her chin with his fingertips to look directly into her eyes.

Why was he tormenting her? Katlyn stared at him through a watery haze. Better to leave her alone in her misery than to make it worse with this empty show of caring.

Case waited a moment then slowly backed away. "I've said the wrong thing. I'll leave you alone. It was an honest offer, though, I promise you."

Honest. The word struck Katlyn like a blow. She couldn't deny that he'd tried everything to help her and her mother, treated her with protective kindness, as a woman and a friend instead of a mere subordinate. But then, to Case, all of his employees meant far more than the word indicated. And each one, in gratitude, in his or her own way, gave back more to Case than he ever demanded.

And how had she repaid him? By returning his efforts with lies.

She reached for him, gripping his hand before he walked away. "No, Case, you've been wonderful tonight. It's just that I—"

Case turned back to her, his hand moving from hers to reach out and brush several coppery strands of hair that had come loose and fallen across her face. Her shimmering curls, now tinted with flames of gold and sparks of crimson in the candlelight, teased his fingertips with their softness, momentarily overtaking any other thought.

"Don't." The effort of restraint to bank his need to let his touch keep trailing down her cheek, left his voice a raspy whisper. "There's no need to explain. Only know that I'll help, however I can."

"You have helped. More than you know."

Case brushed a thumb beneath each eye, wiping away the wetness there. "If you're finished, I'll walk you back to the boardinghouse. Unless you'd rather go to your room. As tired as you are, it might be wiser to stay here. I don't think you can be of much help to your friend now."

Katlyn gathered her tattered nerves, wiped her eyes and cheeks with her napkin and allowed Case to pull out her chair for her. He proffered his elbow and she curled her palm around his muscular arm. He felt so strong, so stable, she longed to lean into him.

She stifled a yawn. "Maybe you're right."

"A little of this may help you sleep," Case said, holding up her wineglass.

She shook her head. *Knowing you care will help me sleep tonight.*

Her small tired steps, the delicate touch of her hand on his forearm, made Case yearn to sweep her into his arms and carry her upstairs to her bed. But tonight, if he took her that far, held her that close, touched the fiery essence of her hair and skin, would only bring the deepest of regrets for them both tomorrow.

He chided himself for the thought, but as they walked slowly up the staircase Katlyn yawned again and leaned her head against his shoulder. She had no way of knowing how that small gesture set his loins aflame, how long it had been since he'd even had any interest in taking a woman to his bed. After the agony of his breakup with his wife, for a surprising length of time it had hardly crossed his mind.

He'd been so preoccupied with Emily and with the hotel, it hadn't mattered—until Katlyn McLain swept into his life. Since that day, he now realized that little by little his senses had begun to awaken to her, from the sweet lilac scent of her hair to the lyrical sound of her laugh, to the gentle sway of her hips beneath those satin and silk confections she wore each night. She was bringing him back to life in ways he'd hoped to never feel again.

Katlyn relaxed against Case's arm, relishing the support. She wished the staircase were a mile long. He'd leave her at her door, all propriety intact. Of that she was certain. But tonight, feeling him so close, needing the power of his soothing touch, she wished he would abandon his cool stoicism and simply hold her.

The tender image filled her mind so vividly, she scarcely heard the first thud strike the lobby door.

In the next instant both she and Case jerked around to face a thunderous ruckus of shouts and pounding. At first the noise came from outside, but whoever it was obviously intended to come crashing right through the front door.

Chapter Seven

Case ran down the stairs, taking several at a time, pausing only to pull his six-shooter from a drawer hidden behind the desk in the lobby. He strode to the front door and yelled above the noise as he grasped the doorknob, "The saloon's closed."

A round of laughter from several revelers answered him, loud even through the closed door.

"We don't mean no harm, mister," a man's slurred voice called back. "We jus' wanna git warmed up and git us some rooms fer the night."

Bucky, roused from the pallet he'd taken to sleeping on in the little nook behind the front desk whenever their father was on a drunken rampage, poked his head up to peer sleepily at Case and Katlyn. "What's happening?"

"Just stay where you are, Bucky. And you—" He turned to Katlyn, hovering at his side. "Wait upstairs until I find out what this is about."

Though tempted, Katlyn didn't argue with his demand. She retreated only as far back as the bottom of the staircase and waited there, watching.

Case unlocked the door, but before he could open it, the men outside flung it back. A mass of drunken, stinking cowboys and painted women stumbled headlong into the lobby, nearly knocking him backward.

"Evenin'!" one of the men said, jovially lifting his near-empty whiskey bottle to Case. "We're lookin' fer a spot to rest our backsides a spell. And we heard this here hotel is the best in town."

Case looked him over, hardly impressed with what he saw. The man stood a gangly six-feet-plus with slicked-back greasy hair, wearing an ill-fitting attempt at dandified clothes. Case had seen the type a thousand times over. And in nearly every instance, it had meant trouble.

Still, antagonizing men with more whiskey in them than good sense would only mean trouble. If at all possible, he wanted to avoid any more bullet holes in the wall—or worse. "I own the St. Martin. What exactly do you want?"

"Why, some empty beds and full bottles," said another of the men.

This one, stocky and strong, in fringed leather chaps with a bright red scarf around his sun-tanned neck, was obviously pure cowhand. Though he wobbled in his boots, he managed to prop up a bleary-eyed blond with red rouge smudged to her cheekbones. The woman in tow, he made his way through the others toward Case.

Katlyn took a few steps forward in an impulse to

support Case, then stopped. Better not to complicate things any further; letting them see her would hardly help the situation. But watching Case face them, so outnumbered, made her nervous.

"We just sold us a herd of mustangs and we're out celebratin'," the cowhand said.

"In the blue chips tonight, ain't we boys!" the first man shouted, toasting again with his now empty bottle. The group answered with cheers and hoots.

Case glanced over the others in the group, then back at the leader. Cattle rustlers. He'd thought as much the minute he'd laid eyes on them.

Trouble.

Maybe, maybe not.

He had to decide quickly whether it was worth the risk to let them stay, although he didn't have much choice. In this territory, the peculiar brand of Western hospitality demanded you feed and shelter your worst enemy if he came to your place, and if you turned anyone away, you might as well close the door on your business.

Still, Katlyn wouldn't know that. He glanced back over his shoulder to where she waited in the shadows in defiance of his order to go upstairs.

Katlyn expected he'd be irritated to find her there. But she suddenly realized he was silently asking her opinion.

The notion both surprised and moved her. He was desperate for the income, she knew. And apart from Emily, nothing meant more to him than the success of the St. Martin. But without income from guests, whatever form they took, he could never hope to revive the hotel.

Yet obviously he was worried about Emily and about how Katlyn would feel with more guests like these under the same roof. He seemed to be looking to her, asking for her approval, before he allowed the men to stay.

She took no time to make up her mind. Case wouldn't let them stay if he thought he couldn't handle them, that much she knew. She'd seen him throw many a rowdy drunkard out into the night, and once he'd neatly relieved two men of their knives before a fight could ensue over whether or not to close a window.

But for some reason, right now he needed her trust and her support before he would take a chance on this group. She mustered a smile and nodded, hoping she looked more confident than she felt.

Case caught her meaning. In spite of her own problems, she was thinking of the hotel, of him. He nodded back, earning himself another fleeting smile.

Turning back to assess the men and their whores, he decided they were so whiskey soaked, once he broke them up and sent them to their rooms, most of them would probably simply pass out.

The hard truth was he couldn't afford to lose the amount they'd let slip through their fingers in his hotel, even if they only stayed one night. And he certainly couldn't afford to give the St. Martin a reputation for turning away travelers.

The bottle-toting ringleader spoke up again. ''We'll

take—now let's see how many of us are there?'' His ridiculous struggle to count on his fingertips frayed Case's patience.

''Nine. You need nine rooms. Pay up front and go on to bed and you can stay.'' Case braced his boots in a wide-legged stance in case what he was about to say ignited the man's temper. ''But nothing else. I told you already, the saloon's closed for the night.''

The man's affable smile turned suddenly sour. ''Closed?'' He whirled around in an off-balance motion. ''Hear that boys? Man says the well's dried up for the night.'' A round of boos and groans fed his cockiness. ''Seems the boys think we might oughta get that pump workin' again 'fore we turn in fer the night. I'm in need of a bottle of the local tangle leg. The kind that'll make a hummingbird spit in a rattlesnake's eye.''

Case took one long stride to stand square in the man's face. He pulled his Colt from his waistband, slid his thumb to draw back the hammer, and pointed it between the man's bloodshot eyes.

Katlyn barely stopped herself from rushing to Case's side. But knowing taking such a risk might only worsen the situation, and recognizing the cold threat in his voice, gave her pause.

''I don't think you're listening,'' he said to the group. ''I said the saloon's closed.''

An uneasy hush fell over them, dousing their high spirits.

Katlyn heard the stairs creak. She glanced toward the noise and spied Becky creeping down to see what the ruckus was. Katlyn lifted a hand in warning, waving Becky back upstairs to the relative safety of Emily's bedroom.

Of all nights for Becky and Bucky to have to have left their house again. She could hardly fault Case for offering them the hotel as a refuge, but tonight it might be more dangerous than their own home. Then again, young as Bucky was, she suspected he'd already learned how to hold his own in a fight and how to handle a gun.

The room deadly still, Case and the other man locked eyes in a silent battle of wills, Case's hand steady on his gun. "If you want to take a bottle to your rooms, you can pay me now. If you want anything else, you won't find it here tonight."

"Are you gonna let him talk to you thatta way, Gar?"

Katlyn picked out a raven-haired woman yelling out from the back of the group. Her dress hung off her shoulders at such a low angle most of her bosom was exposed.

"Ah, shut up, Millie, I'm plum tuckered out," the cowboy to her right groaned.

"Yeah," someone else agreed. "Can't you keep yer woman quiet, Gar? Them mustangs nearly done me in."

"All I wanna do is get outta these damned boots," another man added. "Come on, Gar, give him his money and let's get our whiskey and settle in. There's always tomorrow night."

Gar narrowed his eyes on Case. "No one points a gun in my face and lives to tell about it, mister."

"Then I guess you'll have to kill me. Now, do you want the rooms or not?"

After another tense silence, several men burst out in laughter, cajoling and teasing Gar. Finally, a small twisted smile lifted one corner of his narrow lips. "A jokester, huh? Well, I ain't laughin'. But since my boys are tired, we'll take the rooms. And the whiskey."

Ever so slowly, Case lowered his gun, keeping his trigger finger ready. "And I'll take your money."

"What happened at home tonight?" Katlyn said to Becky and Bucky after Case left with Tuck to see to it the rabble-rousers were all safely in their rooms for the night.

Bucky shrugged. "Nothin' new." He fluffed the pillow on his pallet and lay down.

Becky stood nearby waiting for her brother to settle into his makeshift bed. Emily who, disturbed by the noise, had followed Becky downstairs, looking for her daddy, now rested cuddled in Becky's arms, her head on Becky's shoulder.

"Pa went after us both with a broken whiskey bottle, so we run out and come here," Becky said, sounding unconcerned, as if it had happened so many times it didn't matter any longer. "Mr. Durham lets us do that, you know."

"I know. I'm glad you have somewhere to come."

Case had practically adopted the twins. As demanding and strict as he was at times, he treated them more like his own children than employees. He was a good, solid man and a loving father. And at the same time he could be shrewd and fiercely protective. Somehow, tonight, he'd diffused a highly volatile and dangerous situation and managed to turn a very tidy profit out of it. How could she help but admire him?

She saw an image of him in Emily's frightened eyes now and it made her heart ache for him and for his child. What was the cause of the pain she'd seen in both father and daughter's eyes? They shared so much love, yet a shadow of sadness seemed to hang over them both.

She felt a sudden longing to be able to lift Emily from Becky's arms and cradle her to her own breast. The child looked angelic in her little white cotton gown, her chestnut hair curling down her back in a tangled mass. How confusing and scary all of this commotion must be to her, Katlyn thought, looking down into Emily's innocent face.

"Your daddy is taking good care of all of us," she said softly, hoping to soothe Emily's fears. "He's a very kind, brave man so there's nothing for you to worry about."

Bucky pulled a quilt over himself and snuggled down into the warmth of it. "Yeah, well, he didn't look so nice tonight when he was starin' at that Gar fella," he said, his voice warm with respect. "He'd a taken on all those cowboys tonight, every last one of 'em, if they'd a gave him any more lip. They'd a found out they were foolin' with the wrong man but fast. He had that look in his eye.'' He rose up on one elbow and glanced at Becky. "Know what I mean, Beck?"

Becky nodded. "Yep. We seen him get riled a couple a times. Believe me, Miss Rose, you don't want to."

Her image of Case, looming over Gar, the threat in his eyes a warning without words, backed Bucky's claim. "You're probably right about that. But at least he managed to avoid a confrontation tonight."

"Let's hope he can do it again tomorrow," Becky said.

"I'm sure he can and will."

Bucky gave a mighty yawn and Katlyn bent to brush his wild hair out of his eyes. She kissed him lightly on the forehead, smiling at his grimace at what he considered womanly fussing, and pulled the quilt back up around his chin.

"I think we all could use some sleep," she said.

"I know I can. I'm tuckered out," Becky said. She shifted Emily in her arms and headed for the stairs. "'Night, Bucky."

"'Night, all," Bucky answered, dousing the lamp at his bedside.

Katlyn followed Becky and Emily to the stairs. She smiled when Emily offered Bucky a little wave over Becky's shoulder.

"Emily," she ventured, keeping her voice cautious and low, "I can carry you up to bed, if you'd like. Becky's arms may be getting a little tired."

Becky stopped at the foot of the stairs. "You are gettin' to be an armful, you know that, little girl?"

Emily lifted her head from Becky's shoulder and brushed the hair from her eyes. She stared through the semidarkness, searching Katlyn's face. Katlyn held her breath, hoping with some inexplicable desperation that the child would give her this chance to open her arms to her. She smiled and held out her hands.

Emily started to reach back, then, as though someone or something silently forbade her, she shied away, clinging instead all the more to Becky's neck.

Why her heart sank, Katlyn couldn't have said. She knew Emily never responded to strangers, and she was little more than that to the girl. But the rejection hit somewhere deep in her, in a place where she longed to give the kind of warm, tender love her mother was never able to give to her.

"Are all of you still here?" Case said, coming up from behind them. Immediately Emily wiggled around in Becky's hold and stretched out her arms for Case's neck.

"Come here, you little scamp." Case reached for his daughter and pulled her against his broad chest. "You should be in bed, you know that?"

Emily nodded, then squeezed his neck as if she'd never let him go. "It was noisy and everyone was shouting and I wanted you, Daddy."

Katlyn looked down at her toes, blinking back tears.

The child in her, who never knew even her father's

name, felt the emptiness of never having had that kind of love. The woman in her longed to give it.

Case kissed Emily. "It's all quiet now, honey. Don't worry, everyone in the hotel is sound asleep. Just as you two should be," he said, ruffling Becky's hair, making her smile, and then herding her up the stairs ahead of him and Emily.

Becky chattered at him all the way, telling him about some game she and Emily had played that day. Katlyn marveled that the episode in the lobby only a short half hour ago seemed to have already fled Becky's mind. Emily giggled a little when Case appeared to disapprove upon hearing of her sneaking into his bedroom and making his wardrobe her pretend castle, but he couldn't keep up his stern expression for more than a minute.

Their togetherness made Katlyn feel like an extra wheel on the wagon. She so wanted to be a part of their lives, more than just the singer they relied on to bring in business. I might as well wish for a fairy godmother, she told herself. She could never forget it was Penelope Rose everyone wanted, not Katlyn McLain.

On the landing she turned to her room then paused before going inside and looked to Case, making herself smile. "I want to tell you how impressed I was with the way you handled those cowboys. It could have been—" thinking of the children she hesitated "—much worse."

A low rumble of laughter rose in Case's throat, never quite leaving his lips. "It's hardly the first time, the girls can tell you that, although I'd like to make it the last.''

He shifted Emily so her head rested on his shoulder. ''Are you tired or can you come with me to tuck these ladies in?''

Before Katlyn could think of what to say to his unexpected offer Becky pleaded, ''Please, Miss McLain?''

''This has been an upsetting night,'' Case added. ''Maybe we could talk you into a singing lullaby.''

At that, Emily's head came up off Case's shoulder bobbing enthusiastically, her hair flying every which way. Becky echoed her with a beaming smile.

The sight lifted Katlyn's spirits instantly, easing her sense of not belonging. ''I'd love to.''

Side by side, Case and Katlyn walked to Emily's room and helped the girls back into Emily's bed. Katlyn kissed Becky on the cheek, but hesitated before moving to Emily. The little girl was so skittish and shy, would a kiss frighten her? When she turned to Case for guidance, she found him watching her with an intent expression on his face.

As though he read her thoughts, Case kissed Emily on the forehead and motioned for Katlyn to come near. ''Miss McLain likes good-night kisses, too, sweetheart. Do you think we could share ours with her?''

Emily studied Katlyn for a moment then looked back at her father. ''You first.''

''Happy to oblige,'' Case murmured.

''Oh, that's not—'' Katlyn began.

Words deserted her when Case put his hand against her hair and gently pressed his lips to her temple. His mouth lingered against her skin just long enough to become a caress rather than a brief touch.

Katlyn hoped the dim lamplight hid the flush warming her face. Equally, she prayed it disguised the longing welling up in her at Case's nearness. If he looked closely, she was sure he could see it in her eyes and she didn't want to humiliate herself by letting him see how much he affected her.

"And now it's your turn," Case said to Emily.

"If she wants to," Katlyn added quickly, determined she wouldn't press the little girl into doing something upsetting to her.

"Okay," Emily said in a small voice.

Her heart in her throat, Katlyn stepped close to the bedside and brushed a kiss on Emily's cheek. When she pulled away, she saw a tiny smile.

"Can she sing now?" Emily asked. "I want to hear the princess song."

"Oh, that's my favorite, too," Katlyn said. "I was hoping you would like it."

Case sat back in a nearby rocking chair while Katlyn perched at the foot of the bed and began to sing. Silver moonlight from the window behind him coupled with the diffused gold from the lamp and cast Katlyn in a heavenly glow. It wove through her hair and warmed her skin, and lent her a serenity that enhanced the clear beauty of her voice.

Watching her for a time, he eventually found himself leaning back in his chair and simply listening to her song, feeling the tensions in him ebb. When Katlyn sang like this, from the heart, Case wondered how anyone could be unmoved.

Katlyn finished the last of the lullaby on a whisper. Glancing around the room, she smiled, finding she'd put her entire audience to sleep and for once, was glad to find it so.

After checking to see the blankets were tucked around Emily and Becky, she walked silently to where Case sat, his chair still rocking slightly. Eyes closed, his face was turned toward the moonlight so that the angles of his cheek and jaw radiated in the pure excellence of their forms. He dwarfed the chair, looking almost ridiculous with his long legs stretching far out over the rug at the foot of it.

She hated to have to waken him but she couldn't leave him sleeping in a chair all night. Reaching for his shoulder, her hand slid to his cheek instead. She stroked the bristled side of his chiseled jaw, hoping her light touch would waken him before he realized the cause.

Before his eyes opened, his hand moved from his lap to capture hers. Katlyn swallowed a surprised gasp.

"I needed to wake you, you can't sleep here all night," she whispered, very aware of the pressure of his fingers against hers. "But I didn't know how."

Ever so slowly, Case opened his eyes and moved her palm to his lips. "Yes, my songbird, you did."

Chapter Eight

Katlyn sat on the stage next to the piano and stretched out her legs. After nearly two hours of practicing with Jack, she nearly gave in to her yearning to yank off her shoes and fling them aside.

"Not a very ladylike position for the famous Penelope Rose," Jack observed. He sat at one of the card tables, slouched in a chair, boots propped up on the table's edge, flipping through one of the monte decks.

Katlyn made a face at him. "You should talk."

"Ah, but I'm no lady."

"No, you're incorrigible," Katlyn said, laughing.

Jack grinned back at her. "All part of my charm, ma'am."

The door to the saloon creaked out a few inches and both Katlyn and Jack tensed at the sound, turning quickly to look.

Normally, they took any interruption of their practicing in stride. It wasn't unusual for one of the other staff or hotel guests or even Case to stop and listen.

But for the past two days, since Gar and his companions had arrived, everyone at the St. Martin had been on edge.

Sleep had eluded Katlyn since the other night when after singing Emily and Becky to sleep, Case had simply walked her to her door and bid her good-night with a chaste touch of his lips to her forehead. Her nights had been unsettled, disturbed by disjointed dreams of Case, of her mother, of Emily, of her own childhood and of dangerous outlaws.

The unwelcome visitors had already caused two minor scuffles in the saloon, had Becky in tears with their crude remarks, and disrupted Katlyn's singing with their rowdiness and demands she sing several bawdy tunes. When she refused they joined in to sing them loudly and off-key, driving away several other guests.

Last night Case had finally demanded they leave before noon today, and Katlyn hoped they would be gone by the time she and Jack finished this morning's practice.

The door edging open brought Jack to his feet, but before either he or Katlyn could react, Emily peeked around the corner. She froze when she saw them looking at her.

"It's all right, Emily," Katlyn said as gently as she could. She went to the door and knelt beside the little girl. "Did you come to hear us practice?"

Emily hesitated a moment, then nodded.

"Well, come inside. I was just about to sing our

favorite song, the one about the princess and the prince and the dragon. I know you like that one.''

Getting to her feet, Katlyn stepped back to let Emily edge her way into the saloon. Emily seemed reluctant to go any farther than just inside the door.

Katlyn only smiled and moved back to sit on the stage.

''You know,'' she said, not looking at Emily and keeping her voice deliberately nonchalant, ''I taught Jack this song and he's pretty good at making the dragon sounds on the piano.''

Emily looked doubtfully at Jack and back to Katlyn, who shrugged, barely glancing at Emily. ''It's true, even the fire-breathing sound.''

''You're a good teacher, Miss Katlyn,'' Jack said.

''Mmm…I don't think she believes me. I suppose we'll have to show her.''

Shaking his head at her none too subtle enticement, Jack started playing the melody to Katlyn's princess song. As she sang the words, pausing from time to time for Jack's dragon sounds, Katlyn noticed with delight that Emily began to move a little closer to the stage.

The little girl kept her back to the wall, but by the end of the song, she'd crawled under one of the tables near to where Katlyn sat, watching intently.

''I do like that song,'' Katlyn said. ''You know, I'll bet you have a pretty voice, Emily. Maybe one day you'll let me teach you a song and we could sing together.''

Emily said nothing but looked hard at Katlyn as if giving the idea serious consideration.

Encouraged, Katlyn started slowly singing a little Irish tune about a mischievous leprechaun, giving Emily time to learn the words and melody. Even though the little girl didn't join in, Katlyn had the impression she wanted to, except fear or shyness, or a combination of both kept her silent.

Katlyn thought she even glimpsed the start of a smile on Emily's mouth as she and Jack laughed over Jack's mistake with the chorus when the saloon doors shoved open and Gar and one of the men with him swaggered into the room.

"Ain't this a pretty scene?" Gar sneered.

"The saloon is closed," Katlyn said. She deliberately moved to stand by Emily's table, letting her skirts shield Emily from view.

She met Gar's leer squarely, determined not to let him intimidate her.

"As long as there's whiskey here, it ain't closed." Gar sauntered up to her and looked her up and down. "Maybe you'd like to join us. A shot of whiskey down that pretty throat might make you a little more friendly."

From behind him, Gar's companion sniggered. He was already behind the bar, searching out the whiskey bottles.

"The only thing that would make me feel more friendly is seeing the back of you as you're leaving," Katlyn snapped. Emily gave a whimper and Katlyn stiffened against the impulse to sweep the little girl into her arms. "Now get out before someone throws you out."

"You heard the lady," Jack said, coming up beside her.

"And who's gonna throw me out? You?" Before Jack could react, Gar made a quick turn and swung a fist into his jaw.

Jack fell backward over a table. Katlyn, seeing Gar intended to go after him, snatched up a chair and flung it at Gar, hitting him in the ear and shoulder.

He cursed and whirled on her. But he took only one step in her direction, then a shot rang out, stopping him cold.

Case stood in the doorway, his six-shooter aimed directly at Gar. Tuck and Bat stood behind him.

"All of you out, now. Or I'll be calling the sheriff to haul what's left of you away."

Gar returned Case's unwavering stare and for a moment, Katlyn thought he would refuse and force a confrontation.

But at last, Gar jerked his head to his companion and they pushed out of the saloon. He stopped at the door to glare at Case.

"This ain't over."

"If you're smart, it is. Make sure they leave," Case said to Tuck and Bat.

When they'd gone, Katlyn let go of the breath she'd been holding, relief shuddering through her. She turned and knelt by the table. "You can come out now, Emily. They're gone."

Case strode up to them as Emily scrambled out

from under the table and flung her arms around his neck. He gathered her close and asked softly, "Are you all right, sweetheart?"

Emily nodded into his shoulder then lifted her head to look at him. "She hit him," she whispered. "She's as brave as the princess."

"She did better than the dragon," Jack said, coming up to them, rubbing at his jaw. "You got a pretty good swing, princess." He grinned at Katlyn then winced.

"You're going to have a pretty good bruise," Katlyn observed. Seeing the stony look on Case's face, she said quickly, "I'm not sure how brave it was. If you hadn't come when you did—"

"Oh! Are you all right?" Becky dashed into the room and ducked between Case and Katlyn to touch a hand to Emily. Sally followed behind her, shaking her head when she saw the purpling mark on Jack's face.

"Bat told us what happened," Becky said. "I sure 'nough will be happy to see the backs of those varmints."

"Why don't we go into the kitchen? I think Tuck has some apple cider and cookies," Sally suggested. She motioned to Jack. "I'll see what we can do about that jaw of yours, too."

Emily's eyes brightened at the mention of cookies and Case reluctantly let his daughter slide out of his arms to take Becky's hand. Becky led Emily out of the saloon, chattering to the little girl, followed by Sally and Jack.

Left alone, Katlyn and Case looked at each other, her gaze confused, his cold.

Then he abruptly turned and stalked off in the direction of the door.

"Wait!" Katlyn ran to catch up to him. She grabbed at his sleeve, tugging him around to face her again. "I'm sorry about what happened but you can hardly blame Jack and me for the trouble that rustler and his friend caused. You were the one who said they could stay to begin with."

"I don't need you to remind me of that. But Emily and this hotel are mine to protect. No one is going to take them away from me."

"I never doubted that," Katlyn said, not understanding his declaration. "Jack and I were only trying to help."

"Well, you and your friend weren't much help, were you?"

Katlyn pulled back as if he'd struck her. The hectic color in her face left over from the confrontation with Gar suddenly fled, leaving her pale. "That's not fair," she said quietly.

"No, you're right. It's not."

Case strode over the bar, rummaged for a bottle of whiskey and poured himself a generous shot. He tossed it back, hardly feeling it burn its way down his throat.

He wasn't being fair or honest with her. But the truth was seeing her and Emily with Jack Dakota, imagining what had gone on before Gar interrupted, had provoked an unexpected and wholly irrational jealous anger in him.

After the fight to put the past behind him, to bring Emily here, to make the St. Martin succeed, he refused to let anyone come between him and what was his.

Except he had no right, no reason, to think of Katlyn as his.

"Why did you come here?" Katlyn's soft voice broke into his dark reverie.

Case looked at her, standing a few feet from him as if she was afraid to come any nearer. "Here?"

"To Cimarron, to this hotel. Why is it so important?"

"It's a good investment, don't you think?" Case said with a derisive laugh. "You know what they say about hotel owners, only born fools and educated idiots choose the business. Maybe I was both, coming here. But it was far enough from Silver Springs."

"Why didn't you stay there, in Colorado?"

"Why didn't you stay in St. Louis?"

Instead of retreating from his caustic retort, Katlyn seemed to give it an honest consideration. "I wanted to get away," she said at last. "To find a place I belonged."

"And you didn't belong there, even with all your success? I find that hard to believe."

Katlyn shrugged, glancing away. She ran her fingers over a tabletop, making idle patterns. "You didn't answer my question. Why did you come here?"

"Because of Emily." Case came around the bar and leaned with his back against it. "I wanted to get her as far away from the past as I could make possible. I understand this country, these people, even the worst of them. I couldn't go East. Perhaps you can't understand this, given what you said. But I know where I belong, and I don't belong anywhere east of the Mississippi." He tossed a swig of whiskey back. "Not even close."

"I do understand," she said softly. "And I'm envious."

"You envious of me? You can't know how ridiculous that sounds."

"Why? Because of the past?"

"The past—"

He stopped and Katlyn waited, not daring to press him. She sensed he was weighing what to tell her, deciding if he could trust her with his confidences. Finally, he pushed upright and walked over to her, pulling out a chair for her and taking one opposite her when she sat.

"I married Emily's mother believing she was everything she appeared to be, sweet, innocent, sincere. She was the daughter of a family friend, I had no reason to doubt her when she said she loved me and wanted a life together."

He flexed a hand against the tabletop. Katlyn felt her breath catch in her throat.

"A month after we were married, she presented me with her six-month-old daughter. Her lover's child. She had married me, with her family's connivance, because she needed a name for her child." Case gave a harsh laugh, the bitterness in it bringing tears to Katlyn's eyes. "At least she went that far toward being respectable."

"But...you have Emily. What happened to your wife?"

"I don't know. She abandoned us a few months later, and several weeks after that she had the marriage annulled. As Emily got older, I realized no one in town would ever forget what had happened, so I left to protect her from being hurt by it."

"I can't imagine..." A tear slid down her face and Case realized she was crying for him and for Emily. "How could she just leave you, her daughter?"

"Emily is my daughter. No one will ever know differently."

It was a clear warning and Katlyn tried to think of something to say to reassure him she would never reveal his confidence to anyone.

But crowding out all her other thoughts was a sharpened fear of how much more of a risk her deception really was. She had been afraid of simply losing her job and her means of helping her mother.

Now she feared how much she would hurt Case if he ever discovered her deceit. He'd made it clear from the start how critical honesty was to him. Now she knew why. Even if she meant nothing to him, her dishonesty would scar him, leave him with more reason to fortify the wall he'd built around himself.

"I didn't intend to upset you," Case said. He touched her hand, drawing her gaze back to him.

"You—you didn't. I understand now, though, why the hotel's success is so important to you, why you're counting so much on my singing." And not just to him, she thought, thinking of Becky and Bucky, of Sally and the four boys she supported, and Bat, useless as a ranch hand with his maimed hand.

Case's fingers rubbed absently over hers, almost a caress. He barely touched her but the warm and rough feel of him sent shivers down her spine. Katlyn willed herself to stay still, to not think of all the times he'd touched her, held her, all the times she'd yearned for more than that brief temptation.

She had no right to want anything more from him. But reason didn't rule her longings.

She stood so quickly her chair tipped precariously backward. Case was suddenly too close and she didn't want to embarrass herself again by mistaking his kindness for something deeper.

Case followed her, blocking her retreat. "Why are you running?"

"I'm not running. I—I should go check on Emily and Jack."

He took a step closer so only a hand's breadth separated them. Katlyn wanted to look away from him, to put distance between them that would give her time to gather her wits, to breathe.

The unmistakable glint in his forest-green eyes compelled her to stay because it wasn't kindness or pity she saw there, but desire, pure and strong. It startled her and she had no idea what to do about it.

"What are you afraid of?"

"Nothing. I'm not afraid."

"Then why are you trembling?"

Very gently, Case brushed his fingertips over her face. It seemed to him he had been looking at her forever, but he had never seen her before now.

He had been seeing Penelope Rose, the singer he had only known from her letters, and seeing the woman who drove him to distraction with her attempts to change his hotel and his life.

Tonight he saw Katlyn, who was both, and yet so much more.

"Maybe you should be afraid," he said roughly. "We both should be. Because I can't pretend anymore I don't want this."

He slid his hand into her hair, pushing deep to curve his fingers against her nape and draw her against him, joining his mouth to hers in one fluid motion.

Katlyn forgot every reason she had for not being with Case like this. His mouth moved over hers, gently at first, as if he wanted to test the feeling between them. Then his tongue brushed against her lips, coaxing them open, and she felt her knees weaken, her senses flame in a breathtaking rush of heat.

Nothing she'd known before had prepared her for the potency of Case's kiss. She'd been kissed before but never this deeply, never with this seductive combination of tender and hard, demanding and giving.

Katlyn spread her fingers over his chest, leaning into him even as his hand against her back pressed her closer.

Case dragged his mouth from hers long enough to slowly kiss and taste his way from the sensitive point behind her ear down the delicate curve of her throat. When he returned his attention to her lips she made a small breathy sound of pleasure that turned his kiss hard and hot.

He broke it off suddenly, breathing fast.

Katlyn clutched the edges of his coat, afraid to let go for fear she'd collapse in a boneless heap at his feet.

"Please don't say you're sorry," she said. Her voice came out barely more than a whisper.

"It would be a lie." Case slid the pad of his thumb over her lower lip, watching her eyes darken to violet when he let his fingers skim lower to explore the delicate line of her jaw, the curve of her throat. "Is this the way you look at Jack?" he murmured.

Katlyn laughed shakily then, the uproar of feeling inside her finding some release. "Never. Are you jealous?"

"Never again," Case said and the low husky sound of his voice made her tremble. "I just wanted to hear you say it."

He stole whatever reply she might have made by covering her lips with his. And the moment their mouths joined she stole his reason.

He forgot responsibility, and business, and all his intentions to avoid emotional entanglements. There was only Katlyn, sweet and true and feeling so good in his arms, with her power to tempt him to dare to trust his feelings one last time.

"I lied to you," she whispered when they finally separated enough to breathe again.

The words jarred Case. He stared at her, not sure he wanted to know what she meant.

Katlyn smiled a little but her eyes reflected uncertainty. Her fingertips brushed his cheek in a quick, fluttering motion. "I am afraid. I've never...no one—"

She stopped, shaking her head, unable to tell him what she felt inside. How could she, when she couldn't explain it to herself?

"That's okay, sweetheart, you scare the hell out of me, too." He pulled her close against him, pressing his mouth to her temple. "But it's not enough to keep me away from you."

Not yet, Katlyn thought even as she moved further into his arms. *Not yet, but oh, how I wish it could be never.*

Chapter Nine

A tap at the door startled Katlyn from the musical arrangement she'd been working on at the desk in her mother's room to add to her growing repertoire. "Come in, Mrs. Donaldson," she said softly, trying not to wake her mother.

The door opened slowly and Becky poked her head around the corner. "Mrs. Donaldson let me in. I really need to talk to you about—"

Katlyn jumped from her chair, knocking her sheets of music off the desk. "No! Not here."

"Katie? What's the matter?" Penelope struggled to roll over toward the sound of voices.

"Nothing, nothing at all." Katlyn tried to hide the panic in her voice. "Don't try to sit up. It's someone from the hotel to see me, that's all. I'll only be a moment, I promise."

"But I'm sure I heard—"

"It's nothing, truly," Katlyn insisted. She hurried to the door and practically shoved Becky into the hallway, pulling the door closed behind them. Panting, her heart pounding, she struggled to compose herself, knowing how frantic she must appear to Becky. "Did you need something?"

Betsy studied Katlyn, cocking her head this way and that. "You seem all fussed. Is your friend that sick?"

Katlyn drew a calming breath. Becky hadn't seen Penelope. Of course she hadn't. If she'd so much as caught a single glimpse, even as young as she was she would have recognized the resemblance between mother and daughter.

"Yes, unfortunately, she is very ill. I didn't mean to be rude, but she needs absolute quiet."

"I'm real sorry, Miss McLain."

"Becky, you know you can call me Katlyn."

"Oh, yeah. It's kinda confusin', with you havin' all those names and all."

"I'm sure it is." *More than you know.* "Now, why did you come here? Is something wrong at the hotel?"

"Not wrong, exactly. It's just, me and Bucky found out today is Emily's birthday!"

Katlyn smiled at Becky's deliverance of the news as if it were a catastrophe. "That's not so terrible, is it?"

"Well, it is—not her havin' the birthday, I mean, but the party."

"What party?"

"That's just it! The party Mr. Durham asked me and Bucky to help with." Now that Becky started with her story, the words came tumbling out. "We ain't never had a real birthday party and Mr. Durham was askin' if we'd help fix up one fer Emily. I guess he thought we'd know about stuff like that, but we never had us a birthday party before. We asked Sally and Bat and Tuck, and they said they'd help when they could, but they was busy cleanin' up after all those cowboys and so I told Bucky I'd ask you. We was hopin' you'd have some ideas how to do it up right. Oh, Miss McLain you just got to help. We got all this shoppin' and bakin' and decoratin' to do. Mr. Durham give us some money to go buy what we need. 'Ceptin' we don't know what we need.''

Becky looked so piteous Katlyn put an arm around her shoulder and hugged her briefly. ''I think I can help. Go on down to the mercantile and tell them about the party. I'll be there in fifteen minutes and we'll decide what we need.''

''Oh, thank you! This is gonna be fun now!'' Becky said, her sunny nature restored the moment she had Katlyn's cooperation. ''I knew you'd know what to do.'' She turned and skipped downstairs.

Katlyn went to check on her mother, relieved to find Penelope had fallen asleep despite the unexpected visitor. She made sure Penelope was comfortable, then hurried out after Becky.

Here was her chance to do something for Case and Emily beyond her work at the hotel and she jumped at it. Somewhere in her heart, she realized she welcomed the chance because it brought her closer to them.

Her mind wouldn't admit that, though. Because

then she would have to admit how much she longed
for Case to see her as much more than just the St.
Louis Songbird.

And she could never let that happen.

"'Buy whatever you need to make the party special. Put it on my account.' That's what Mr. Durham
said." Becky's head bobbed in certainty.

Katlyn eyed the pile of ribbons, candies, toys and
ingredients for punch they had chosen from the store.
Their purchases lay in a heap on the counter, waiting
for Katlyn to give her permission for the sale. "This
seems extravagant."

"I think Mr. Durham'd get riled if we ain't done
it up right," Becky said. "He felt real bad about
nearly forgettin' Emily's birthday."

"Forgetting? Oh, I'm sure he didn't forget,
Becky."

"But he did! With all that trouble those cowboys
caused, he was so worried over everything he told us
her birthday just plain skipped his mind."

If Becky was right, Katlyn could well imagine how
Case must be feeling, Case who prided himself on
always being in control of everything around him.
She fingered a length of bright pink ribbon, already
thinking how she could use it to decorate the dining
room.

"All right. We'll take everything, then. After all,
this is a party!"

Several minutes later, their arms laden with packages, Becky and Katlyn walked alongside the bustling

street back toward the hotel. The early afternoon high country air was brisk, scented with the earthy smells of pine, horses and dust, the sun and scattered clouds making warm and cool patches on the worn sidewalk boards.

As they strolled along the plank walkway past the shops, a few people, mostly men, nodded toward Katlyn and Becky offering greetings to Katlyn as "Miss Rose." Katlyn felt uncomfortable responding, but what else could she do but smile and return a friendly, "Good day to you, too."

"What's the matter?" Becky scrunched up her nose and looked at Katlyn's flushed cheeks and stiff shoulders, perplexed. "Ain't it grand bein' famous and all?"

"I'm hardly famous," Katlyn said, her laugh a bit too wry. "I'm more likely to be thought of as infamous."

"Huh?"

"Nothing," she returned, eager to change the subject. "Oh, say, which is the other saloon Mr. Durham talks about, the Crooked Pony?"

"That rat trap? It's over there between the blacksmith's and the jailhouse. Why would you want to look at a place like that? The miners and cowboys only go there 'cause they got sportin' women."

"Becky!"

"Well, it's the truth. But our saloon's got you."

Katlyn shifted her packages and laughed. "I'll take that as a compliment," she said, shoving open the door to the St. Martin. They looked around the door to make certain Emily was nowhere in sight before slipping into the dining room to set down the party goods.

Bucky and Sally were there already, busily moving chairs aside and pushing tables together to make one long party table. Bucky looked up and wiped his forehead with a crumpled bandanna when he saw Katlyn and Becky.

"'Bout time you got back, Beck. Mr. Durham's gonna jump out of his skin if we don't get this place fixed up quick."

Katlyn tossed her shawl aside and began unwrapping packages. "Where is he? And where's Emily?"

"He's tryin' to keep her busy in her room, but she ain't dumb. She knows somethin's goin' on and wants to come down and have a look."

"We would have gotten a bit further along," Sally added, "but no one knew anything about a party until this morning. And Bat's still busy trying to get the saloon cleaned up."

"Well, don't worry. We'll have this place looking like a room out of a fairy tale in no time," Katlyn said. "Has Tuck started baking a cake yet?"

Becky and Bucky looked at each other and shrugged, and Sally shook her head.

Katlyn made a little *tsking* sound to herself, doled out instructions to all three as to where and how to drape the ribbons, place the favors, and start getting the games ready, then rushed out to the kitchen to talk to Tuck about the cake.

An hour later Katlyn went to hunt down an old

tablecloth Sally said was in an upstairs closet, and met Case coming down the stairs.

"You're here," he said, hurrying toward her.

Katlyn nearly laughed at how ruffled he looked, as if they were readying for a grand opening and expecting royalty, rather than a child's party. But she also remembered what Becky had said about his nearly forgetting Emily's birthday and guessed he must be feeling guilty at leaving all the preparations to his employees, rather than taking on the task himself.

She found herself wanting to soothe him and to let him know how good, how needed, it made her feel to be able to help organize this party for him and for little Emily, whom she'd grown to care for so deeply.

Case ran his fingers through his hair, shoving it away from his brow. "Did Becky find you?"

"Yes, and I know all about it. We'll be ready for Emily in about half an hour. Can you keep her occupied that much longer?"

Relief washed over Case's face, smoothing out the lines of tension. He took her hand and squeezed it. "Thank you. This day has to be special for her. You can't know how much she needs to feel important today, and I almost ruined it because I was so distracted by those damned rustlers."

"You were watching out for her, protecting all of us. Don't be so hard on yourself. Anyone could have forgotten."

"You wouldn't have."

"Oh, so you think I'm that organized, do you?" she said, laughing.

"No..." Case looked straight into her eyes. "I think you understand, better than anyone, how important it is to feel loved."

Unexpected tears sprang to Katlyn's eyes. She shook her head and looked away so he wouldn't see them. Drawing in a breath, she looked back at Case and smiled, her eyes bright with unshed tears. "Well, I do understand I'd better get back to decorating or there isn't going to be a party. You just keep that daughter of yours busy for a little while longer. Oh, and tell her to put on her best dress but don't tell her why. And make sure her eyes are covered when she walks into the dining room."

"Yes, ma'am. Anything else?"

"If I think of anything, I'll let you know." Impulsively, she reached up and kissed his cheek. "Thank you."

Case looked astonished. "What for?"

"For trusting me to do this. For making me feel I belong. You don't know how much I need that."

She pulled away from him then and hurried back to the dining room, leaving Case staring after her, struck by a satisfaction so sweet he hardly dared to trust it.

Case and Emily stood in the doorway to the dining room, Case's hands covering Emily's eyes. All the staff, Sally's boys, and two families with children

Emily occasionally played with stood waiting beside a table fit for a fairy princess.

Using techniques she'd learned from growing up around entertainers, Katlyn had ransacked the hotel for paper, paste, paints, bits and pieces of cloth, and all manner of bric-a-brac to create what amounted to a stage set for a little girl's fantasy party.

Case couldn't help but admire her talent as he scanned the amazing scene Katlyn had conjured from odds and ends. The chandeliers were all hung with bright ribbons and paper cutouts of stars and moons and hearts. The plain white linens had been altered in some way with ribbons and some floral fabric to look like a magical flower garden had bloomed all over the long guest table.

Big poster-like pictures hung on the walls, some for decoration, some obviously put up to use in games. Each chair was draped in ribbons and bows, and at the head of the table one chair had been decorated to look like a princess's throne.

His eyes met Katlyn's and he tried to tell her without words how much her effort meant. She smiled and gave him a wink, and then gestured for him to uncover Emily's eyes.

"Okay, honey, one, two, three—"

As Case took away his hands from Emily's eyes, everyone in the room shouted, "Surprise!"

Caught off guard, Emily whirled and grabbed hold of Case's leg.

He bent and gently lifted her chin. "This is for you, Emily. A birthday surprise. Miss McLain and the others made all of this for you because you're a very special little girl.''

Slowly, Emily turned back to look over the room, her eyes growing wide and round in utter amazement. Finally her smile broke through and she beamed up at Case.

''Oh, Daddy, it's beautiful,'' she whispered, awestruck. ''It looks like the palace in the song she sings about the princess and the dragon.''

Case lifted Emily into his arms and carried her to her make-believe throne. ''Well, today, this is your palace, sweetheart.''

Katlyn made her way to where Emily sat and pulled out something she'd been hiding behind her back. It was a false diamond tiara her mother had found stuffed in a roll of stockings after their arrival in Cimarron. Luckily, it had escaped the notice of the stagecoach robbers that day.

With reverence, Katlyn gently placed the tiara on Emily's head. ''And today, as the princess, you'll wear this crown. A treasure just for you.''

A round of applause followed and Emily was quickly swept up into the excitement of the party. Before he was drawn into the lively group, Case bent and whispered in Katlyn's ear so only she could hear.

''Emily may be the princess today, but you, Katlyn, are the queen.''

''Fine entertainment, that. You plannin' on spendin' the rest of the night here?''

Gar ignored Jed's taunt and kept his eyes fixed on

the St. Martin Hotel. Through windows he could glimpse snatches of the ongoing party. He spat out a long stream of tobacco before answering.

"Too many people there now. That bastard ain't worth getting' myself filled with lead or tossed in a jail cell over."

Jed shrugged. "You'll be lucky if it don't happen anyway. But you please yourself. I'm goin' to find myself a bottle."

Gar stayed still a moment longer then followed Jed in the direction of the saloon at the far edge of town. "I'll have one myself to pass the time. Then I plan on comin' back to teach Case Durham a lesson. No one points a gun in my face without learnin' to regret it."

Case pulled down the last of the ribbon streamers from the doorway of the dining room and tossed it into the crate Katlyn had left for him. She sat on the bottom stair with her chin resting on her palms and he smiled at the picture she made.

Her hair, which usually resisted any attempt to tame it, had half escaped from its pins and curled wildly around her face. Pink icing smudged her dress and the yellow calico looked as limp and faded as a waterless flower.

"You look as if you could use a restorative," he said, coming over to her and offering her a hand.

"I'm not sure you have anything reviving enough," Katlyn said as she allowed him to help her to her feet.

Case laughed as he led her to the couch in the foyer. "Wait here, I'll see what I can do."

He returned a few minutes later carrying two mugs of coffee and handed one to her. "Extra honey and cream and Tuck said he brewed it twice as strong, just for you." Waiting until she had taken a sip and sighed in blissful appreciation, Case said, "I want to thank you for today. Everything went perfectly."

Katlyn bent her face over her mug to hide her flush of pleasure. "You're welcome. I'm happy both you and Emily were pleased." She shot him a mischievous glance. "You haven't always been so happy with my interference."

"Your interference hasn't always been the most practical," Case countered, any sting in the words diluted by the teasing glint in his eyes. "Wanting to extend the dining room wallpaper to Tuck's kitchen, for example."

"Well—" Katlyn shifted, a little embarrassed. "I'll admit, I get carried away sometimes."

"Sometimes?" Laughing at her indignant expression, Case held up a hand to ward off her protest. "Okay, I'll admit, I like most of your ideas. But I also have to be sure I'm getting my money's worth."

"Well, except for your questionable taste in curtains, I don't think you've done too badly."

"Just look at my choice of singers. You've done more for my business than any other investment I've made. I was right to trust your ability."

Katlyn blushed and couldn't quite meet his eyes. "I hope you'll never regret hiring me. And I have to thank you for letting me be a part of something so worthwhile. There's so much potential here. Why, a year from now, no one will ever remember the St. Martin's shady past.''

She rushed into an explanation of an idea she had for redecorating the upstairs rooms, trying to cover her confusion at Case's unexpected warm praise. She didn't deserve it or his trust. But having someone appreciate her for talents that all her life most people had considered impractical and frivolous filled her with a rush of satisfaction.

It rested like a warm golden glow inside her, overshadowing the guilty whisper reminding her she had no right to it.

Case suppressed a smile as he listened to her, finding her enthusiasm infectious. The way she described his hotel, it seemed more flesh and blood and soul than an investment in wood and stone.

Watching her, her color high and her eyes dancing, he believed at that moment that she alone had breathed life into the St. Martin. And into his spirit.

''You know, you've made yourself almost indispensable,'' he said thoughtfully when she finally paused for breath. ''With your singing, the restoration, and now this party. Today was the first time I've seen Emily really enjoy herself in a long while.''

Katlyn chewed at her lower lip then asked, ''Has she always been so—withdrawn?''

She nearly regretted the question when Case's face took on the tenseness she knew so well. ''She's been that way for about a year. A few months before we left Silver Springs, someone told Emily her mother had abandoned her. That's one of the main reasons we left. I was afraid Emily had begun to feel she wasn't important to anyone. No one, especially a child, should ever feel they're not worthy of being loved.''

Tears pricked at Katlyn's eyes. She fussed with putting down her now-empty mug on the table beside her. ''You were right, before. I do understand,'' she said in a voice she struggled to keep light and level. ''I never knew my father and it always made me feel different, separated from other people. My mama was always so busy with her work, I missed being part of a family.''

She brushed at an imaginary speck of dust on her skirt then flashed him a smile that was over-brilliant in her attempt to appear nonchalant. ''I used to sit alone in my room and invent a family and make up conversations for them. I'm sure people thought I was crazy, talking to myself.''

Her forced brightness drew no answering smile from Case. ''Not crazy, just lonely. That's what I'm afraid of, that I can never be enough for Emily.''

''But you've done a wonderful job with Emily! It's so obvious you love each other and that's all that's important.''

In her anxiousness to convince him, Katlyn reached out to grip his arm. Almost instantly, a heated intensity flashed in his eyes, changing her intent to reassure and comfort into sudden longing for something darker and forbidden.

"You really believe that, don't you?" he asked. He searched her face as if trying to convince himself she was real. "How have you stayed so innocent, after all you must have experienced? It's as if none of it touched you."

Katlyn jerked her hand back as if burned. She didn't need to guess what experience he referred to. He rightly thought her worldly, provocative, expected she had known other men.

Just like Penelope had been. While she loved her mother and would do anything to protect her, Katlyn had no illusions about Penelope's past. Her mother was well aware of her attraction and had used it to her advantage. And Katlyn knew she'd had several suitors, although none of them had been allowed to become too permanent.

But I'm not Penelope, she thought. The longing to tell him rose up fiercely inside her. *I'm not like that, and he'll never know.*

And suddenly, despite the impossibility and the consequences, she wished more than anything that he did.

Chapter Ten

"I do know."

Katlyn wasn't aware she'd spoken the last words out loud until Case's deep voice came into her thoughts.

"But you can't! I mean—"

Case took her hand and very slowly drew her closer to him. The need and desire in his eyes, hers alone, was so compelling Katlyn couldn't have resisted even if she had wanted to.

"I know more than you realize," he said softly. "And right now, the rest of your secrets don't seem that important."

Though the very air between them was charged with anticipation, at first he did nothing more than stroke the length of her fingers with his.

She quivered at the bare touch. When he lifted her hand, palm up, and pressed a kiss against her wrist, his tongue flicking at the delicate skin, Katlyn let go a shuddering breath. Closing her eyes, she tried to think, but could only feel.

Case forced himself to move slowly. He lightly kissed her shoulder, her throat, and felt her pulse skitter and her breath quicken at the caress of his mouth.

Smiling to himself, he grazed the corner of her mouth with the lightest of touches once, and again until she trembled, part impatient, part needy. Only then did he claim her lips, abandoning seduction for desire when she gave a little moan and opened her mouth to his.

Katlyn's hands flattened against his chest as Case gathered her into his arms. He had earlier shed his jacket and vest and his shirt was a thin barrier between her palms and the hardness and heat of him.

His tongue swept the inside of her mouth, tangling with hers, as his kiss grew more demanding. In a part of her mind, Katlyn heard a faint voice warning her from letting this go any further, any deeper.

But she deliberately ignored it and instead let herself be drawn into the storm Case started inside her. Her whole body felt taut and restless, needy for something she knew only he could give. She wound her hands around his neck to bring them closer.

Case responded immediately, in one motion pulling her up against him and guiding her back until she lay against the arm of the sofa. His mouth never left hers and he continued kissing her until Katlyn believed she would melt inside.

Vaguely, she felt his hand move over her, sliding down her shoulder, the hollow of her throat, then to her breast. The intimate touch shocked her senses like a lightning strike. She felt her nipple harden under his palm and her lower belly clench and quiver even as her mind confronted her with what she had invited, what she wanted.

What she could never have.

Case felt her hesitation though he didn't understand it. He swore from her response she wanted this as much as he did. But at the same time she reacted like an innocent, unprepared for the full force of passion.

He realized, too, he had been close to making love to her in his foyer, in plain view of anyone who happened to come into the hotel or down the staircase. For someone who prided himself on his control, he had shown a distinct lack of it the moment Katlyn looked at him with longing in her eyes.

Sitting up Case brought her with him and cradled her against his chest, stroking her tumbled hair to give some outlet to his need to touch her as much as to soothe her.

"Case..." Though her face pressed against his shirt, muffling her voice, Case heard the hurt she couldn't quite disguise. "I—I'm sorry, I—"

"Don't be," he said. He took her face in his hands, willing her to look at him. "I don't want to take you anywhere you're not ready to go, no matter how much I want to."

I am ready, Katlyn told him silently. But the truth was she had no idea what admitting that meant and no right to want it to begin with. How could she ever think of surrendering herself, heart and body, to him when she was living this lie? When she knew she would one day have to leave him to give her mother the care she needed? She could never allow herself to love Case Durham.

Except she feared it might already be too late.

"It's late," Case said, his words jolting her. Reluctantly, he let her go and got to his feet. He held out a hand to help her up. "I'll walk you to your room."

Katlyn wanted to say something to him, but anything short of the full truth seemed either dangerous or foolish.

In silence, she walked with him up the stairs, pausing with her hand on her doorknob to tell him goodnight.

He stopped her from going in by bending and kissing her. It started as a light caress but Katlyn easily released the knob to wrap her arms around his neck. He pulled her to him almost at the same time, and it flared quickly into a passionate embrace.

After a minute, Case ended it, not trusting himself to be near her any longer and resist temptation. He took a step back.

"Good night, Katlyn," he said, his voice not quite steady.

"Good night." She said it quickly and then rushed inside her room, shutting the door in a hurry against the longing to throw herself back into his arms again.

Leaning back against the door, Katlyn wrapped her arms around herself in a vain attempt to stop the trembling inside. She listened for the sound of Case's footsteps moving away but he didn't go.

Instead she heard the slight rattle of the doorknob

as if he reached out a hand to fling open the door then drew back. She closed her eyes, imagining him there, wishing he would come to her, praying he would leave before she begged him to stay.

Finally she heard him stride down the hallway and down the stairs. And then she heard nothing but the rapid pulse of her own heart.

Gunshots and the crash of splintering wood and the shattering of glass jolted Katlyn awake shortly after midnight.

She tumbled out of bed and into the hallway, not stopping for her robe or to wonder if it was wise to venture beyond her door.

She met Case halfway up the hall. He had his six-shooter already in hand and Katlyn didn't need an explanation when he held her gaze for an instant then glanced back at the door to his rooms.

Without a word between them, Katlyn nodded and hurried to stay with Emily, answering Case's unspoken entreaty.

Katlyn found Emily huddled in her bed, all wide, scared eyes and quivering mouth. She climbed into the bed with the little girl, wrapping her in blankets and holding her close.

What seemed like hours later, after more gunfire and earsplitting shouts and crashes, silence finally settled over the hotel.

Easing back from a now-sleeping Emily, Katlyn moved to a chair by the stove in the sitting room and waited what seemed an endless time. Her imagination running amok, she braced herself to face the worst of whatever had happened.

Case eased the door shut behind him and moved quietly into his sitting room. Curled up in a chair by the stove, Katlyn had fallen asleep. He stood just looking at her for a moment.

In her white cotton nightdress, her hair loose and tumbled around her face and shoulders, she looked impossibly young and innocent. He brushed a curl back from her cheek, just grazing her skin, and she sighed, murmuring his name.

Case felt something twist in his chest and he quickly stepped away, going into Emily's room to check on his daughter. Satisfied she was sleeping soundly, he tucked the blankets up around her and gently kissed her forehead before leaving her to her dreams.

At Katlyn's side he again hesitated, then touched her shoulder and softly said her name.

Her eyes fluttered open and she blinked sleepily. When she focused on him she bolted upright in the chair. "Oh, thank heavens you're back. What happened? It sounded so awful down there, I've been having nightmares."

Case gave her a brief, humorless smile. He sat heavily in the chair next to her, leaning his head against the chair back. "Everything is quiet, and that's the best I can say for it right now."

Fully awake now, Katlyn took in how tired and battered he looked. A bruise was beginning to darken the side of his jaw, and the knuckles of both his hands were scraped and bleeding.

Any awkwardness she might have felt, being alone with him, dressed only in her nightgown, after what had happened between them earlier, instantly vanished.

"Case—" She knelt beside his chair. "What happened?"

He shifted in his chair to look at her and she saw his involuntary wince of pain. Katlyn frowned but he shrugged it off.

"It's nothing. I need to learn to duck."

"You're a bad liar. I hope whoever did this looks worse than you."

"Gar. He decided to pay us another visit." Case told her as briefly as possible, skimming over the damage to the downstairs rooms, although he knew she guessed from what he didn't say how bad it was.

"The sheriff has them now," he finished. "But they've shut us down for a few weeks at least. The saloon is the worst, which means we're both out of business." He shoved a hand through his hair, shaking his head. "I just hope we can survive this. It's going to take a helluva lot of time and money to repair everything."

Case looked at her fully, trying to gauge her reaction. Her face told him nothing. She remained motionless beside him, her hand on his arm. "Look, I'm sorry, I know you didn't expect any of this when you agreed to come here."

He waited and still she stayed silent, her eyes abstracted as if she were lost in thought. "Katlyn—"

"Yes, I was thinking...there's probably space in the dining room, although it would take some maneuvering," she said more to herself than him. "Tuck will probably complain but that can't be helped. If we—"

She broke off as Case started to laugh, holding a hand to his aching ribs. "What is it?"

"I'm sorry." Though it tasted bitter, the laughter eased the tight knot of tension in him enough for him to appreciate Katlyn's stubborn optimism. "But only you would start making plans to renovate the dining room sitting here in your nightgown at 3:00 a.m., with the downstairs of my hotel practically in ruins. You truly are a treasure, Katlyn McLain."

"You need a drink," she said, secretly smiling to herself as she went to pour him a generous measure of whiskey. She waited until he'd drunk it back before insisting on tending to his various scrapes and bruises.

"I'm only just beginning to realize how talented you are," Case said, as she finished binding up his ribs.

"My half sister is a healer. I guess I learned a thing or two when I lived with her," she said, pulling snug the last wrap of bandage. She tried to keep her mind on nursing and not how good it felt to put her arms around him. Without his shirt, the sleek, hard muscle she'd pressed herself against just a few short hours ago was clearly defined, inviting her exploration.

She sharply reprimanded herself for her straying

thoughts, especially now, and focused on completing her task as quickly as possible. "I'm hardly as talented as either Isabel or Dr. Garrett. You'd be much better off with either of them. But I'm all you've got tonight."

"I'm not complaining."

When she straightened to move away from him, Case caught her hand and with a quick tug, pulled her into his lap.

He covered her mouth with his, silencing her yelp of surprise as he took advantage of her parted lips to kiss her deeply. The feel of Katlyn in his arms, warm and vibrant and responsive, kept at bay the black despondency he felt weighing on him, knowing the worst of what waited for him downstairs.

He wanted to bury himself in her sweetness, to forget for a few hours that, this time, nothing and no one might be able to rescue the St. Martin.

Caught defenseless, Katlyn tried to slow her slide into complete surrender. But with the feel of him under her hands, skin to skin, she knew it would be like trying to stop a runaway train.

"Case," she gasped as he worked free the first buttons of her high-necked gown and pushed the material aside to kiss her bared shoulder.

Case released two more buttons. He kissed the hollow of her throat, spellbound by the enticing whisper of lilac that clung there. "I need you, Katlyn. My beautiful songbird."

His words tore Katlyn's heart.

To know he needed her evoked a sweetness so intense it almost hurt.

To be reminded of her duplicity stabbed her with shame.

She put her hands between them, stopping his tormenting caresses. "I—I can't... Case, not here. I'm not—and Emily..."

Floundering for the right words, she couldn't meet his eyes when he pulled back to look at her. "I want...but not now. Not with everything—" Katlyn stopped, finally giving up. There was no way she could explain without telling him the truth. Her eyes pleaded for understanding.

Case stared at her, still bemused by the lingering sensual haze. He let her slip out of his arms and take a few unsteady steps away. "Katlyn—"

She turned her back to him as she fumbled with the buttons of her gown. When she looked back at him the misery on her face brought Case up out of his chair to her side.

"I won't apologize for wanting to make love to you," he said bluntly. "But this was the wrong time and place."

Color stained her pale cheeks but she held her ground. "Maybe it will never be right. I'm not who you think I am."

"I know the woman I want. And it will be right." He touched her cheek as if memorizing the curve of her face. "I promise you that. Because no matter how much you try to run from it, you want this as much as I do."

* * *

The first pale tendrils of dawn threaded through the cracks in the saloon windows as Case heaved a heavy oak table back onto its pedestal leg. He straightened and tried to ignore the ache in his ribs. Raking a hand through his hair, he took a long hard look at the remains of the saloon.

The damage was bad enough. It would take every cent he had left and far more to make repairs.

Worse, he didn't know if he could put the St. Martin back together and pay his staff at the same time. Becky and Bucky, Sally, Tuck, Bat—they all depended on the salary he paid.

And Katlyn, his songbird who sacrificed to save every penny to help her friend. What would she do when she discovered the full scope of the ruin?

One way or another, he would make certain that she and the others wouldn't have to worry. Righting a chair beside the table, Case decided the long night, toiling in the stench of sour whiskey, the wreckage of broken glass and splintered wood, had at least made one thing clear. If he had to sell his soul, everyone who depended on him would be paid and paid on time.

Katlyn stood in the doorway of the saloon, watching Case test the unsteady balance of a damaged table, her heart in her throat. A dark bristle of beard shadowed his jaw, partly concealing the bruise there, and he looked disheveled.

She could tell he hadn't slept. And she knew why.

Even from a distance, she read his thoughts as though they were her own. It wasn't the broken table at his fingertips or even his hotel commanding his attention now.

He was worrying far more about his daughter, and about everyone who worked for him, everyone who counted on him, everyone he was responsible for. Her eyes blurred with tears. The success of the St. Martin meant everything to him yet his concern was for the people he had adopted and given a place to belong, a purpose, a reason to be proud.

"Oh, Case…"

She hadn't realized she'd spoken his name until Case turned toward her voice. "Katlyn." He glanced around him, then gave her a twisted smile. "Not exactly a setting for respectable guests."

"I didn't realize this was so—" She followed his gaze around the broken room and couldn't keep the dismay from her face.

Sidestepping the debris around them, Case moved to her side. He reached out and touched a gentle finger to her lips. "Don't. There's nothing to say."

"But there is." Katlyn put her hand over his and brushed a kiss against his palm. "There's a great deal to say, and do."

"Yes, and I'll find a way to get it done," Case murmured, distracted by her enticing caress. "I promise you that."

"I don't need a promise. I know you will. You're a rare man, Case Durham. The sort of man I didn't think existed."

"Careful, or I'll start to believe you."

"You should. I've never known anyone like you."

It was true. Her mother had warned her she couldn't trust any man to act with his heart, but Case had proven Penelope wrong time and again.

From his loving care of an abandoned child to his concern for everyone who relied on him, he showed her daily the kind of man he was.

And, looking at him now, his hair ruffled as though he'd just rolled out of bed, his shirt carelessly unbuttoned and revealing a tempting mat of dark curls, his broad shoulders straining the material, he was so much more. He was everything male.

Everything any woman could want.

Everything she did not deserve.

"Don't worry, Katlyn," Case said, mistaking the emotion filling her eyes as fear. "I'll take care of everything. You don't have to wonder about your future, now or ever."

"*My* future is the least of my worries right now. We're going to start rebuilding, all of us."

"Today?"

"Right now. I've looked at the damage to the rest of the hotel. This is by far the worst."

"Can't argue there."

Squaring her shoulders and lifting her chin, Katlyn nodded briskly. "Then let's not waste time reminding ourselves how terrible it is. We have more important things to talk over. I have an idea."

Case laughed despite himself. "Why am I not surprised? Don't you always?"

"Hear me out, please."

"Do I have a choice?"

Hands on her hips, Katlyn raised a brow. "Do you still need to ask, Mr. Durham?"

Chapter Eleven

A loud gasp interrupted Katlyn's explanation, and both she and Case turned to the door, where Becky and Bucky stood gaping at the destruction.

"It looks like a cattle drive come through here," Bucky blurted. "Who got into a fight this time?"

He yelped when Becky dug her elbow into his ribs. "They don't want to talk about fightin' right now. Anyone with a brain can see that."

"What anyone can see is we got us one helluva mess here," Tuck said, he and Bat coming up behind the twins. Tuck pushed between them and gave the room a sweeping look. "Seems the devil had a party and invited all his friends. Everyone all right, Mr. Durham?"

Case waved the group inside. "As right as we're going to be under the circumstances." Briefly he told Tuck, Bat, and the twins about the night's events. He'd barely finished when Becky asked to go check on the still-sleeping Emily. Case let her go with a nod, then turned back to the others. "And now Katlyn is about to reveal her master plan for putting us back in business.''

Katlyn glared at him, irritated at the sarcastic edge to his words. ''Maybe you should save your judgment until you hear me out.''

''Maybe.'' He looked at her a moment, then shoved a hand through his hair and offered her a tired smile. ''Sorry, it's been a long night.''

''I know,'' Katlyn said softly. She touched his arm in understanding before facing the others again. ''Okay, here's what I have in mind. We can't use the saloon, maybe not for weeks. But that doesn't mean we're out of business.''

''Could've fooled me,'' Bat muttered, glancing around.

''It's not going to be easy, but the dining room is more or less intact. If we all pitch in, we can have it back in decent shape by Friday night. I propose we offer a dinner show, like the big hotels in St. Louis and San Francisco do. Granted it'll be quite a change, but my instincts tell me there are plenty of people who'll be willing to pay a fine price for a fancy dinner and a fine show.''

Pleased with her spur-of-the-moment solution, Katlyn looked at the faces of the others in anticipation. Their expressions weren't encouraging.

Bucky stared at her as if she'd lost her wits. Bat frowned and Tuck scratched his ear and made a harrumphing sound indicating his reluctance to tell her straight-out she was crazy.

Only the thoughtful expression in Case's eyes offered any hint that at least he saw possibilities in her idea. "A dinner show. In Cimarron."

"Well, yes. Why not?"

"Why might be a better question, Miss Katlyn," Tuck answered for Case. "I never heard of such a thing in these parts."

"It's just a fancier way of entertaining people, that's all. And it means we can ask for more money when they come in for the evening. Or, better yet, if we can draw from surrounding towns, they might stay the night. And it would only be temporary," Katlyn quickly added in hopes of convincing them all, "until we can get the saloon opened again."

"There are a lot of wealthy ranchers living outside this town whose wives rarely come to town because they don't think there's a decent place to go," Case said, turning the idea over in his mind. "They're the kinds of folks I'd hoped to appeal to when I bought this place. Lots of money and nowhere to spend it that's less than a day or two ride." Somehow, when Katlyn talked about it now, it didn't seem as outrageous, as if the suggestion had come from someone else.

"Well, I've heard 'em say their women complain there's no place around here worth dressing up for," Bat added.

Katlyn nodded. A growing enthusiasm for her project fizzed through her veins. "We can change that. But we'll need to get the word out to bring them in, advertise in the newspaper and post handbills. And we'll have to work on some special menus.'' She looked appealingly at Tuck.

''Now, Miss Katlyn, fancy food ain't exactly my strong point.''

''You can do it, I know you can,'' Katlyn said. ''I'm no cook, but I've seen enough elegant dishes prepared to show you how to present them. With your wonderful cooking and my decorating, we can't go wrong.''

Tuck gave up trying to resist her and grinned. ''Well, if you think puttin' ribbons and frills on my beans'll bring 'em runnin', then I'm willin' to give it a try.''

''They take one look at this and they'll be running for cover,'' Sally said from the doorway. She pulled off her bonnet and picked her way around the overturned tables and chairs to stand next to the others. ''What in the Lord's name happened here?''

''Them rustlers happened,'' Bucky said as she approached.

Briefly, Case told her about the fight.

Sally *tsked,* patted Bucky's shoulder as if to assure herself he was all right. ''I can't say I'm surprised. That one fella was a mean-spirited sort. I saw it the minute I laid eyes on him. So what are we going to do now, Mr. Durham?''

Case looked at the people who were depending on him, one by one. All eyes fixed on him, waiting. Katlyn held her breath.

Leaning over slightly and planting his hands on the back of a chair, he faced them all directly. ''None of you should worry,'' he began with a confidence he hoped sounded more far convincing than it felt. ''You all have a place here. We may have to shut down for a while, but you're still on my payroll.''

Katlyn watched him, her heart filled with an aching tenderness. His caring made her long to tell him here and now she would work for him without pay, help him rebuild his dream simply for the reward of seeing him succeed.

But her love for and duty to her mother put her in the most agonizing quandary she'd ever faced.

Beside her, Tuck slapped a hand down on a nearby table, nearly toppling it. ''Well, you can count me in for the work but I ain't gonna take a cent from you 'till there's money comin' in. I expect with Miss Katlyn behind us, that won't be long.''

''We were doin' fine before this,'' Bat said. ''Tuck's right. Folks'll be back just to hear Miss Katlyn sing.''

Bucky nodded a silent agreement. ''Becky and me don't need nothin', either, Mr. Durham. We'll get by. Just means Pa'll have to find his own whiskey money fer a while,'' he added with a laugh. ''We'll do just fine long as Tuck keeps feedin' us.''

Case held up a hand. ''No, I can't let you—''

''Yes, you can,'' Sally interrupted. ''I'm with the others. Times have been lean before, and they'll be lean again, we just make do. You're a good man, Mr. Durham. There isn't anyone else I'd rather work for. And my boys feel exactly the same way.'' She laid a hand atop his and smiled. "At least we all know we always have a place to sleep if we need it."

Katlyn wished the floor would open and swallow her whole. The others' willingness to sacrifice for Case, and their belief in her should have been inspiring. Instead, she felt guilty and ashamed.

She so wanted to belong but any sense of her being a part of the family of the St. Martin was a charade, just like her singing and her reputation as Penelope Rose.

She realized everyone looked at her expectantly and hot color flowered on her face. Obviously they all expected her to echo them in refusing Case's money until the hotel was back in business.

They didn't know it was the one thing she couldn't do.

But before she found the words to try to defend her apparent selfishness, Case spared her that agony.

He straightened and stepped over to stand in front of her. Looking directly into her eyes, he lifted her chin and forced her to face him squarely.

"You can't go without pay. Your companion depends on you and we all know how ill she is," he said firmly. "We all understand."

"But, Case, I want—"

"Katlyn, it's all right. Isn't it?" He drew away from her and turned to the others.

Murmurs of approval answered him all around but Katlyn's conscience forced her to try to justify herself.

"I don't need the money for myself. No matter

how much I would like to turn it down, I have no choice. She may die if I can't pay for the care she needs.''

Sally moved over to her then, taking Katlyn's hand between her work-roughened palms. ''We all know that, honey. We believe you. You don't need to say any more.''

We believe you... Those words of faith, the comforting smiles at every side, the look of absolute understanding and trust in Case's eyes were her undoing.

Her heart in her throat, her eyes filling with tears, she managed to choke out, ''Thank you all. I'll find a way to make this up to you. I'll work twice as hard, I swear.''

Bucky laughed then, easing the tension. ''Miss McLain, you already do that!''

After putting Emily to sleep with yet another story of castles and brave princesses, Case headed back downstairs to finish one last job he'd started earlier, repairing a corner of the bar counter. When Jack had shown up later that morning, he and Bat had tackled the job of hauling out the broken furniture and glass, while Case began prioritizing repairs.

He shook his head in amazement at how much Becky and Bucky and Sally had accomplished in the foyer already. Cleaned of debris and scoured of dust and dirt, it was bare, but no longer resembled the backside of a stampede, as Bucky had put it.

Katlyn spent most of the day in the dining room

and kitchen with Tuck, reorganizing and working on new menus. He'd seen little of her during the day, but as he crossed the foyer, the soft strains of piano and an angelic voice he knew well reached his ears.

His songbird.

Following the soulful melody of her mournful Irish ballad, he stepped into the dining room and saw her there, sitting at the piano alone in the shadowy stillness.

Her hair tumbled down her back as if she'd recently untwisted her braid and run her hands through it to comb it. She leaned a little over the keyboard, her eyes closed, lost in her song, and she sang as if every word cut at her heart.

"'And the waves and the wind,
Tossed his ship to and fro',
But his heart ne'er did fail,
For his love would he hail,
Through the storm did he strive,
To his lass, to his love,
Rocky coast, sandy shore,
Ne'er to leave ever more.'"

Katlyn let her fingers slide from the keys, the last notes fading to an echo. Her head bent, she sighed and brushed quickly at her eyes.

The gesture tugged at Case's heart. He offered a quiet applause as he walked slowly to her side, the sound drawing her eyes to his.

"That's one I haven't heard before," he said softly. "It's moving."

"Yes…" Katlyn cleared her throat then smiled a little. "It's one for dining by candlelight, I think."

"Mmm, I believe you're right." Drawing a cheroot from his shirt pocket, Case went through the motions of clipping and lighting it, then leaned against the piano and took a long draw before adding, "We'll have to make certain we have candlelight."

Katlyn followed the motion of his hands, marveling at the combination of strength and grace. She had witnessed both, when he defended the people he cared for and his hotel, and when he touched her in that slow, supple way with desire in his eyes.

Quickly she glanced away from him, not wanting him to see the longing she was sure must be clear on her face.

Case didn't miss the glimmer of need in her eyes. He said nothing, only smiled to himself.

"I see you've already taken it upon yourself to have the piano moved here."

"Oh, Jack did it, with a little help from Sally's oldest," Katlyn said, glad to have a distraction to her illicit thoughts. "And I told him to buy a new shirt, and do away with that scarred-up leather vest of his. He'll need to look presentable for the kind of audience we want."

Case blew out a series of perfect smoke rings and smiled. "Sounds like you have everything under control."

Katlyn couldn't hold back a sigh. She gazed into

eyes that looked dark and fathomless in the dim light, unable to read his expression. "Case, I wish...I feel so badly about having to take what money you can pay me."

"I told you I understand."

"I know, but—"

"But nothing. We're not discussing this any more. I will say, though, this friend of yours must be one special lady to have earned such devotion. I hope to have the privilege of meeting her someday."

Katlyn just kept from flinching. She shrugged, toying with the piano keys. "She's far too ill for visitors now, but maybe one day."

"Definitely one day."

Not liking the determination in his tone, Katlyn hurriedly began rattling off ideas for converting the dining room, just as determined to change the subject.

"...and thank heavens the white linens weren't damaged, and we still have all the china," she was saying when Case bent and stopped her prattle with a kiss.

At the touch of his lips, she melted. She yielded, helpless to resist, when he pulled her to her feet and into his arms, craving the feeling only Case could give her.

Her response tempted Case to press further. But remembering her hesitation before, he kept his caresses light and stroking, teasing them both with a taste of the fire between them.

He finally broke the kiss when his teasing started

to become torment. Cradling her against his heart, he held her close.

"I think we've both done enough planning for one day," he murmured. "The real work begins tomorrow."

"Was that your idea of planning? If so, I don't think it's going to be too good for business."

"You're my business, Katlyn," he said, lifting her chin so their eyes met. "So I happen to think it's very good."

And when he joined his mouth to hers again, Katlyn had no reason to disagree.

The stranger held a hand to his eyes, blocking out bright morning sun streaming through a broken window. "Excuse me, I'm lookin' for Penelope Rose. I heard she was singin' here."

Case looked from the broken window frames he was helping Bat pry off to the man who stood just inside the saloon. Tall and elegant in his finely tailored suit with its elaborate gold-and-red silk vest, his silver hair brushed into a smooth cap, he looked as if he'd taken a wrong turn from San Francisco to end up in Cimarron.

"Miss Rose is singing here," Case said, coming up to the man. "I'm Case Durham, I own the St. Martin. What's your business with Miss Rose?"

"Well, now," said the man, smiling broadly. "I like a man who comes right to the point. But I promise you, Penelope will be pleased as punch to see me.

You just tell her Luck Connor is here, all the way from St. Louis. That'll bring her runnin'.''

Will it now? Case wondered, not liking the easy assurance of Luck Connor or the implication behind the older man's wink and grin. Bat, who had paused in his work, now avoided Case's backward glance and began industriously yanking at the window frames again.

"I'll find Miss Rose," Case said, striding past Connor to the door to call sharply for Becky. When the girl came running up he said shortly, "Go and find Miss Rose and tell her I want to see her. Now."

Katlyn came a few minutes later, wiping her hands against her skirts. She looked perplexed and a little concerned at his summons. "Case, what is it? I was in the middle of finishing—"

The instant Luck Connor turned to greet her, she stopped cold. Case thought it would take a blind man not to recognize the naked fear in her eyes. He took a step forward in an instinctive move to protect her. But in the next moment she flashed a brilliant smile and rushed up to Connor, putting a hand on his arm. "Luck, it's so wonderful to see you! I had no idea you were coming to New Mexico, and here, of all places." She whirled to Case. "Luck is an old friend. He owns one of the riverboats I sang on for oh, so many years. Why, he was the one who started calling me the St. Louis Songbird, weren't you, Luck?"

Katlyn turned back to Luck Connor, careful to shield her face from Case. With her eyes and a hard squeeze of his forearm, she begged Luck to hold his tongue long enough for her to get him alone and explain.

Seeing Luck here shocked her to the core. She prayed her face hadn't betrayed her terror to Case, and more that her mother's old friend would keep their secret. Luck had been one of Penelope's many lovers, one she kept returning to over the years, and the only one who ever stayed a friend.

A good friend, Katlyn hoped now, for both her and Penelope's sakes.

"You're lookin' fine, honey. Younger and prettier than ever," Luck said with a spark of mischief in his eyes. "This wild country must agree with you. You'll have to tell me all about it. You hightailed it so fast out of St. Louis, I never got the chance to hear why." He put an arm around Katlyn's waist, the pressure of his fingers daring her to object. "We got us a lot to talk about."

Inwardly, Katlyn groaned. Case looked as if he wanted to commit murder with his bare hands and she wished she could tell him she shared his sentiment.

Extricating herself from Luck's hold with a wide smile that never reached her eyes, she said sweetly, "Oh, we sure do. Come and have a drink with me in my suite and we'll catch up on old times."

She would have preferred to talk to Luck anywhere but in her rooms, but she couldn't think of a place more private. She couldn't risk being interrupted or overheard.

"I won't be long," she said, risking a look at Case and immediately wishing she hadn't.

His face was set in that stony coldness she remembered so well from her early days at the St. Martin. It had been missing lately, replaced by tenderness and the heat of desire.

With a sharp pang, Katlyn knew it would be a long time before she saw that in him again and cursed Luck's untimely arrival.

Case let her move past him and to the door before he could control himself enough to speak.

Anger and suspicion warred inside him, but above all he felt an irrational rage against the man who touched Katlyn as if he'd done it many times before and had the right of possession.

Obviously, Luck Connor was more than an "old friend," although he was hardly the man he would have pictured Katlyn with. Years older than her, with that insincere, patronizing attitude toward her, Connor was the kind of man he could envision with the Penelope Rose he had imagined in the beginning.

But not the Katlyn McLain he knew by heart.

"Miss Rose," he said sharply, stopping Katlyn on her way out the door.

Keeping his expression carefully controlled with sheer will, Case looked straight at her, ignoring Luck Connor. "Bring your guest to dinner with us, won't you? I'm sure we'll all enjoy talking to your old friend."

Katlyn came downstairs less than a half hour later, Luck on her heels.

After explaining her mother's situation, it had taken a considerable amount of cajoling and pleading on her part to wring a promise from Luck to keep their secret. He had agreed only on the condition she take him to see Penelope.

Katlyn wanted to refuse. Even more, she wanted to shove Luck Connor onto the next stage to anywhere.

But when Luck wanted something, he would resort to anything to get it. He'd betray her in an instant with a smile and a tip of his hat. Which left her no choice but to take him to the boardinghouse.

She hoped to at least escape running into Case on her way out. He came out of the saloon just as she reached the bottom of the stairs, though, as if he'd been listening for her footsteps.

"Are you leaving us, Miss McLain?" Case asked.

Katlyn inwardly winced at his cold, formal tone. "Only for a short time. Luck insists on visiting my— Beatrice."

"Ah, the mysterious companion. I thought you said she refused all visitors."

"Beatrice has known Luck longer than I have. I'm sure she would be disappointed if she didn't get a chance to see him before he leaves Cimarron." She took Luck's arm and pushed him toward the door. "I won't be long."

Seeing the ice in Case's eyes, Katlyn thought it would be long, though, before she could convince him Luck Connor was nothing more to her than an unwelcome surprise from the past.

* * *

"How lovely for your ma to have a visitor, and such a handsome one, too." Mrs. Donaldson beamed at Katlyn as she refilled her teacup. "I'm sure she gets lonely, not able to leave her bed and all."

"Yes, I know she does," Katlyn said, glancing at the stairs for the umpteenth time in the past hour. She'd left her mother to her reunion with Luck.

At first Penelope balked at allowing Luck to see her. But Katlyn pressed her, knowing if they wanted Luck to keep their secret, Penelope would have to suffer through at least a brief visit.

After Penelope reconciled to the inevitable, though, Katlyn swore her mother started to like the idea of meeting her old lover again. At Penelope's insistence, Katlyn helped her dress in a gold satin negligee that complimented her coloring, brush her hair, and touch a little color to her sallow cheeks.

When Katlyn at last let Luck in her mother's room, she found herself dismissed, reluctantly agreeing at Penelope's request to have a nice cup of tea with Mrs. Donaldson.

She suspected her mother was still a bit uneasy about meeting Luck again from her sickbed and wanted Katlyn there in case it all went wrong. After an hour, Katlyn decided whatever was happening, Penelope apparently was pleased.

She was ready to give up her vigil in the parlor and go back to the hotel when Luck appeared at the top of the stairs. "Can you come up for a minute, honey?"

Katlyn braced herself for the worst but when she

went into her mother's room, Penelope greeted her with a dazzling smile. Propped up on several pillows, Penelope still looked fragile. But her eyes sparkled and the flush on her face was more nature than rouge.

"Oh, Katie, I've been having the most marvelous time," she said. Penelope stretched out a hand and Katlyn took it, coming to sit beside her mother on the bed. "How silly of you to be worried about Luck keeping our little secret. Why, he's been just wonderful. We've had so much to talk about."

She turned her smile on Luck and he grinned back. "Still a lot more where that came from, honey." He glanced at Katlyn. "You tell that Mr. Durham for me, Katie, that I'll have dinner at his hotel some other night. Your mother and I are going to have us a little party right here."

Katlyn quickly looked at Penelope. "Mama, are you sure you're—"

"Don't fuss, Katie," Penelope said, lifting a lank hand to wave away her concern. "I'm not a total invalid, no matter what that wretched doctor may say. You go on back to the hotel. Aren't you singing tonight?"

Katlyn didn't bother to answer. She didn't want her mother to know about the disaster at the hotel. Kissing Penelope's cheek, she wished her mother and Luck a good evening, then left them to their party. Maybe a little male attention was the best medicine her mother could have right now and Luck Connor certainly had plenty of that to give.

The afternoon shadows had lengthened into evening when she reached the St. Martin and let herself into the foyer with a sigh. Caught up in her thoughts, she didn't see Case step out of the saloon until she nearly cannoned into him.

"Miss McLain—you're alone," he said.

"Yes," Katlyn snapped, tired and afraid and not ready to do combat with him tonight. "I'm sorry if you're disappointed. Now, if you'll excuse me, I'm going to my room. I need to get some sleep so tomorrow I can make up for the time I lost today. I have a list of things a mile long to do around here."

Case put his hands on her shoulders, stopping her move toward the staircase. "Not yet. Not until we talk about Luck Connor."

Chapter Twelve

Case expected her to refuse. Facing him now, stiff with anger, her eyes hot, she looked ready to turn her temper loose on him.

He couldn't blame her. He had no right to ask about her past and she owed him no explanations. She had done her part and more to help the St. Martin. Beyond that, they had made no promises to each other.

Except that seeing Luck Connor had rekindled the fear in her he'd seen from the day she arrived. He didn't understand it, but suddenly he wanted to, more urgently than ever before.

"I want to help you," he said at last.

Katlyn wilted. She wanted to be furious with him, she *was* furious with him. But it was hard to sustain her aggravation at his high-handed demands when he looked at her as if everything about her truly mattered to him, and offered to help in that low, husky voice that plucked a chord of need deep inside her.

Slipping from his hold, she walked into the saloon

and sat at one of few tables still standing. Bat had left two of the oil lamps lit and they cast a dim uneven light over the broken room.

Case sat opposite her with his back to the lamp glow. The shadow masking his face made it impossible for Katlyn to read his expression.

Katlyn didn't give herself time to think about what deep waters she might be diving into but plunged ahead. "You want to talk about Luck. There's very little to say. He was never my lover, although I know that's what you believe. He owns a riverboat and he created the St. Louis Songbird to entertain his customers. He was a friend, nothing more."

"And he came all the way here just to say hello?"

"He came because he wants Penelope Rose back."

Her words struck him like a blow. "I see."

"No, you don't. His riverboat is failing and he thinks he can save it by bringing the St. Louis Songbird back. He's wrong. I won't go back, ever."

"Did he threaten you?"

"Threaten?" Katlyn frowned, truly confused at the question though Case had never looked more serious. "Luck? Of course not."

"Then why are you afraid of him? Don't deny it. I saw your face when you first recognized him."

"I wasn't afraid. I was—startled to see someone from my past here in New Mexico." She said it confidently, as if she expected to be believed. She kept her hands under the table though, so Case wouldn't see them shaking. "I thought I had left St. Louis behind and made a new start here."

Case busied himself with lighting a cheroot before replying. He took a long draw on it, blew the smoke to the side, then looked straight back at her. "You seem determined to forget St. Louis ever existed."

"Just as determined as you are to forget Silver Springs."

"I left Colorado to protect Emily. What are you running from?"

"I'm not running, from anything or anyone."

"Aren't you?"

"No," Katlyn said firmly. That, at least, she didn't have to lie about. "I told you before, I came here because I was looking for a place to belong, a place I felt needed. Is that so hard to understand?"

"It is because it seems you had everything you could aspire for as a singer. Connor still needs you. Why give it all up to come here?"

To her horror, Katlyn felt tears sting her eyes. How could she explain that the way Luck needed the St. Louis Songbird was hardly the way she yearned to be needed? Everything had become so convoluted between them because of her deception, trying to unravel her feelings in a way that would make any sense to him was futile.

She didn't want to be at odds with Case, not now, not after all they'd shared. She couldn't afford to be weak. Yet all she wanted right now was to fling herself into his arms and ask him to hold her.

She blinked and fixed her gaze on her lap and Case's coolness immediately fell away. He couldn't stay detached, nurse his suspicions of her when she looked so small and vulnerable and alone.

"I shouldn't have asked," he said. "It doesn't matter."

Katlyn raised her head. The lamplight caught the sheen of tears in her eyes. "Do you believe me, about Luck?" Impulsively, she reached across the table and put her hand on his. "I would never deceive you about something like that, or about how I feel. Never."

"I believe you," Case said, not knowing whether he was right or a fool to trust her. But it didn't matter now. Maybe it never had and never would.

"Thank you," Katlyn whispered and squeezed his hand.

She started to pull her fingers away but Case took her hand in his and, getting to his feet, drew her up and into his arms.

He held her close and she clung to him tightly. They stayed together, in the stillness and the shadows, both wishing there was nothing else between them but the feeling this was where they should stay.

Hours later Case paced the floor in his sitting room, wondering what to do about Katlyn.

He could argue with himself that her past was none of his business. Many people came west to escape their mistakes and start over. Whatever secrets haunted her shouldn't concern him.

Except everything about her concerned him and he

knew it wasn't simply because he had invested the future of his hotel in her.

He was in danger of loving her.

He believed Katlyn when she said she would never deceive him. But he didn't know if he could trust Penelope Rose. And he wasn't about to commit his heart and his daughter's future to another woman who was nothing she appeared to be.

Never before had he dealt backhanded with anyone. Katlyn, though, wasn't about to tell him the truth.

A friend in St. Louis had recommended the riverboat songbird when he was looking for a singer. Perhaps Penelope Rose had left something more than her reputation behind when she abandoned her career there—rumors at least of why she suddenly departed.

If he knew, maybe he could help Katlyn. Maybe he could help himself before it was too late and he gave his soul to her.

Sitting at his desk, Case started writing a letter, determined to finish before he changed his mind.

The bite in the late-morning air prompted Katlyn to grab a blanket from the barn and drape it over Becky's legs. The chill bite of autumn in the country breeze swept through the tattered sides of the old wagon Becky and Bucky were using to drive outside of town to invite ranchers and their wives to the new dinner show at the St. Martin.

"Now be back before dark and don't forget those handbills. Please drop them at the general store, and the barbershop, and Mrs. Donaldson's boardinghouse on your way back here. Oh, take some by the livery, too. And you might tack a few up here and there, too. It couldn't hurt.''

''We won't forget,'' Bucky said with a grin. ''You've been tellin' us enough the last two days.'' Clucking his tongue, he snapped the reins against the back of the spotted mare and the wagon lurched up the dirt road leading out of town.

''We'll keep tellin' them it's real fancy, Miss McLain,'' Becky called to her as the wagon rattled past. ''This town ain't never seen nothin' like what you're puttin' on, that's for certain.''

Katlyn raised a hand and waved after them. ''I know. That's what I'm gambling on,'' she answered, mostly to herself, hesitating to add out loud that she hoped her gaming instincts weren't anything like her father's. If she had inherited his notorious bad luck, they were all about to land in deep trouble.

Too late to think about that now. Tugging her shawl around her shoulders, she headed back toward the hotel, ticking off a list of things yet to be done before the dinner show opened. For days she'd worked herself and everyone else to the bone, practicing, preparing, cleaning, polishing and planning.

There'd been some good-natured grumbling from Tuck and Bat, and Jack had teased her about her prowess as a general. But all in all, everyone fell in with her plans, trusting she knew enough to carry off her most elaborate performance yet.

Case had said little, seemingly willing to let her manage everything, offering only a suggestion here and there in between his long hours spent making repairs. Katlyn didn't know whether his silence meant he believed in her or he was biding his time until she fell flat on her face.

And right now, she didn't know which alternative seemed the more daunting.

Pushing in through the back kitchen door, Katlyn found Tuck hard at work arranging food on a plate to look the way she had described it ought to be presented. He looked up when she came in, exasperation written in his furrowed brow.

"It ain't workin', Miss Katlyn, this fuss and fanfare just ain't me."

Katlyn made her way around a sack of potatoes and a crate of canned fruit, angling herself between the big black stove and a haphazard stack of unwashed pots and pans on the dry sink to peek around Tuck's wide girth at the worktable. Dozens of oddly cut scraps of carrots and radishes lay tossed aside in a heap. She glanced at the delicate pale green china plate at his burly fingertips, smiling at the contrast.

"Tuck, you're doing fine. Here, if you'll allow me to invade your kitchen for a moment, I'll show you a trick with the radishes and carrots. A few cuts here and there and you'll have just the right garnish for the ham."

Tuck moved aside. With a heavy breath, he shook his head and handed her the paring knife. "Invade all you want. I sure ain't gettin' the job done."

Katlyn tossed her shawl onto a chair. "You're doing a wonderful job. I learned this from a cook on

Luck Connor's riverboat a long time ago. Here, watch this.'' In a few deft slices, she turned a simple radish into something akin to a blooming flower, then created curly strips from thin slices of carrot. ''Now if we put these in water and set them out in the evening air, by the time we serve dinner, they'll be crisp as new lace.''

''Here, you try,'' she said, offering him the knife.

After a few tentative cuts, Tuck mastered both techniques and held up his finished radish blossom with a grin. ''Well, now, maybe you can teach an old dog a few new tricks.''

''There's not much I can teach you. All I can do is add a few frills to what's already the best food in town.''

''That may be,'' Tuck said with a grin, ''but you're the best thing that ever happened to the St. Martin, Miss Katlyn. They don't come truer than you.''

Katlyn's smile drained away. She made a pretext of turning to gather up her shawl. ''I'm just doing what I have to do,'' she said quickly. ''We all need this place up and running again.''

Case drew a handkerchief from his back pocket and wiped the sweat from his brow. ''Ready?''

At the other end of the refinished bar counter, Bat gripped the ends and nodded. The two men hefted the weighty mahogany slab, shifting and sliding it slowly into place.

Katlyn watched from the door of the saloon, her eyes fixing on the muscles flexing in Case's arms.

He'd rolled his sleeves up until they caught and held snugly, and as he squatted to lift, she saw the sinuous length of his thighs and backside tighten beneath his denim pants. Knowing he didn't realize she was there, she allowed herself the luxury of staring.

Before the destruction at the hotel, she'd most often seen Case at his elegant best, groomed to perfection, dressed in fine, tailored clothes. He'd always struck her as impossibly handsome, commanding attention and turning every woman's eyes his way. To deny her attraction to him would be a lie.

But lately, working long hours on the renovations, his usually meticulously kept hair looked permanently mussed. Each day he'd put on the same denims that with time and wear had molded perfectly to his body. The comfortable old white cotton shirt he wore, he left carelessly unbuttoned, tempting her to slide her fingers through the dark mat of curls that caressed his broad chest. For days she'd been watching him, discovering a side of him she found irresistible.

Looking at him now, a trickle of sweat sliding down one side of his brow, muscles taut, eyes intense and focused on his task, he aroused something deep and intimate in her. No man, not even her former fiancé, had ever provoked such an impatient yearning in her. But it happened every time she so much as glanced Case's way, causing her stomach to clench with excitement and a heady warmth to fizz through her blood.

Case pounded the last nail into the counter and tossed his head back, wiping the sweat from his face with the underside of his forearm. As he did, he caught Katlyn staring at him from the doorway.

"Come to check on the hired help?" he teased.

For a moment she only looked at him with an odd expression on her face.

"Katlyn? Are you all right?"

"All—yes. Yes, of course." She shifted her shoulders as if throwing off some unsettling thought. "I...I was just watching—I stopped to see how you were coming along."

"I see," Case said, though he didn't. She seemed nervous, rubbing her palms down her skirts, shifting her gaze everywhere but to him. "Are you sure there's nothing wrong?"

"What could be wrong?"

"Where you're concerned, I have no idea," Case muttered, shaking his head as she started picking her way through the piles of wood and sawdust to his side.

"Daddy, look what I made!" Emily, who'd been sitting on the stage with a pile of wooden blocks, now commanded his attention.

"Those are wonderful!" Katlyn exclaimed, coming up beside him to admire Emily's handiwork. "Emily, you can build a castle with those."

Emily looked up to Katlyn and nodded. "I already am. For the princess. See?"

Katlyn closely examined the little girl's "castle," a hodgepodge of wood squares heaped this way and that. "It's beautiful, sweetie," she said, bending to brush a kiss atop her head. "The princess will be very happy there."

Katlyn straightened to find Case just behind her, so close she felt the heat of his body through her thin cotton dress.

"Your song inspires her imagination," he murmured in her ear, his breath warm on her neck.

"She's making good use of your wood scraps."

"Well, every princess should have a castle, don't you think?"

"Oh, definitely." She turned, and finding herself at eye level to the rise and fall of his chest, looked up at him, a shaky little smile on her mouth. "And a knight in shining armor to defend her."

"Will you settle for a more tarnished and slightly less heroic version of a champion?"

"Tarnished? Mmm...I don't think so. A bit battered, maybe," she murmured. She skimmed her fingertips over his bruised jaw. "No less heroic."

She teased him but Case heard the note of longing in her voice she couldn't hide. He felt a thrust of pure satisfaction remembering her expression when he'd caught her watching him before. He might not understand everything about Katlyn McLain but one thing she couldn't keep secret was her feelings.

And if he didn't move away from her, his own feelings right now wouldn't be a secret, either, from anyone in the room.

Katlyn ran the tip of her tongue over her lips. Case stared a moment too long, then took a quick step back. "I'd better get back to work."

"Yes," Katlyn agreed. "We've got so much to do."

"Quite a bit."

"Well, then…"

"I should—"

"And I have to—"

They both spoke at the same time, stopped and then Katlyn burst out laughing. She sidestepped around him and went to sit on the edge of the stage near Emily, stretching her legs out in front of her.

The tension broken, Case shook his head at her, smiling. "So, are we going to be ready to open on Saturday night?"

"As ready as we'll ever be."

"We're in luck at least in one respect. The stage comes into town early afternoon so we should be able to draw in a few customers from there. Have Becky and Bucky had any luck with the ranchers?"

"Yes, several of them seem curious and their wives are eager to have a reason to parade their finery. And a couple of the mine owners and local businessmen are all interested in what we're trying to do here."

Case let out a wry laugh. "I have to say, I'm curious, too."

Katlyn couldn't mistake the concern in his voice. "Don't worry," she insisted with more confidence than she felt. "This is going to work, I know it."

"You have a way of making me believe that," Case said with a sincerity that warmed Katlyn.

"Oh, by the way, since I couldn't pay Mrs. Donaldson for the alterations on the clothes for the staff,

I'd like to invite her to the show. I think she'd enjoy the treat.''

Case nodded. ''Of course. You ought to invite your companion, as well.''

Forcing her eyes to not turn from his, Katlyn returned what she hoped was an appreciative smile. ''Thank you. I don't think she'll be well enough to leave her bed, though.''

The flatness of her tone, so at odds with her usual vivacity, knotted Case's gut. Why was it that every time he mentioned the mysterious companion, everything about Katlyn changed?

Questions, doubts, suspicions plagued him each time the subject came up. But with all of the hard work and sacrifice she'd shown him, his daughter, his staff and his hotel, how could he suspect her of anything but honest dedication?

Why couldn't he simply trust her?

In the silence, the letter he'd sent answered him when his heart could not.

On the eve of the first dinner show, Katlyn bustled about checking on Tuck in the kitchen, straightening Bucky's black jacket and string tie, adding an extra petticoat to smooth out the lines beneath the dress she'd altered for Becky.

Passing Jack in the hallway, she tried in vain to persuade him to attempt to do something to his hair to keep it tame and away from his brow in a dignified fashion, but he merely brushed her aside with a wicked smile that made him look anything but dignified. Giving up, she went to give the dining room tables one last look.

If she didn't fall asleep during her performance it would be nothing short of a miracle, she mused, hiking up her skirts to rush downstairs. She and Becky had done a quick job on her makeup and hair, but as she stole a glance in the foyer mirror at the bottom of the stairs, amazingly, it all seemed to her eyes to come together well.

The deep golden velvet dress suited her coloring, after Mrs. Donaldson removed all the excess lace and the ruffle around the neck, the now-simple design made it look like her dress, instead of one of Penelope's castoffs.

For the first time since she'd come to the St. Martin, Katlyn felt comfortable. She might still be called the St. Louis Songbird, but tonight it was Katlyn McLain who would perform.

Inspecting the dining room, table setting by table setting, a deep sense of pride filled her.

"The room is magnificent. And so are you."

Katlyn turned to find Case leaning against the broad pine frame that outlined the double pocket doors to the room. The last breath of smoke from his cheroot slid from his lips and she watched as he turned aside to grind out the butt, his motions slow, lithe, confident. Dressed in a perfectly fitted black suit, a few easy long-legged strides brought him face-to-face with her.

"I'm glad you're pleased," she murmured. "With everything."

Gently he lifted her fingers and brushed his lips to the back of her hand. "You please me."

"I hope I will, tonight of all nights. I so want this night to be a turning point for the hotel, for you. You don't know how much I want this to be a success."

"A turning point?"

"Yes, for everyone."

"For us?"

"Case, I don't—" Katlyn faltered. "You don't know…"

Sally burst into the room then, tugging at her ruffled skirts as she tried to navigate between the tables. "Drat all these petticoats! Mr. Durham, the guests are starting to come in. And, oh, they are a sight! Silks and satins and jewels and furs! My, oh, my, just wait until you see!"

"I'll be right there," Case said, scarcely turning from Katlyn to respond. "It looks like you're going to get your wish tonight, songbird. And if we're a success, it will be because of you."

"No, Case, I don't deserve that."

"You deserve so much more. I've been unfair to you."

Katlyn stared at him in disbelief. "Unfair? How can you say that?"

"I didn't believe you when you told me about Luck Connor. I half expected you to tell me you were going back to St. Louis with him."

"I'm never going back," Katlyn said quietly. It hurt to know he hadn't trusted her. But she couldn't be angry at him for it because she didn't deserve his trust.

"Katlyn." Case slid his hand under her chin and lifted her face to his. "All of it is in the past. I believe you, I've seen how much all of this means to you. You could never deceive me about that."

"I don't want to ever deceive you," Katlyn said, the words spilling out of her heart before she could stop them. "I wish I could—"

She stopped suddenly. *I wish I could tell you the truth. I wish there were no lies between us.*

"I know," Case said softly and for a moment, Katlyn wondered if he truly did.

Then he kissed her cheek and drew back smiling. "Nothing else matters now, my songbird. We're going forward, ready or not. It's show time."

Chapter Thirteen

Still buzzing with pride and satisfaction from the previous nights' dinner show successes, Sally and the rest of the staff plunged into their morning chores with zeal.

"You'll come, won't you, Katlyn? And get Mr. Durham to bring Emily?"

Katlyn looked up from the pile of napkins she was helping Becky to sort and fold. "Come where?"

"The rodeo, of course," Becky said, giggling at Katlyn's blank expression. "You've been here all morning, but I don't think you've heard a word anyone has said."

"I'm sorry, I—I've got a lot to think about, with the new show and—and everything." Everything meaning Case, the thought of him enough to start a familiar warmth coiling inside her. She fixed her attention back on the napkins, hoping her face didn't look as flushed as it felt.

Sally eyed her for a moment then said, "Yes, I'm sure you do. We were talking about the rodeo out at the Amos's ranch on Saturday. They've been having it every year there for as long as I can remember.''

"Everyone goes," Becky put in. "You just can't miss it.''

"My boys talk about it weeks ahead," Sally said. "I know Emily would love it, too. It would be so good for her, she hardly ever leaves the hotel. If you say you're going, I'm sure Mr. Durham would agree to bring Emily.''

Before Katlyn could protest she hardly had that much influence over Case, Becky blurted in excitedly, "Of course he would! He really likes you, anyone with eyes can see that. You'll ask him won't you, please?''

Ten minutes later Katlyn hesitated at the doors to the saloon where Case was working, wondering how she had so easily let Sally and Becky maneuver her into tackling Case about the rodeo.

She'd agreed partly out of self-defense, wanting to escape Sally's knowing look that implied several things, all of them unsettling.

But more than that, she had decided to talk to Case for Emily's sake. Too well, she knew what it was like to grow up in a hotel or on a riverboat, with little opportunity to befriend others her own age and enjoy childish play. Emily needed to get away from the hotel for a while, especially now, after all the days of chaos and frantic rebuilding.

Determined now, she started into the saloon just as Case came out.

He stopped short, then smiled, a warm, intimate

gesture that turned Katlyn inside out. "Were you looking for me?"

"Oh, yes," she said, in the next instant blushing furiously. "I mean, I wanted to talk to you, to ask you something."

"This sounds interesting." Case led her to the couch in the foyer and sat beside her. "I'm all yours."

I wish, Katlyn thought. She banished the enticing images the idea conjured and hurried out her request about the rodeo. "I know Emily would love to go, and it would be so good for her to get out."

She expected him to hesitate and even argue with her. Instead, he seemed to mull over the idea before nodding in agreement. "It would be good for us, too," he said finally.

"'Us'?"

Case smiled at her startled expression. "Mmm... we can show people we want to be upstanding members of this community. That last fracas we had here didn't exactly help our reputation, but the first few dinner shows have been such a success, we could be on our way to making this place respectable."

"Are you saying people might expect me to show up in low-cut lace and satin garters?" She tapped her chin and appeared to consider the idea seriously. "Of course there could be advantages to an act like that."

"I can think of several."

"Why, Mr. Durham, I thought you wanted to be *respectable*."

"Respectable isn't the way you make me feel, Miss McLain," he said, reaching out to brush an errant curl back from her cheek. Touching her, he was suddenly intent again, his expression sober. "I need respectable, though, if I'm going to get the money I need to keep this hotel afloat. The rodeo might be a good place to court investors, or to at least broach the idea of a loan."

"Investors? You've never said that before. Are things that bad?" Katlyn asked quietly.

Case stood and paced to the windows and back. "If I can't find some way of raising money, I won't be able to pay the staff past next month no matter what promises I've made, to say nothing of supplies."

"But you can't give up! The hotel means everything to you."

He moved over to her and gently lifted her chin with one finger, bringing her eyes up to meet his. "Not everything, Miss McLain." He paused, let his meaning sink in, then added, "I'm not giving up. But there's a big distance between a dream and the hard truth. And the truth is, right now I need those investors or there will be no more dream."

"Then we'll get them."

Katlyn put her hand on his arm in a gesture of support and Case recognized the determined light in her eyes.

It had been there all along, almost from the first moment she'd arrived at his hotel, and it nurtured his faith in his ability to beat the odds and succeed despite his setbacks. Only Katlyn could do that for him and he was beginning to wonder if he could ever live without it. Without her.

"I'll also use this chance to coax people into coming to our dinners," she was saying. "Although, I warn you, I won't resort to lace and garters. Well—maybe a little lace."

"A pity. I have an image of you in midnight blue..." He punctuated his words with the slide of his fingertip down her cheek to the hollow of her throat.

Katlyn found it hard to think of anything but the seductive promise of his touch. She tried for his sake, though, to keep her mind on business. "We'll be a success without them, I promise you."

"I know we will," Case said. "I have my songbird, don't I? What else do I need?"

The horses and riders came thundering past them in a whirl of dust and Emily clapped her hands in delight as the spotted Appaloosa she'd picked to win nosed out a victory over a big bay stallion.

She tugged on Katlyn's sleeve, pointing. "Did you see? He did win! I knew he would because he has spots."

"Well, I should have listened to you. My gray one came in last," Katlyn said, laughing. "I suppose this means I owe you another ribbon."

"A pink one this time."

"Pink it is. But if I don't stop making bets with you, I'm going to have to buy you every ribbon in the shebang."

"Teaching my daughter to gamble, are you?"

Katlyn started at Case's deep voice in her ear. Distracted by watching the race with Emily, she hadn't seen him approach. Now as he scooped Emily into his arms and listened to her happy description of the race, Katlyn couldn't help but notice the air of satisfaction around him. He looked relaxed, pleased with himself and his work today.

And well he should, she thought. Since they'd arrived this morning, Katlyn had watched Case moving among the ranchers, businessmen, and mine owners here, as charming and compelling as she had ever seen him. He commanded attention, yet was so adept at persuasion he managed to leave people convinced it was their idea to invest in the St. Martin.

"From that smile of yours, I'm guessing we're still in business and Monday you'll be working us all off our feet again," she said, smiling at him.

"Any objections?" Case asked.

"I can't think of anything I'd like to do more."

And she couldn't. As Katlyn looked around at the people milling around them, waiting for the next race, talking, laughing, their children playing around them, she thought of the life she might have had if she'd stayed in St. Louis. Standing in her mother's shadow and keeping men like Jack at arm's length, she mused, smiling a little to herself as she saw him flash that wicked smile of his at two young women, making them giggle and blush.

Watching other women and their families, Katlyn felt a little pang of envy. She realized suddenly how much she loved working at the hotel and singing and the feeling she was helping Case build something of value. But these women had what she could never have: they had something that would last.

All too soon, she would have to leave Cimarron— and Case. And when she did, Katlyn knew she would never be this happy again.

Case saw the wistful look on Katlyn's face and wondered what had put it there. She had seemed happy enough today, charming everyone with her laughter and wit, and genuinely pleased to share his good news about the investors. Since Luck Connor had left, he'd been watching her for any signs she was sorry for not taking Connor's offer to return to St. Louis. But she only acted relieved at his leaving.

"Katlyn," he said softly. He shifted Emily to one arm and put his hand lightly on her waist, drawing her slightly closer into his family circle. "Is something wrong?"

"Oh, no." She hurriedly put on a smile. "No, of course not. It's been a wonderful day. I was just thinking—" she said, with a wink at Emily. "We've been here for hours and Emily and I have yet to see the famed Amos pigs. Sally's boys say they're the biggest in the world, but Emily and I want to judge for ourselves."

"We don't believe those boys," Emily said with a touch of scorn.

"Then by all means, let's go and see for ourselves," Case agreed, rewarded by his daughter's delighted smile and by Katlyn taking his arm and leaning into him a little to share Emily's happiness.

Caught up in the sweet warmth of being together, Case set aside his concerns about Katlyn. But as they walked side by side to the barns, he vowed to find a way to banish those shadows that haunted her eyes as well as any doubts she had about belonging here in Cimarron with him.

A cool whisper of breeze rustled through the ponderosa pines that ran along the edge of the pasture used for the rodeo grounds, forming a barrier to the woods beyond. The light wind stroked Katlyn's cheeks, turning them pink. She pulled her woolen shawl closer around her shoulders, and glanced at the deepening twilight.

"It's getting late. We should take Emily back to the hotel soon."

Case snapped a twig and rolled it idly between his thumb and forefinger as they strolled together along a path that wound through the pine forest back to the backyard where most of the families now gathered for dinner. "I know. But she's had so much fun today being with other children, I hate to see it end. I'll never forget the look on her face when that huge pig snorted at her."

Katlyn laughed, recalling Emily's almost comic expression of horror. "She climbed up you like a cat with its tail afire."

"I'm glad you invited us. She'll never forget this

day." He tossed the twig aside and turned to her. "And neither will I."

She looked up at the genuine appreciation in his eyes and it pricked at her conscience. "Well, actually, the whole staff wanted you to come," she admitted, ducking beneath a low-hanging branch. "They just nominated me to do the asking."

"Ah, I see the plan now. They knew I couldn't refuse you."

"But, Mr. Durham, you're always saying no to my requests."

"Since when, Miss McLain? It seems to me you've been having your way with me from the day you walked into my hotel."

"I haven't heard you object," she teased. "Well, maybe once or twice."

"Only when you tried to wallpaper the kitchen."

"I could have made that work."

"Knowing you, I believe you could have," Case said, thinking how true it was.

From almost the start, Katlyn had brought something to the St. Martin he, for all his experience and business prowess, could never have created alone. Everyone at the hotel willingly worked hard for him, but Katlyn's spirit, her unflagging optimism, spurred them to believe in themselves and what they could accomplish together.

She'd given so much of herself to all of them, so much more than he ever expected. How could he doubt her commitment to him?

He thought of the letter and was glad he'd hadn't

received any answer. Maybe he never would. He should never have written the damned thing to begin with, and wouldn't have, if he hadn't been poisoned by memories of Silver Springs.

"What are you thinking about?" she asked softly, tentatively, as if she feared intruding on his privacy.

"You," Case answered truthfully. "How glad I am you came to the St. Martin."

Katlyn sharply drew in a breath, glanced away from him, and let it go slowly. "You don't know how much it's meant to me, being here."

"You sound as if it's over. Are you planning on leaving me?"

"Not until I convince you to wallpaper the kitchen," Katlyn said lightly. She pretended to focus on the expanse of deepening sky overhead, shaded from blue to nearly black and just beginning to show glints of starlight. The forest's shadows lengthened all around, enveloping them in the mysteries of the magic hour, the last glimmer of light before night's cloak ends the day.

Case followed her gaze and they paused for a moment to share the view. "Then it looks like you're going to be here forever."

Forever. Oh, how she wished that were true.

She had never been so satisfied and content in a place in all her life. Always, she'd felt like an outsider, never fitting in. Penelope had her singing, her admirers, her lovers; Katlyn's sister, her family, her work, her patients.

But Case made her feel she belonged at the St.

Martin, that without her, the hotel would be lacking a vital spirit.

Except it was a lie. She would never belong here because her place was at her mother's side, wherever that might lead. And it would never lead her to stay in Cimarron.

This was only a temporary haven. It could never be a permanent home.

Lost in her own thoughts, Katlyn didn't realize at first Case had stopped walking. "Are you leaving me behind?" he asked.

"What?" Katlyn turned to find him sitting on a fallen log, watching her, an amused smile playing at the edges of his mouth. She walked back to him, easing down beside him. "I'm sorry, I was lost in my own thoughts, I guess."

"From your expression, I wouldn't call them happy ones. What's troubling you?"

"Nothing. I was just thinking about everything we have yet to do, how important it all is…" She shifted her shoulders and fixed her gaze on a spot of moss clinging to the pine bark, worrying it with her fingertip.

"Katlyn—" Case reached over and took her hands, warming them between his palms. "You're chilled. Come here." Pulling her close, he wrapped her in his arms.

Katlyn didn't think of resisting. Instead she leaned into him, taking comfort in the warmth of him, the strength of his arms enfolding her.

When he touched her cheek, she tilted her head

back to look at him and saw the smolder of desire in his eyes he made no attempt to hide.

"Katlyn, you've come to mean so much to me," he said, his voice low and rough with emotion. "I never believed I'd find a woman like you, so caring and giving and honest."

Honest. "Oh, Case…" Katlyn couldn't bear to hold his straightforward gaze. "Please. Don't say that. You don't know…there are things about me—"

"There's nothing you could say that would change my mind about you. Not now, when I've seen the woman you really are."

If only that were true, Katlyn thought, and then she had no time for thoughts or worries when Case took her face gently in his hands and touched his mouth to hers.

Her lips parted in response to his, inviting the moment to last forever, casting aside for one sweet interlude her guilt and the lies she knew would soon destroy them. She kissed him deeply, and he returned her kiss with growing passion.

He held her in a sweet embrace, his lips sampling the delicacies of her cheeks, her eyes, her nose, her neck. She moaned with the need he roused in her, every new touch of his lips on her skin kindling a warmth that threatened to become fire.

She met him kiss for kiss, returning every caress with one of her own design. Her response threatened his restraint, and Case pulled her up hard against him.

It would be easy to have her now, here in the secret

shadows of the wood. Her response told him that, as clearly as if she'd begged him to make love to her.

But surrendering to temptation would mean everyone in Cimarron would know she was his lover by tomorrow morning. He knew better than most how being at the center of gossip and speculation could ruin all their diligent efforts toward gaining respectability.

Even as he listened to the voice telling him to stop, Case moved his hands over her back, her arms, her waist, memorizing every curve with his touch. She locked her arms around him, pulling him closer still.

Breathless, they clung to each other, the forest around them speaking in hushed whispers as the evening darkness slipped in and around it.

"We have to go back," Case finally managed to say, his voice deep and graveled from desire.

Katlyn sighed. "I know. But right now, I wish there was nothing to go back to." She brushed her fingers against his cheek. "Because here, there's every reason to stay."

"It's so dark, I don't know how they can keep from stumbling," Katlyn told Case, peering into the gloom to make out the children still playing in the pasture, oblivious to the fact the sun had gone.

Beside Katlyn, Case kept his eyes on his daughter. Emily giggled as she tried to master the art of jumping rope amid a group of young girls. "A few more minutes and they'll have to call it quits. Look at Emily, I don't know when she's enjoyed herself more."

"I know. She needs to do this far more often. She needs to be around other children."

Katlyn had noticed Case's little girl struggling awkwardly, trying to figure out the complexities of jumping rope. Katlyn had stopped herself from interfering, and simply stood by, rooting for Emily silently, remembering her own embarrassment from her ineptness at games and sports that seemed to be second nature to other children. Emily had to find her own way, though, or she would never feel at ease with her peers.

"She's been wrestling so long with that rope, I can't believe she hasn't given up," Case observed.

"She's her father's daughter, isn't she?" Katlyn said, then caught herself, a flush creeping into her cheeks. Quickly she put her hand on Case's arm. "I'm sorry. I didn't mean to—"

"It's all right. I take that as a compliment. Besides, Emily is my daughter, in every way that matters."

"Well, your daughter is precious," a woman's voice spoke up behind them. "She's so well mannered, and has a lovely smile. You two should be very proud. She's going to be a beauty."

Katlyn turned to face an older woman's welcoming smile. But before she could correct the lady, Case answered for both of them. "Thank you. But we are a little afraid she may never learn to jump rope."

The woman laughed, the wisdom of experience in her voice. "That little girl will do anything she puts her mind to, mark my word. All you have to do is look at the determination in her eyes. Believe me, after raising seven of my own, I ought to know. And with a mama and daddy like the two of you, nothing will stop her.''

Katlyn and Case exchanged a look, his amused, hers disconcerted.

She admitted to herself the idea of she and Case and Emily being a true family sounded wonderful. But it wasn't true and she waited for Case to correct the woman's impression, knowing how important honesty was to him.

He said nothing, though, merely continuing the light conversation with the woman, ignoring her mistake as if it wasn't a mistake at all.

''Well, it's time to round up my grandchildren and head home,'' the woman said finally. ''You take care of that darling little girl of yours now, you hear?''

''Yes, ma'am,'' Case said with a respectful tip of his hat and a charming smile that brought a blush to the woman's face.

When she'd gone, Katlyn turned to Case, torn between exasperation and laughter. ''Now, you've done it. You're going to have everyone talking about us and what's really going on under the roof of the infamous St. Martin. So much for respectability, Mr. Durham.''

Case shrugged. ''A few minutes ago I would have agreed. But the idea of us as a couple, as Emily's parents, seemed too right to refuse. Perhaps you've corrupted me, Miss McLain, because all I can think now is to hell with it. Let them talk.''

''I can't believe you said that. I thought you hated

deception. Why didn't you tell her we aren't married?''

Taking Katlyn's hand, Case put it in the crook of his arm and led her toward Emily. ''Because I found something about the image of us as partners more enticing than telling her we only work with each other. Besides, we haven't done too badly in business together. Is it so difficult for you to think of us as more?''

Katlyn ignored his last words. They meant too much for her to consider right now. ''I'm not really your partner. I'm just another employee with a louder voice than the others.''

Case stopped then, turning to take both her arms in his hands. ''You're much more than that. I respect your ideas and your spirit as much as I would any *real* business partner's. You're a resourceful, talented woman, whom I care about very much. Why is it so hard for you to believe that?''

His sincerity touched her somewhere so deep, Katlyn found it difficult to speak.

''I want to believe it,'' she said finally, the words coming hard and shaky. ''You don't know how much I do.''

''Then believe it. We can do anything, be anything together.''

''You deserve to succeed. You deserve to see your dream come true, more than any man I have ever met.''

Case caught and held her gaze, the intensity in his

eyes both daunting and welcome. "My dream may be more ambitious than you know."

"Daddy, Daddy! Katlyn! Look at me! I'm jumping! One, two, three!" Emily shouted at them with a gleeful joy.

"Hurray, Emily!" Katlyn cried back, clapping wildly. Relief flooded through her at the interruption. She couldn't listen to Case telling her how much he wanted her, needed her. Not now. Not ever.

"That's my girl! You did it!" Case strode over and swept Emily into his arms, spinning her 'round and 'round. "You didn't give up, did you?"

Emily shook her curls wildly. "No, not once. Princesses never give up, do they, Katlyn?"

Katlyn stepped close, brushing her hand down Emily's tumbled hair, her heart aching. "No, sweetheart. They never do."

Chapter Fourteen

Katlyn walked back and forth across the landing by her mother's room, fidgeting first with the sleeve of her dress, then with the framed sampler on the wall. It seemed like hours since Dr. Garrett had closeted himself in the room with Penelope. He'd asked Katlyn to be here today so he could talk to her after he finished examining Penelope, but Katlyn hadn't expected the waiting to be so long and so unnerving.

It would have been easier if this once her mother had allowed her inside with the doctor there. Penelope, though, always insisted on seeing Dr. Garrett alone. Katlyn suspected it was easier for her to deny the truth of her illness without a witness.

At last the door opened and the doctor came out, carrying his bag. Motioning Katlyn to the far end of the landing, he faced her, his expression grim. "Your mother isn't getting any better, I'm sorry to say. There's not much else I can do for her here."

"Is she well enough to make the trip to Las Vegas?"

Dr. Garrett hesitated. "Under other circumstances,

I would say no. But if you don't make the trip soon, the snows will make the trail from here down the mountain impassable. Otherwise, it'll be spring before you can get there. By that time your mother is likely to have deteriorated to the point that the trip will be useless.''

Katlyn felt her heart constrict painfully. "I understand," she said.

"I am sorry there's not more I can do," the doctor said, putting a hand on her arm.

"No, you've been wonderful to her. I—I just wasn't expecting to have to make the decision to leave so soon. I don't have enough money saved yet and…well, it doesn't matter." She faced the doctor resolutely. "I will get her to that hospital and soon. One way or the other. Please tell me what I owe you so we can settle before I leave."

Nodding, Dr. Garrett patted her arm. Katlyn waited until he was down the stairs and out the front door before slumping against the wall. She felt like screaming and crying and railing against the choices she had to make.

But feeling sorry for herself wouldn't change reality or help Penelope. Her mother depended on her. She had to make plans to leave Cimarron.

Once the thought of staying here had terrified her. Now she was more frightened of leaving because she knew when she left, her heart would stay here.

Penelope barely glanced at her when Katlyn let herself into the room. "I suppose that wretched doctor told you how hopeless it all is."

"Oh, Mama." Katlyn sat on the edge of the bed and took Penelope's frail hand. "It isn't hopeless. We just have to get you to Las Vegas. We'll be able to leave by the end of the month, don't worry." She hesitated. "I'll have to tell Case I'm leaving. And why."

"What do you mean, why?" Penelope demanded, for the first time a spark of her old self coming through the dull apathy on her face. "Just tell him you got a better job. Tell him you've decided to go back to St. Louis and work for Luck. What does it matter? He doesn't need to know about me. It's bad enough Luck saw me like this. At least I convinced him I was only recovering from influenza. But if you confess, everyone will know I'm like—*this*."

Penelope's voice had steadily risen in pitch, ending on a note of panic Katlyn well knew. Katlyn took her mother's hand and tried to be both gentle and firm.

"Mama, I have to tell him. I owe him the truth, at least."

"Why? Why? You can't ruin everything for me now, Katie. Not after all this time. You can't!" Penelope eyed her with sudden suspicion. "Why is the truth suddenly so important? Oh, Katie—what have you done?"

"Nothing. Only pretended to be you." Katlyn abruptly got up and paced to the window. She stared unseeing at the street below.

"I may not be the best mother, my dear, but I know when you're upset and when you're lying. You get that tight little look on your face. You've never been any good at hiding your feelings."

"I'm not upset, Mama. Just—tired. We've been busy at the hotel, with the new show and all the renovations."

"What renovations? What new show?"

Katlyn cursed herself for slipping. She'd never told her mother about the disaster the rustlers had caused, lest it give her mother reason to worry.

She glanced away. "Oh, Case is doing some remodeling to make the hotel more desirable to wealthy guests. And we've worked on adding material for the shows in accordance, that's all."

Turning back to her mother, she forced a smile. "I wish you could see the show just once before we leave. I'm not you, but I think you would like it."

"Yes, I'm sure I would. Don't try to distract me, my mind isn't gone yet," Penelope said sharply. She hitched herself up in the bed and frowned at Katlyn. Then her face cleared. "You haven't gone and fallen for that man, have you?"

"Of course not. Here, let me adjust those pillows for you...."

Penelope caught her hand and squeezed it tightly. "Please, Katie," she said, her mouth trembling. Tears welled in her eyes. "Please, don't tell him. Let me pretend for a little while longer. No one will be hurt."

A pain welled up in her so keen that for a moment Katlyn couldn't speak. *Oh, Mama, it's too late for that.*

Kissing her mother softly on the cheek, she made herself smile. "Don't worry about anything, Mama. I'll take care of you, I promise."

Before Penelope could say anything else, Katlyn got up and bustled around the room, making her mother comfortable, tidying up a bit, fetching a tray of tea and biscuits for Penelope—anything she could think of to stop more questions from her mother about Case.

She couldn't tell if Penelope believed her when she denied any feelings for Case. *Small wonder if she doesn't, I don't believe myself.*

Which made telling Case the truth so much harder.

And she had to tell him soon, at least that she was leaving. Except then he would demand to know why.

Despite Penelope's pleas, Katlyn didn't know if she could stomach leaving Case with yet another lie. It was bad enough she was deserting him when he and the hotel needed her most. Didn't she at least owe him the truth?

The truth…the idea of telling him twisted her up inside. All during the short walk back to the St. Martin, Katlyn tried out several approaches, but none seemed right. They all ended with her confessing her deception, and how could she do that, knowing she would be breaking her vow to her mother?

And knowing the pain it would cause Case. How could she watch the shadow come down over his eyes, separating him from her forever, as the realization dawned in him that she was no better than his wife? That she, too, had lied to him, had pretended to be someone she was not.

The image of Case withdrawing from her tortured her heart and soul as she pushed open the door of the hotel, Katlyn nevertheless made up her mind she had no choice but to tell him. Now, before she changed her mind.

"Oh, Katlyn, finally!" Sally rushed up to her, out of breath and looking unusually ruffled. "Maybe you can figure out what to do."

Katlyn tossed off her hat and shawl, her dilemma temporarily set aside. "What's the matter? Is there—"

Before she could finish, a loud scrape and thud came from the dining room.

"We've got five new guests staying, they came in unexpectedly and nothing was ready. And there's going to be another six for dinner, as well," Sally said in answer to Katlyn's raised brow. "Tuck is all out of sorts because now there's not enough chicken for dinner, and Mr. Durham and Jack are trying to rearrange the tables so there's room for everyone and the piano. And then Becky accidentally broke the lamp in the big bedroom when she was cleaning. That odious Mr. Miller left with two of our blankets and a clock, and his friend threw up on the rug this morning. Oh, and, we're running low on wood and—"

"I get the idea," Katlyn said. She hurried into the dining room, stopped short by the chaotic scene there.

Case and Jack, tables and chairs haphazardly bunched around them, stopped as she came into the room, Sally behind her. Perched on Jack's piano stool, Emily smiled and gave a small wave.

"Ah, reinforcements," Jack said. He grinned at her, motioning to the chair he was trying to squeeze into place between the wall and table. "Be prepared to sit on my lap tonight, Katie."

"Oh, I'd never come between you and your keys." Katlyn briefly glanced at him, but her eyes fixed on Case. She suddenly felt as tongue-tied as she had the first moment she'd met him in her newly assumed role as Penelope.

Case put down the chair he'd been moving and came over to her, frowning. She'd gone pale and when he touched her arm, a tremor went through her. "Are you all right?"

"Y-yes. Yes, of course." With an effort, she seemed to regain control over herself. "Sally says we're going to have a full house. How can I help?"

"You'll be singing. That's enough." Concerned by the look of her, Case was about to suggest she go to her room to rest before the dinner show when Sally broke in.

"It's everything, if you ask me. Before she came, I was getting worried about how I was going to feed my boys, but the way Katlyn sings, we can't keep people away. You sure knew what you were doing, Mr. Durham, bringing her here."

"Katlyn is a princess," Emily piped up from behind Case. "She came to rescue us, Daddy says so."

Katlyn smiled at their praise and gently caressed Emily's cheek in thanks. But Case saw how stiffly she held herself, as if she were afraid moving would break something inside her.

"Becky said she was going to need some help moving one of the dressers upstairs," he said, looking sideways at Jack. "And I'm not sure if she was quite finished with the feather duster."

"Oh, your favorite, Emily," Sally said, taking the hint along with Jack. He was already heading toward the door, and Sally took Emily's hand, leading her out behind him. "Let's go see if we can make some dust fly."

Katlyn gave him a rueful smile and walked a little away from him. "You didn't have to send them all away."

"I want to talk to you. What's wrong, Katlyn?"

"I want to talk to you, too." She stopped, biting her lower lip.

Case felt a prick of uneasiness. It wasn't like Katlyn to be hesitant about speaking her mind. He reached out a hand. To draw her back to him or to offer her reassurance? He didn't know which.

Before he touched her Tuck marched into the dining room carrying three limp chickens. "Don't ask me where I found 'em, but at least we won't be servin' beans and biscuits tonight. Glad you're back, Miss Katlyn. I was gonna ask you to help with them radishes and carrots again."

Katlyn nodded and as Tuck pushed his way into the kitchen, Case turned back to her to ask his question again.

"Daddy?" Emily poked her head into the dining room. "Jack got the dresser stuck in the door."

Case sighed and Katlyn shook her head, smiling. "I'll be there in a minute," he said to Emily. He took Katlyn's hand when the little girl scampered off upstairs again. "What did you want to talk to me about?"

"It's not important right now," Katlyn said softly. "We both have things to do, we can talk later."

Instinct told Case it was important. But he wouldn't find out what it was now, with them likely to be interrupted at any moment. "We will talk later," he promised.

Pulling her closer to him, he leaned down and kissed her. She responded instantly but with an urgency that surprised him. It touched off a warning in him even as he took her in his arms and deepened his kiss.

Katlyn fought an upsurge of panic that became a desperate need to be with Case and forget everything but the way he made her feel—soft, hot, hungry, alive.

When he held her like this there was no denying her feelings. She loved him, heart and soul.

And when he discovered her deception, she would be the last woman on earth he would want.

Katlyn slammed her hairbrush down on her dressing table, causing Becky to jump. "I'm sorry. It's just that my hair is hopeless tonight. You've been trying, I've tried, and it just won't work!"

"I think it looks real nice," Becky ventured. She

stood a step back from Katlyn as if expecting her to throw the brush at any moment. "It's such a pretty color, it doesn't matter if the curls aren't just right."

"They're far from just right, but they'll have to do. Thank you for trying." Katlyn pushed away from the mirror to go and get her gown from the armoire. Her satin dressing robe swished and caught around her ankles, annoying her further.

"I can manage the dress myself tonight, Becky. I'm afraid I'm not fit company. Why don't you go and get yourself ready?"

"But—"

"Please. It's all right, really. Just leave me alone for a few minutes."

Katlyn turned away, not wanting Becky to see the tears welling in her eyes.

"Well, if you say so." Becky backed out of Katlyn's bedroom, confused. She'd never seen Miss McLain in such a state. Sure the lady could be emotional and she always spoke her mind, but she'd never been so irritable. Becky headed for the sitting-room door, shaking her head.

Temperamental, that was the word Sally said they used for fancy actresses and singers, wasn't it? Maybe tonight the St. Louis Songbird decided to be *temperamental.* Whatever the problem was, Becky hoped it wouldn't last. Mr. Durham'd never put up with it, no matter how much he liked her.

The object of her thoughts surprised her on the landing outside Katlyn's door. "Is she in?" Case asked, shifting one hand behind his back.

Becky nodded. "Oh, she's in, all right, Mr. Durham. But she's, um...*tempermental* tonight."

"Ah, I see. Well, maybe I can cheer her up."

With a shrug Becky stepped past him. "I sure hope so. We got a full house again tonight. I don't think it'll be too good a show with her like this."

"Katlyn?" Case rapped on the half-open door, letting himself inside before she answered. "I wanted to see you."

"Oh, Case, wait a moment," she called from the bedroom. Wiping the tears from her cheeks, she scurried to the basin and dipped a cloth in the tepid water to dab the smeared makeup from her eyes and face.

Wiping her cheeks before her mirror, she knew, despite her best efforts, Case would know she'd been crying. What would she say? How could she explain?

"Are you all right?"

"Yes, of course. I'm just—I was dressing." She tugged the belt on her robe closer and tied it securely. With a toss of her head, she braced herself to face him.

"Come in," she called. "I have a few minutes before I have to be downstairs, but I need to finish my makeup first."

Katlyn watched in her mirror as Case strode into her bedroom. The sight of him in black formal attire never ceased to stir her. In a few lithe moves he was at her side, bending to touch a light kiss to the top of her head. "What's wrong? Becky said you weren't yourself."

Katlyn busied herself touching up her cheeks and lips. "I'm fine. I was just abrupt with her, poor girl. It wasn't her fault."

"That's not like you." Case pulled a chair close and sat, his knees touching her thighs. "What is it, Katlyn? Please tell me."

Katlyn dropped her gaze from the mirror to hide her eyes from his keen appraisal. "Nothing I want to talk about right now, if you don't mind. I have a performance to give in a few minutes."

"Is it your companion?" He reached out and stroked her cheek with the back of his hand, then gently tipped her face to his. "You've been crying. Katlyn—"

"Case, please. It's not important right now. I'm just…tired."

Case studied her face for a moment then decided to let the matter drop, for now. "I brought you something," he said. "For luck, I suppose, although you hardly need it." He handed her a rectangular velvet box. "Open it."

Tears blurred Katlyn's vision again. "Oh, Case, I can't."

Case put the box in her hands and closed his fingers over hers, imprisoning his gift there. "I insist."

Hesitating, Katlyn ran the tip of her tongue over her lips. Then, taking a steadying breath, she carefully lifted the lid on the box, revealing the most exquisite necklace she had ever laid eyes on. The artisan who had crafted it had bent and twined delicate strands of silver and carved gems into a chain of sapphire leaves and silver roses, each so perfectly formed they looked as if they would be warm and supple to the touch.

Katlyn caught her breath. "Case, it's beautiful," she whispered. In the next instant she took his hand and put the box in it. "And it's out of the question."

"I didn't mortgage the St. Martin to buy it, if that's what you're thinking," Case said with an indulgent smile. "This was my mother's. I've saved it and a few other pieces since her death. This one seemed to be made for you." He held it up to the light near her eyes. "Look," he said, gesturing to the mirror, "tell me it's not a perfect match for your eyes."

Katlyn followed his gaze to the mirror. Except, reflected there, she didn't see the gems but the expression on Case's face that told her more clearly than words how much he cared.

"It is a perfect match," Case was saying. "I knew it the first time I looked into your eyes."

Now tears slid down her face unchecked. "Case, I can't. You don't understand—"

"No, I do understand. I understand this—"

Setting the box aside, in one easy swoop of his arm, he pulled her atop his lap. He covered her mouth with his, tasting and tempting at first, then demanding far more when she responded eagerly.

Emotion overwhelming all trace of reason, Katlyn never thought of resisting. She wrapped her arms around his neck and returned his kiss with a need laced with desperation.

"Katlyn, I need you," Case murmured against her neck.

"And I need you," she returned before their words became unnecessary, swept aside by a deep, consuming communion of desire.

He tugged at the belt of her robe and it fell away with little coaxing. Wanting, craving his touch with an abandon she couldn't explain, Katlyn arched back, inviting him.

Case brushed his lips across the tempting swells of her breasts above her corset and with a little moan, she moved restlessly in his lap, nearly driving him crazy. Fumbling with the laces of her corset, he finally freed her of it and flung it aside.

The thin cotton of her shift scarcely concealed the fullness of her breasts, taut with the evidence of her want of him.

His hands roved, caressing her through the material until the temptation to feel her skin became too much. With trembling fingers he lifted it over her head, silencing her surprised gasp with his kiss.

Bared to his touch, Katlyn could hardly breathe. She ached in places she never knew could feel so much, wanted him to caress her in ways she couldn't name. She shouldn't be here with him like this. But at this moment she couldn't bring herself to break away.

Why shouldn't she, just once before she left him, know the full meaning of loving Case?

Not content to be still, she ran her hands down the breadth of his broad back under his coat, over his firm buttocks and down his hard thighs. His clothes suddenly became an irritating barrier to everything she craved, the feel of skin to skin, passion to passion.

With one hand, Case pressed her to him, the other skimmed up her bare thigh, beneath her drawers, teasing close to the most intimate part of her. Katlyn nearly begged him to go further.

"Case, please...I need you."

"My sweet Katlyn," he whispered. Forgetting where they were, that they had a hotel full of guests waiting for the St. Louis Songbird, Case shifted to pick Katlyn up in his arms and carry her to the bed.

"Miss McLain! It's gettin' late!"

Becky's call jolted him back to reality. Case inwardly groaned at her timing. He looked at Katlyn, seeing her eyes smoky with passion, her hair tousled, her skin flushed from his touch, and he nearly said to hell with it and told Becky the guests would have to wait.

Instead, Case lifted her from his lap and back onto her chair. Handing her the discarded robe, he went to fend off Becky while Katlyn wrapped the satin around her and tried to smooth her hair with an unsteady hand.

Becky gave him an odd look when he closed Katlyn's bedroom door behind him but she was too flustered to say anything. "I'm sorry, Mr. Durham, but everyone's waitin' on Miss McLain. It's gettin' late and the crowd's mighty restless."

"I'll take care of it, Becky. Tell Jack to say Miss McLain will be down in a few minutes. He can entertain them while they're waiting for her. And have Bat offer them a round of free drinks for their patience.''

When he went back into the bedroom after sending Becky off, he found Katlyn in her shift and corset, pulling on a deep blue satin dress. ''Thank you,'' she said, giving him a grateful smile.

''It's the least I can do, since I'm responsible for the delay of the show.''

''You'll have to share the blame, Mr. Durham. I don't recall you being alone here.''

''No.'' Coming over to her, he slid his fingers down her bare arm, making her shiver. ''Definitely not.'' Before either of them could consider temptation's offer, Case went to the dressing table and picked up the necklace from its cushioned box. ''You will wear this, won't you?''

Katlyn turned and indicated her dress, her cheeks flushed with anticipation. ''That's why I've chosen this dress.''

''Then please allow me the pleasure of placing this around your beautiful neck,'' he said, turning her around.

He clasped the silver chain and turned her back to face him again. With a satisfied smile he said, ''I can't decide what has more fire. The sapphires or your eyes.''

''It must be my eyes. Because they hold a reflection of you.''

Chapter Fifteen

Jack plucked his whiskey glass from the top of the piano and saluted Katlyn as she accepted the last accolades from the audience. "Here's to another rousing success," he said with a wink.

Katlyn smiled and motioned the audience's attention his way. "A round of applause for my piano player," she asked, leading the clapping herself.

Jack downed his whiskey in a single drink and returned the audience's praise with a jaunty, deep bow, a sun-splashed wave of overlong hair falling over one eye as he did.

Laughter and more applause followed, gradually dying down to a pleasant hum of conversation among the guests in the crowded dining room. Rising at their leisure from their tables, appetites well sated with Tuck's cooking, minds mellowed with Case's choices in fine wines, they mingled with one another, satisfied with the evening.

Katlyn stepped down from the stage, thanked Jack and tried to slip to the side door that led to the saloon, which was still closed while Bat and Case worked at the restoration. As usual, her attempt at an early escape was quickly thwarted. A friendly couple she recognized from the rodeo caught up with her, hands extended, faces beaming.

"Mr. and Mrs. Erickson, how nice to see you here," she said, putting on her best smile when they approached.

Richard Erickson, sixtyish, distinguished but ruggedly handsome, self-made, and now a man of great means and prominence in the territory, bent to lift her fingers to his lips. "Why, I'm only here to protect my investment, ma'am," he said with a sly grin.

The attractive woman at his side slapped his arm playfully. "Now, Miss Rose, don't you pay him any heed. He came to hear you for the same reason we all did. You're the best show in town."

Katlyn laughed lightly. "Thank you, but from what I'm told, I'm also the only show in town unless you fancy the entertainment at the Crooked Pony."

Looking a bit flustered, Mrs. Erickson fidgeted with her ruby-and-diamond wedding ring. "You must know we all simply love your singing. Especially those sad Irish tunes. And this hotel has never served finer food or looked so elegant." She leaned in closer to Katlyn. Her sharp eyes narrowed with curiosity. "Something tells me you had a say-so in the new decor."

"Indeed she did," the familiar resonance of Case's deep, velvety voice sounded close behind Katlyn, sending a warm thrill through her. "Miss Rose is not only our resident songbird, she is also our resident decorator and culinary advisor.''

''My, my, your talents do have a wide range,'' Mr. Erickson said, the hint of suggestiveness in his voice earning him a tight-lipped grimace from his wife.

''Oh, don't embarrass yourself, Richard. Miss Rose is young enough to be your granddaughter.''

Undeterred, the older gentleman continued to smile at Katlyn, shamelessly appreciative of her beauty.

Taking a step nearer to Katlyn, Case rested his hand at her waist. Mrs. Erickson glanced at Case, speculation in her eyes over the possessive gesture.

Case only smiled. Let the woman think what she wanted. He didn't worry Richard Erickson would take his admiration of Katlyn any further than looking, but he also felt compelled to make it clear anything beyond admiration from any other man in the room was unwelcome.

Katlyn smiled to herself, a little amused by Case's determination to stake his claim. If he only knew she had no desire to look anywhere but in his eyes.

A few more guests joined the little group and Case and Katlyn chatted with them a few minutes, accepting their praises for the show and the hotel renovation.

''My wife and I are staying the night, too,'' a young man with sleek black hair, wearing a finely tailored suit volunteered. ''Janie doesn't want to ride all the way back to the ranch this time of night.''

Twisting her hands nervously, a pretty little woman at his side nodded. ''If the Indians don't get you out there, the *banditos* will. I told Gavin I'd only come tonight if we stayed safe and sound under this roof until daylight. Oh, and we've booked a room for my mother, too.''

She wrapped her arm protectively around the small elderly woman next to her. ''Your young man at the front desk assured us you have two adjoining rooms on the first floor so Mother won't have to climb the stairs. And I need to be able to hear if she calls in the night.''

Though Katlyn quickly decided Janie was the nervous sort, the young woman's devotion reminded her of her own situation. From the beginning, she'd been uncomfortable with the promise she'd made to Penelope. But was her mother asking so much that Katlyn not take her dignity by revealing her illness?

It sounded so simple put that way, yet Katlyn knew it was so much more complicated.

''Miss Rose?'' A tap on her arm brought her back from her musings. ''I'm trying to find out where you came by that exquisite necklace. Do you mind?'' Mrs. Erickson bent close to examine the sapphires in the necklace Case had given her. ''I've never seen anything like it.''

Katlyn glanced to Case and he smiled.

She steeled herself, knowing his expression would quickly change. ''Actually, it belongs to Mr. Durham. It was his mother's and he was gracious enough to lend it to me tonight.''

Katlyn didn't have to look at Case to see the coldness settling over his face. She could feel the chill from him as if winter had suddenly blown in through the windows. He was insulted by her rejection of his generosity. But she absolutely would not accept such a priceless gift knowing that soon she'd be leaving him.

"Yes, Miss Rose has difficulty accepting her due," Case said.

Quickly looking up, Katlyn caught his eye and they looked at each other, cool challenge in his gaze meeting stubborn defiance in hers.

"I know what belongs to me, Mr. Durham."

"You know, Miss Rose, I don't think you do. Now, if you'll excuse me," he said to his guests. "My bartender is trying to catch my attention. Enjoy the rest of your evening, please."

Then, without so much as a backward glance, he was gone.

Somewhere in the middle of the night an icy wind came from nowhere, stealing under Katlyn's quilt. She curled up, reaching blindly through the darkness and what had been a deep sleep, for the bedcovers. How could her window be open?

The cold swept over her and Katlyn awoke with a start, shivering. She grabbed all the bedding she could and buried herself under it, trying to warm away the chill that seemed to have settled in her bones.

"Wretched drafty hotel," she muttered.

She punched at her pillow and was just about to settle down to sleep again when mingled sounds of laughter intruded into the stillness of her room.

Who would be up at this hour? As far as she knew, the guests this time were all respectable families and couples. Katlyn shivered again, but this time from a strange feeling that crawled over her.

"You're being ridiculous," she told herself.

The laughter grew louder, a woman's voice more raucous. She heard the rustling of cards and the slide of poker chips across a table.

"I should know better than to drink coffee before bed." She spoke out loud to the darkness, hoping to dispel the odd dreamlike quality hanging over it.

"Straight flush! I win again. Better luck next time, cowboy!"

"Oh, yeah? Well, woman, my luck's about to change. Now git on over here."

Katlyn sat bolt upright, straining in the dark to see something, anything.

As surely as if she were in the saloon, standing next to Jack as he played out a winning hand, she heard the flip of cards, the scrape of dozens of chips across a table, then a burst of loud playful laughter, a swish of petticoats and the stomp of heavy boots in rapid pursuit.

The sounds slowly faded somewhere in the black distance, only a waft of whiskey and cheap perfume lingering like a whisper in the air.

With the silence, the room seemed warmer, the darkness less impenetrable.

It was a dream, Katlyn said to herself, brought on by too many tense hours, too much worry, and too many stories of Rattlesnake Cooper and his hauntings.

She'd nearly convinced herself when the sound of doors opening and raised voices completely eliminated any vestiges of a dream.

These sounds and voices she recognized all too well.

Not bothering with her lamp, Katlyn snatched up her robe and hurried out to the landing.

Sleepy-eyed guests with mussed hair, wearing all manner of nightdresses and robes, long johns and nightshirts had begun to gather, clamoring about the noise. Someone said the word "ghost," and Katlyn didn't know whether to laugh or groan.

Cooper's midnight antics might be amusing if they didn't threaten disaster for the St. Martin.

Case appeared then at the rear of the crowd, Emily clinging to his neck. Somehow he'd managed to toss on a pair of black trousers and a gray flannel shirt. Katlyn recognized worry written in the lines furrowing his brow, but he gave the impression of calm control.

Even in the middle of the night, he maintained the dignified composure that inspired others' confidence in him. At first he was so absorbed with his guests, he didn't see her watching him.

"There's nothing to worry about," he said, pitching his voice to reflect the right balance of amusement and reassurance. "I'm sorry they disturbed your sleep, but I think they've had their fun for the night."

Mrs. Erickson slapped a hand to her mouth. "Well, I'll be! So this place *is* haunted. I've always heard the stories, but I never believed them until now." She turned to her husband and beamed. "Richard, isn't this exciting!"

"Well that's one way of looking at it. And I hope for Durham's sake and the sake of my investment here, the other guests see it the way you do."

"Oh, of course they will. Real ghosts! How often do you get the chance to see, or hear, that! It's positively thrilling! I can't wait to get back home and tell Maribelle and Suzanna! They'll be dragging Irwin and Henry up here before the week's out. Maybe we could come back with them, Richard, and have one of those séances?"

Mr. Erickson smiled indulgently at his wife and wrapped an arm around her shoulders. "Slow down there, honey. I think I've had my fill of late-night visitors."

Case turned from the Ericksons, glancing up at the landing to see Katlyn there.

When she saw him looking at her, she smiled and lifted her hands as if in surrender to Cooper's willful tricks. Case couldn't help but smile back, shaking his head.

For the next few minutes he walked through the crowd listening to the guests as they talked and shared what they'd heard. To his relief, the main reaction to the night's disruption was laughter.

The guests seemed excited by the experience rather than frightened, eager to boast to all their friends that they had witnessed the antics of the infamous St. Martin ghosts firsthand.

Katlyn, watching, wondered if Cooper and his

friends would actually wind up being *good* for business.

But before the thought fully formed, the sound of Janie's shrill voice drowned it out. "I demand to see the owner! We want our money back."

Janie, fully dressed, suitcase in hand, stood at the bottom of the stairs shouting. At her side, her husband tried to silence her, no understanding patience in his voice this time.

Katlyn hurried downstairs, taking Emily from Case as he went over to the young couple.

"I can understand why you're upset, ma'am," he began.

"Upset! Why I'd rather ride out tonight and face the Indians, *banditos* and the devil himself than stay in a haunted hotel!"

The old woman who'd shuffled up next to Janie, laid a hand on her arm. "They were nice ghosts, honey. Not like Uncle Redeye." She turned a kind smile to Case. "I'm sorry, my daughter is a little anxious."

"Mama!"

"My mother-in-law is right. Janie doesn't get out much. She would probably be more comfortable at home."

"It's your choice, of course," Case said. Business or no business, he wouldn't mind seeing the back of the over-anxious Janie. "But if you'd like to stay, we'll be offering all guests a free breakfast in the morning."

"Breakfast!" Janie screeched. "We're not paying one cent—"

"Yes we are, *dear*. We had a wonderful evening here and the accommodations are first-rate. And if you'll bother to take note, all of the other guests seem to find this little incident amusing. Now let's go."

After settling the bill, Case escorted the trio to the lobby and summoned Bucky to ready their horse and buggy.

By the time the three had gone, the other guests had drifted back to their rooms and Case climbed the stairs in search of Katlyn.

He found her, Emily on her lap, asleep in the rocking chair in Emily's room. Gently, he bent and lifted his daughter to tuck her into bed. The motion woke Katlyn and she yawned and stretched, giving him a sleepy smile.

"Let me walk you to your rooms," he whispered when he'd settled Emily.

Nodding drowsily, Katlyn rose and leaned easily into him when he wrapped an arm around her shoulders and pulled her close.

Case walked her to her rooms and Katlyn sighed when he moved away from her to open the door, missing his heat and the firmness of his body against hers.

"It's been quite a night," he said.

"Well, at least you can't say it's been dull. I guess Cooper missed all the shooting and fighting. All this respectability probably bores him."

"That gives us something to look forward to. By the way—" Case reached into his pants' pocket and pulled out the necklace. He made the gesture casually enough, but inside he tensed. "You left this in my room."

"On purpose," Katlyn said. She refused to take the gleaming silver from his outstretched palm. "I told you, I can't accept it."

"Why? If you don't like it, I'll have the gems reset."

"Oh, Case, it's not that. It's the most beautiful piece of jewelry I've ever seen. But I don't deserve it."

"How can you say that? You've been a partner and more with me in all of this. You're like a mother to Emily. I want you to have it."

Putting the necklace into her hands, Case closed her fingers around it, lifting them to his lips to seal the giving with a kiss. "You deserve much more than this, Katlyn."

To his surprise, her mouth began to quiver and then she burst into tears, rushing inside her suite. A moment later he heard her bedroom door slam.

She left him there, staring at the place she'd been, wondering if he would ever fully understand Katlyn McLain.

Katlyn glared at the blank sheet of paper in front of her and fought the urge to throw it, pen and ink out the window. It wouldn't resolve a single thing but it would feel good to do something because she wanted to, not because a tide of events she couldn't control swept her toward decisions she didn't want to make.

She sighed and picked up her pen again. The sooner she got the details of the trip to Las Vegas, her mother's admittance to the hospital there, and a job for herself settled, the sooner she could begin rebuilding her life. At the very least, she needed to send a wire to the hospital today to make sure they would be able to take her mother at month's end.

Dipping the end of the pen into the ink, she started to write a few words of the message, hesitated, then threw her pen down. She hated everything she was doing, the lies, the leaving.

Most frustrating, she hadn't been able to tell Case anything. With the hotel full, and the dinners and her performance to cope with, she'd had no time alone with him. It made her impatient and nervy, and at the same time, part of her was secretly glad to have an excuse to put off the inevitable.

"This telegram is one inevitable I can't put off any longer," she muttered to herself. She started again and just touched her pen to paper when a furious pounding rattled the door.

Katlyn's hand jerked and the pen tip skittered over the page, leaving a trail of ink drops. Abandoning the wretched task altogether, she got up to answer the door.

Before she could reach it, Becky flung it open and rushed up to her. Tears streaked her face, making trails in the dusting of red dirt. "Oh, Miss McLain, you have to help us. Please! I didn't mean for it to happen, I really didn't! But if Mr. Durham finds out, he'll throw me out, I know it. I just know it!''

"Becky, it's all right," Katlyn said. She put an arm around the distraught girl. "Take a deep breath and tell me what's happened."

"It's Emily!" Katlyn's heart constricted and seeing the sudden tension in her Becky wailed, "Oh, I never thought she'd git into trouble like that, really I didn't. It was just fun! You have to believe me!''

"I do believe you, Becky. But what's happened to Emily?" Katlyn pressed.

"She's stuck!"

"Stuck? Stuck where?"

"I-in the t-tree. Behind the h-hotel. Bucky and I like to climb it and Emily don't git out of the hotel much, and I thought she'd like it, too, and, oh, I never thought she'd go and git herself s-stuck!" Becky gave a hiccuping sob and wiped at her eyes with her sleeve.

"Well, what's important now is that we get her down. Have you tried to find Mr. Durham?"

"Sally said he was with Tuck and Bat, gettin' supplies. Bucky went to find him, but I was hopin' you could git Emily down before he gits here." Biting at her lower lip, Becky shot her a pleading look. "Maybe he won't be so mad then."

"I'll see what I can do," Katlyn said, giving Becky a reassuring pat. "Now show me this tree."

Katlyn followed Becky outside and behind the hotel. There, a short distance from the building, was a large, gnarled chestnut tree. Reaching it, Katlyn peered up into the twists and turns of branches. "Oh, my," she said softly.

About halfway up the tree, Emily straddled a large branch, one foot caught in a crevice made by a vee between the branch and trunk.

"Emily, honey, are you all right?" Katlyn called up to her.

Emily nodded, barely moving her head. Katlyn could see she clutched the branch so tightly her fingers looked glued to the wood.

"What're you gonna do?"

Katlyn glanced at Becky, touched by her faith. She looked back at Emily, then at the distance up the tree. "Go get her," she said. "How hard could it be?"

Flashing a smile at Becky's wide-eyed look, Katlyn knotted up her skirts as well as she could before grasping the lowest handhold and hoisting herself up.

"Um…Miss McLain," Becky called up as Katlyn wrestled to find a place to put her foot, "have you ever climbed a tree before?"

"I climbed down the arbor outside a second-story window once when I was twelve," Katlyn said, panting. "It can't be that much different."

As she flopped her arm over the branch closest to her head, Katlyn noticed Emily's expression had turned from pure terror to a fascinated interest in Katlyn's progress.

Well, at least I'm entertaining someone, Katlyn thought as she hoisted herself a little higher.

A few feet from reaching Emily, Katlyn heard

voices behind her—Bucky's, fast and excited, and Case's, deeper and tense.

Case got to the foot of the tree just as Katlyn stretched her fingers up and touched Emily's leg. For a moment he could only stare at the sight they made: Emily sitting astride a branch of the first tree she'd ever climbed, and Katlyn, her skirts hiked up to her thighs, climbing up after her.

He supposed he should be surprised. But then Katlyn rarely stopped to ponder before acting, and it was that unexpected quality in her that made her so alive, so appealing.

"Katlyn," he said at last, "do you need help?"

"Well—" She dared a look down at him. "Not right at this moment. But I have a feeling getting Emily down is going to be a lot harder than getting me up."

She hadn't been exaggerating, Case thought half an hour later when he finally put his hands around Katlyn's waist and lifted her down from the tree. Emily, standing close to Becky, clapped excitedly and ran to them, hugging Katlyn first, then her father.

"You rescued her, just like she rescued me!"

"No one would have needed rescuing if you hadn't climbed that tree in the first place, young lady," Case said, trying to look severe. But his relief at having both his daughter and Katlyn safe on the ground made it difficult to maintain a suitably hard expression.

"It's my fault, Mr. Durham." Becky spoke up behind them. She scuffed the toe of her boot in the ground and watched the dust kick up when they looked her way. "I'm the one who said it'd be fun to climb the tree. I thought she'd like it. I never thought she'd go'n git stuck. Never!"

She ended up turning a look both fearful and sorrowful on Case and it was obvious she expected him to reprimand her, and even throw her out of the hotel.

Instead, Case, with Emily in his arms, walked up to her and lifted her chin so their eyes met. "I know you meant well, Becky. But I think Emily needs a little more practice before she's ready to climb that high in a tree again."

"Oh, I promise, Mr. Durham, I'll never let her do that again!" Becky said fervently.

Bucky lightly cuffed her arm. "If you'd told me what you were doin', I'da never let you do it to begin with."

"I think Becky's had her share of tree climbing, at least for a day or two." Case glanced at Katlyn and found her trying to hide a smile. "Would you like to give it another try?"

"No, thank you," she said, then added with a mischievous smile, "not today, anyway."

Case gave up trying to remain serious, laughed and took Katlyn's hand as they followed Becky and Bucky back to the hotel. Sally met them at the door, fussing over Emily and Becky, raising her brows at Katlyn's disheveled dress and hair. When she'd satisfied herself they were all more or less in one piece, she herded Becky and Bucky to the dining room for apple cider, leaving Case and Katlyn to tend to Emily upstairs.

"It doesn't seem serious," Katlyn said a few minutes later, after they'd both examined Emily's slightly swollen ankle. "Cold compresses with aloe should make it as good as new," she added, remembering her sister treating a similar injury to one of her boys.

Case nodded. Sitting next to Emily on her bed, he put his arm around his daughter. "You're lucky Katlyn was here to rescue you."

"Katlyn rescues everybody," Emily said, then reached up and put her arms around Katlyn's neck and hugged her tightly. "I love you, Katlyn. I want you to stay here forever and ever. Say you will. Please?"

Katlyn sat on the bed and held Emily close. She put her cheek against the little girl's soft curls and closed her eyes against the tears that burned her eyes. "Oh, Emily," she whispered. "I love you, too."

"Then don't ever go away and we can always be together, you and me and Daddy. Just like a real family. Will you stay, Katlyn?"

A real family. Katlyn's throat tightened painfully. But it was nothing compared to the hurt inside her, so keen and pure she wasn't sure she could bear it.

She finally managed to speak, though her voice came out rough with unshed tears. "Sweetheart, there's nothing I'd love more than to stay with you and your daddy."

Emily's smile flashed like sunlight and Case, watching Katlyn with his daughter, was struck by how much he loved them both.

It seemed, with Katlyn, it was something he had known for a long time, but only now admitted. Emily wanted Katlyn with them forever and he wanted it, too. It all seemed so simple now. No matter what lay in her past, surely he couldn't be wrong about Katlyn's feelings for Emily and for him. Not this time.

"Daddy," Emily piped up. "I'm hungry!"

Case laughed and stood with Emily in his arms, pulling Katlyn up with them. "I think it's time I fed both my ladies. I'm sure Sally saved us something."

Katlyn smiled and tried to share in their lighthearted mood as they all went downstairs and joined Sally, Becky and Bucky in the dining room. Bat and Jack came in a few minutes after them, and even Tuck came out of the kitchen to hear Emily relate her adventure in the tree.

Sitting next to Case, Katlyn ached every time his leg brushed hers or he casually touched her hand or draped his arm over the back of her chair in a possessive gesture that everyone seemed to accept as natural.

She belonged here and every time Case looked at her she saw that thought reflected in his eyes. How could she think of leaving the one place she was wanted, needed? How could she leave the one man she loved?

But even as the words formed in her mind, Katlyn knew there was only one answer to those questions. She had made a commitment to her mother and she would honor her promise.

A little while later, when Case was distracted by

Emily's animated telling of climbing the tree, Katlyn slipped out of the dining room. Pulling her shawl around her, she left the hotel and made her way to the telegraph office.

The clerk looked up as she came in, his smile fading a little seeing the bleak expression in her eyes.

"I need to send a wire," Katlyn said shortly. "To Las Vegas."

Chapter Sixteen

Case leaned against the front desk, finishing the last of his cheroot, waiting. He'd seen the last of the dinner guests out; those that were staying had gone to their rooms and most of the staff had either gone home or departed to their own beds. All but Katlyn.

In the late-night stillness, he could hear her moving about the dining room and the occasional now-familiar sound of her shuffling sheets of music or adjusting chairs perfectly back into place around tables. She was obviously biding her time until she was sure everyone had left or gone to bed. What wasn't so obvious was why.

Ever since lunch today, when she'd slipped away unnoticed, he'd been aware of an air of sorrow around her, as if she were grieving. It wove its way into her music tonight so every song had a bittersweet quality, so keen at times it brought several women in the audience to tears.

It touched him, too, but made him uneasy and restless. Crushing out his cheroot, Case started for the dining room. Just as he did, Katlyn walked out, stopping abruptly when she saw him.

Their eyes locked and held, suspending time and space for a moment. Then Katlyn blinked and looked away.

"I thought everyone had gone to bed," she said quietly.

"Not everyone. I waited for you."

"I know. Everywhere I've looked this evening, there's been you." Katlyn avoided his direct gaze, afraid he would recognize the longing in her eyes. And he was watching her with that intense, perceptive look that at times like this would melt her completely if she so much as let her eyes meet his for more than a moment's glance. She felt the weight of his eyes on her like a heated caress.

She wanted to be with him. But by being with him, she felt compelled to tell him she was leaving. And right now, after all the emotional upheaval and an exhausting performance, she couldn't do it.

Case, very slowly, walked up to her. He trailed one fingertip from her temple to the curve of her jaw. "I missed you at lunch."

"I—I had to run an errand for my...my companion," Katlyn stammered. Even so simple a touch made her heart leap.

"You're wearing your necklace again," Case said. He ran his finger between the cool metal and her throat, finding the combination of cool hardness and warm silk an intoxicant. "I'm glad. This is where it belongs."

"Case..." She stopped, licked her lips, then tried
again. "I need to talk to you."

"No. I don't want to talk anymore tonight."

"But—you don't understand. I have to talk to you
about—"

"Not tonight, Katlyn. Whatever it is doesn't matter. I just want us to be together tonight. I don't want
us to talk about the past or the future. Just the present."

Case moved slightly closer and from the glint in
his eyes, Katlyn thought he would kiss her. And, oh,
how she wanted his kiss. Her whole body ached for
it and, forgetting her confession, she leaned toward
him, anticipating.

Instead he smiled and lightly brushed his lips
against her hair, then took her hand in his.

"Where are we going?" she asked, baffled.

"You'll see." Case smiled as they neared the saloon doors and Katlyn's eyes rounded. With a flourish, he flung open the doors and ushered her in.

She stared at the refurbished room, wood and brass
polished and gleaming, the bar rebuilt, and new card
and billiard tables, chairs and curtains in place. A glistening mirror lined the wall behind the bar, reflecting
each gleam of lamplight back into the room. On one
wall hung a huge painting of *Custer's Last Fight* Case
said one of his investors had donated.

"You've been so busy with everything else around
here," Case said, "Bat and I were able to get it done
without you knowing it. I thought I'd surprise you."

"You have done that. Oh, Case, it's beautiful! It's really perfect."

Katlyn let go of his hand and stepped farther into the room, turning around and around, catching her breath a little. "It's even better than before. Truly, Case, you've done a wonderful job."

"I'm happy you're pleased. I wanted the perfect setting for my songbird."

"I—I don't know what to say." Katlyn flushed and looked away from him.

"Say you'll dance with me."

"Dance?" The low, caressing note in his voice, the slow slide of his hand down her cheek, flashed an image in her mind of Case holding her in his arms, loving her. A warm, sweet longing tremored through her, all the more keen because she could see he easily read her thoughts.

"Are you such a magician you can create music from the air?" she asked lightly to dispel the persistent, tantalizing vision.

"Maybe I am."

Case moved away from her, and taking his time, went around the room, dousing all the lamps save for one. Finally he went to the bar and came back with a small box, sitting it on a table near them.

Katlyn looked at it curiously, understanding when he opened the lid and the tinkling notes of a waltz began to play. As if in the dream from which she never wanted to wake, she stepped into his arms.

He held her close and the press of her breasts against his chest kindled a slow heat that rolled through her in a wave. They swayed together, his thigh brushing hers, her hand rubbing over his shoulder, his lips teasing the edge of her ear, neither of them aware when the music box wound down and the waltz stopped.

Katlyn tipped her head back to look at him, tempting Case with her parted lips and the longing in her eyes that turned them the color of twilight. Still, he denied them both the kiss she invited and instead moved around behind her and started pulling the pins from her hair.

"Case..." she breathed his name on a sigh.

The pins fell to the floor with a soft click as he slowly removed them, one by one, and let loose the coppery ripple of her hair. When the last one dropped, Case threaded his hands through her curls before lifting the silken mass to one side and kissing her nape.

"You smell like a summer meadow," he murmured. "Sweet and wild."

Katlyn let her head fall back as Case continued kissing her neck while his hands caressed her shoulders. When he finally turned her in his arms and covered her mouth with his she responded with all the fire and storm he'd incited with his slow seduction.

Heartache honed her desire for him to an almost painful sharpness. This might be the only time she could be with him like this, to love him as his touch made her ache to do. She would never feel like this again and this once, she wanted more than anything to catch and hold every sensation so she could have the memories to cherish when she was alone and lonely.

Case tried to gentle their embrace, to give Katlyn time to decide how far she wanted to take this dance they'd started. But she seemed determined to rush them headlong into the fire and Katlyn, bold and willing, drove him to the edge of his control.

She pushed his jacket off his shoulders and he shucked it along with his vest. His hand cupped her breast and teased the peak through the slick satin of her dress as his tongue probed the depths of her mouth, foreshadowing a more intimate joining.

Knowing she had aroused him made Katlyn daring and intensified her need for him. She fumbled with the buttons of his shirt. When the first few gave way she rubbed her palm against his bare skin and felt a clenching low in her belly when he gave a low groan.

''Katlyn—'' His breath came hot and fast in her ear. ''Are you sure this is what you want?''

Katlyn stilled her hands, suddenly unsure. Had she been too brazen? ''I...yes. But—'' She hesitated, then, ''Is it what you want?''

''Is it what I want?'' Case took her face between his hands so their eyes met. ''I've never wanted anything more in my life. I love you, I want to be with you, now and always.''

Tears welled in her eyes. ''Oh, Case.'' Her voice cracked and broke.

''Sweetheart, what's wrong?''

The tender concern in his voice and touch released

Katlyn's tears. "Nothing. Nothing, this is right. I know it is, it must be, because I love you, too."

Reaching up, she pressed her mouth to his and even as he tasted her tears, Case's hunger for her hit him full-force. His intention to gently woo her burned away as their kissing grew harder and hotter.

Finally, in danger of laying her down on one of the tables, Case scooped her into his arms and carried her up the stairs to her suite. Kicking the door open, he shoved it closed behind them and strode into her bedroom.

He lowered her to her feet. The look in his eyes made Katlyn feel both vulnerable and strong. She wanted to tell him how good he made her feel, how she yearned to be with him, how much she loved him. She knew she should tell him he would be her first lover; with the certainty of love she knew he would be her last.

But when he began unfastening her dress, inching the satin off her body until it pooled at her feet, Katlyn couldn't think of anything except the exquisite rough and firm feel of his hands stroking her body.

Case undressed her slowly, with tender reverence, until she wore only his necklace. Her hair curled like spun fire against the cream of her skin, the contrast like Katlyn, fiery and sweet.

"You're everything I dreamed of, and so much more," he murmured, kissing the hollow of her throat where the silver roses lay cool against her warmth. Cupping her breasts, he caressed her softness, stroking her nipples until they peaked, then taking one into his mouth and suckling her.

The intensity of the pleasure caught Katlyn by surprise. After all her imaginings, how should she have expected it would be like this?

The little moan she made sent a tremor through Case. He laid her on the bed, pausing only to strip off the rest of his clothes before joining her there.

For a moment, only his eyes made love to her. Katlyn wriggled a little at his intense scrutiny, not from modesty but from anticipation. He appeared to be contemplating every way he would touch her and she felt her body tighten and tingle in response.

Katlyn let her eyes linger over him, too, relishing the masculine strength stretching across his broad shoulders and narrowing to his strong but slender hips. She knew well the power swelling in the muscles of his arms and legs, had felt it beneath her fingertips, had seen it when he worked. What a perfectly formed work of art his body was, she thought, her fingers aching to caress every magnificent part of him.

Case abandoned his indulgence when she reached out and stroked her hand over his chest and hip, coming tantalizingly close to his arousal. ''I've waited so long for you,'' he said hoarsely, nuzzling her throat. ''Katlyn...''

Moving over her, Case kissed her deeply, touching her intimately between her thighs and feeling her shudder when he brushed her moist heat.

When he parted her legs and Katlyn felt him hard against her, she sucked in a breath at the first jolt of uncertainty. But then he was inside her in one smooth thrust and the stab of pain quickly drowned in a flood of exquisite sensation.

Case hesitated for a moment. He stared at her with a look of confusion but Katlyn gave him no time to think. Wrapping her legs around him, she drew him back into her again, craving something she couldn't name, something only he could give her.

Centered at their joining, the feeling built and swelled inside her until just when she thought she would die from the wanting, Case thrust deeply into her and she shattered. Slowly it subsided and left her shaking so she barely realized it when Case stiffened above her, groaning her name as he found his own release.

He held her for long minutes afterward, his forehead resting against her shoulder, panting. At last, he rolled onto his side, pulling her close so he could cradle her against him.

"I love you," he whispered, lifting her chin to kiss her slowly and deeply.

Katlyn kissed him back, clinging to him. She held to him tightly long after Case pulled the bedclothes up around them and drifted into a light sleep. And in the darkest hours of the night, she wept, for what she had lost, and what she could never have again.

Dawn came with the first bite of a winter chill, spurring Case to reach out and pull Katlyn's warm body against him. In the gray light, he stretched out a hand for her, seeking the comfort of her embrace, the pleasure of touching her again.

He supposed he ought to get up and relight the fire, but holding Katlyn close and coaxing the heat from her body was a far more enticing thought. He reached across the bed—to emptiness.

Jolted fully awake, Case stared at the rumpled bed-clothes, momentarily stunned to find the obsession of his thoughts not in his bed.

Something deep in his stomach clenched into a fist.

He shoved upright, searching the shadows for her. "Katlyn?"

Cold silence answered.

Swinging his legs to the icy floor, Case tossed on his clothes and headed back to his rooms. Maybe Katlyn had gone to check on Emily? Walking through his sitting room, he moved quietly to Emily's bedside. She slept soundly, her child's breathing quick and deep.

Gently he closed the door behind him and went back to Katlyn's bedroom, finding it just as he'd left it. He sat on the edge of the bed, not sure what to feel.

Surely she wouldn't leave him in the middle of the night, not after what they'd shared. But then, where had she gone, without even a word to him?

He was about to search downstairs for her when he heard the slight sound of her door opening and cautious footsteps moving across the sitting room.

Katlyn hesitated in the middle of the room, trying to steel herself for what she had to say to Case this morning.

Waking hours before dawn after a few restless hours of sleep, she'd slipped away from his arms and gone to the kitchen to make herself some coffee, and to sit and think. Though so far, thinking had done her little good.

She'd lain awake long after their rapturous love-making, torn hopelessly between a sort of awestruck wonder at the depth, the beautiful intimacy of her love for Case, and her despair at knowing she was about to destroy everything they had shared, everything they had built together.

But one thing was certain now. If she didn't take advantage of this moment's courage it would surely fail her again.

Before she could make herself walk to the bed-room, Case came out. He stopped when he saw her, his expression a mix of delight at seeing her and un-certainty at her leaving.

"I wondered where you'd gone," he said. "And why."

Katlyn clasped her hands tightly together, her nerves so raw her whole body shook. She forced her fingers apart and pulled her shawl tightly to her as if it could shield her from the hurt to come. "I need to explain."

Case strode up to her side and touched her cheek. Her skin felt chill and trembling. "I'll start a fire. You're freezing."

"No—" Katlyn grasped his arm. "Please. It's not the cold. It's what I have to say."

The resolute tone in her voice peaked the apprehension knotting every muscle in Case's body. "I'm listening."

Katlyn's heart began to pound. In her mind, she could already hear the pain and anger in his voice, even though it was yet to come. *Give me strength...*

"Whatever it is, know that it won't change the way I feel," Case said. "If it's something about your past—" He stopped when she shook her head. Sorrow hung over her like a shroud, but it confused him because he couldn't understand the reason. "Do you regret making love?"

"Oh, no," she said softly. A tear slid down her cheek. "Never. How could I regret something so wonderful?"

"Then what is it?"

"I have to leave Cimarron." She hurried on before Case could interrupt. "My companion has to go to a hospital in Las Vegas for treatment before the snows set in. She's too ill to wait until spring. I have to go with her."

Katlyn faltered as she watched the realization of what she was saying change Case's expression to stunned disbelief.

She turned away, unable to bear looking in his eyes any longer. "I have to stay with her."

An endless, agonized silence fell between them. Case turned and paced across the room. Stopping in front of the desk, he slammed a fist down hard then whirled on her so suddenly Katlyn jumped.

"Why are you telling me this now? You knew last

night before we were together, probably long before that. Couldn't you have been honest with me?''

Katlyn flinched at the raw anger in him. ''I should have told you sooner. I know. I—I just couldn't.'' A sob caught in her throat, stealing all her voice but a whisper. ''I didn't even have the courage to tell myself. But Dr. Garrett forced me to face the truth yesterday. I don't have a choice. I have to leave now. Please, try to understand.''

''I don't understand. It doesn't make any sense. Why couldn't you just tell me? And why do you have to go, too? I can hire someone perfectly trustworthy and responsible to see that she arrives at the hospital and is settled safely in Las Vegas.''

''You don't understand.''

''You're damned right I don't understand! What is this companion to you? You act as if she's blood and not just someone who works for you.''

Wiping at the tears she couldn't hold back, Katlyn tried to face him without breaking down completely. ''She's never been just someone who works for me. She never will be. And you're one to talk about treating employees like family!'' she added with a spark of her old spirit.

''Katlyn…'' What could he say to the woman when she seemed so hell-bent on ruining both their lives? Looking away for a moment, he finally walked back to her side and gently put his hands on her shoulders. ''Who is she, this so-called companion of yours? Why is she so important to you?''

Even with the pain cold inside her, her skin warmed to his touch, the scent of him recalling with disturbing vividness their loving only hours earlier. Katlyn breathed him in, momentarily overwhelmed by images of the most perfect night of her life.

"She's—someone very close to me," she answered at last. "That's all I can say. I made a promise, I won't break it. Please don't ask me to tell you more."

"Then let me go with you to Las Vegas."

Katlyn pulled back slightly. "Case, thank you, but I can't accept, no matter how much I want to. You can't leave the hotel."

"Can't I?" He let out a short cynical laugh. "The St. Martin is nothing without you."

"That's not true and you know it. There are dozens of singers who would fill my shoes gladly and easily. You've made the St. Martin the best hotel on the Santa Fe Trail. This is your dream, Case. You've made it come true. I'm not going to be responsible for making you risk losing it now."

Slowly, Case's hands slid away from her and he took a step back, an odd distant look replacing the hurt in his eyes. "I've already lost. Because you made me believe it was your dream, too."

Mrs. Donaldson led Katlyn upstairs to her mother's room, chatting as she went. "She's still sleepin'. I tried to bring her a tray of sweet rolls and coffee earlier, but she didn't so much as stir so I left it on her nightstand."

"Thank you," Katlyn said, quietly opening the door to her mother's room. "You've been so good to her. We owe you a great deal."

The older woman waved Katlyn's words away. "Now, don't you go talkin' about such things again, lass. Why hearin' you sing that night was a finer gift than all the coin you could ever give me." With a pat on Katlyn's hand, Mrs. Donaldson turned and headed back downstairs.

Katlyn took off her bonnet, cape and gloves and set them aside. She stepped over to her mother's bed and took her usual seat beside her. Penelope's face looked as white as her bedclothes, her breath came deep and slow, and Katlyn hated the thought of having to wake her to give her the news they were leaving.

Leave... The word sounded more bitter than ever after last night. How could she leave Case, who was now the other half of herself?

She had given herself willingly and completely to a man for the first time in her life and it felt so perfectly right. They were joined now in the most intimate of expressions. Leaving him meant spending the rest of her life incomplete, for the best part of her would always remain here in Cimarron in Case Durham's arms.

Katlyn let go a long breath, shoving aside bittersweet thoughts of last night, and gently touched her mother's hair. "Mama, it's Katlyn."

Penelope stirred, then softly sighed. "Katie, is that

you?'' She opened her eyes and rubbed them with the tips of her fingers. "I can hardly see you, it's so dim in here. Pull the curtains, won't you?''

Katlyn glanced to the bright streams of morning light pouring in from the window across the room. "Mrs. Donaldson already did. Your eyes are weak, like the rest of you and—''

With great difficulty, Penelope struggled to sit up. "Nonsense, I'm simply not awake yet.''

Katlyn fluffed the pillows behind her mother's head and helped her to a comfortable position. "Mama, that's not the reason you're having trouble seeing or walking. I know Dr. Garrett has told you about your illness. It's time we both faced the truth of it.''

"The truth of it?'' Penelope lifted a frail white hand and pointed a finger toward her daughter. "Now, you listen to me, young lady—''

"No. Today, Mama, you listen to me.''

After a moment's pause Penelope sank back into her pillows without further fight. "All right, Katie. What is this truth you simply must tell me?'' she asked, weariness edging her voice.

"We have to pack and leave for the hospital as soon as possible before the snows start. Dr. Garrett says you can't wait until spring to get treatment. And the trail down the mountain from here can be impassable in winter.''

A long silence followed, then Penelope whispered at last, "I see. So you've decided I've become an invalid now.''

"Mama, you know Dr. Garrett can't do any more for you than he has already. I'll make the trip as comfortable as possible for you, don't worry."

Sounds of the front door opening and closing below momentarily distracted Katlyn. She'd left the bedroom door ajar, and a deep voice she recognized all too well resonated up the stairwell to her ears.

"Oh, no," she said without thinking.

Penelope perked up then, her ears more keen now that her eyes were fading. "Who is that?"

"Mama, please—"

"Don't treat me like an imbecile! There's nothing wrong with my hearing. That man is asking for you. And your companion! Who is he, Katie? Tell me!"

Katlyn wished herself anywhere but here, caught squarely between her mother and the man she loved.

"It's Case," she said flatly. "He's come to find us."

Chapter Seventeen

"I should have known he'd be determined to find out about you after—" Katlyn stopped, biting at her lower lip.

"After what?" Penelope sat bolt upright. "Katie, what's going on? What haven't you told me?" She grasped for Katlyn's arm, her voice rising with panic.

"Calm down, Mama, please, it's nothing."

"Don't you dare let him see me! You haven't told him, have you? You didn't—you wouldn't break your promise! I'm going to get well and be back on that stage, you know that. You promised you would never let him or anyone see me like this."

Katlyn took her mother's thin shoulders and gently eased her back down. "Mama, please! I hear him on the stairs. No, I haven't told him who you are. I've kept my promise." She knew her frustration came through, but couldn't worry about that now. "But I have to go close the door, or it won't matter what promises I've made."

"I can't have that! Keep him away from me! Keep him away!"

Case heard the wail from upstairs and brushed past Mrs. Donaldson, taking the stairs two at a time.

He'd never felt so powerless to control his feelings. He had to find out who this companion was and why Katlyn would go to any length to protect and care for her. Even to the extent of sacrificing her own—and his—happiness.

"Mr. Durham, this is my boardinghouse and I owe my guests their privacy," Mrs. Donaldson called after him, panting as she tried to catch him on the stairs. "My livelihood depends on keepin' my payin' guests happy. Surely you of all people know that's the truth."

"I apologize," Case said over his shoulder, "but this is important." He was on the landing. "Katlyn!"

Case reached for the doorknob just as Katlyn slammed it shut. Anger and frustration rose in equal measure in him, but the sound of muffled weeping from behind the door gave him pause and stopped him from shoving his way inside. "Katlyn, are you all right?"

Penelope yanked the quilt to her chin, her eyes nearly bulging. "He's just outside the door. Stop him, Katie. Stop him!" She started to sob, burying her face in her hands.

"Yes, Case. What are you doing here?"

"We have to talk."

"Case, please. Not now. I can't, not here."

Small, high gasps followed spates of sobbing from inside the room. Case's gut twisted. It couldn't be Katlyn, but something was obviously very wrong in there.

"Dammit, Katlyn, what's going on?"

"Case it's—wait a moment while I talk to her. Please, just wait."

Case stood outside the door, balling his fists so tightly his knuckles turned white. The temptation to kick down the door nearly overwhelmed him.

He loved Katlyn. He had a right to know what, and who, inside that room affected her life—and now his—so profoundly.

Or did he?

When Katlyn left him waiting, doubt crept into his thoughts. Maybe last night didn't mean to her what it meant to him. Maybe she thought their loving was only for one night, the end of a pleasing relationship, not the beginning of a future. Or had it been his reward for giving her a job and trusting her to revive the St. Martin?

Confusion, disappointment, or was it enlightenment—stopped him cold.

"Katlyn?"

He heard her move back to the door but she didn't open it. "I can't leave right now," she said, and Case could picture the look in her eyes from the strained sound of her voice.

"Is there anything I can do to help?" he asked.

Despite the cool distance he tried to convey, Katlyn

heard the resignation in his words. He obviously believed she didn't care for him enough to share her secret, and the realization pierced straight through her heart.

If only he knew she shared the same anger, the same frustration. Having to hold it all in, unable to comfort him or to reveal the truth of her love for him left her feeling broken.

"No," she said, not bothering to stop the tears from coursing down her cheeks. "There's nothing you can do. But thank you. Your offer means a lot to me."

How inadequate that sounded when she wanted to tell him how much she loved him instead.

"I'll go then. Goodbye, Katlyn."

Facing him, Katlyn placed her palms on the smooth white pine that kept him from her view. Through the barrier he didn't hear the whisper of her heart crying out, *You'll never know how sorry I am for us both, Case. I do love you. Oh, how I love you.*

Jack's fingers flew from one end of the keyboard to the other, deftly pronouncing each note just long enough to check its tune. He glanced up to where Case stood leaning against the side of the upright piano.

"I'm the last person you should be asking about Kate," he said.

"Why? You seem to know her better than almost anyone here."

"I wouldn't say that. But I will say I don't think Kate wants to leave the St. Martin."

"Want to or not, she seems determined enough to go because of that companion of hers. But something about that situation just doesn't ring true with me."

Jack shrugged, keeping his eyes on the keyboard as he tapped out a quick, jaunty bar. "Maybe the lady's waiting for a proposal. It wouldn't tempt me, even though she's a beauty, but it may be the one way to convince Kate she belongs here." One more slide across the keys to limber his fingers for the night's performance and he added, "The thought of being tied to one woman the rest of my days makes me want to catch the next stage to anywhere, but it's your choice, *compadre*."

Case let out a wry laugh. "No, I don't see you as the marrying type. I hope you're right about Katlyn, though, because propose is exactly what I intend to do. But I need your help."

Jack's fingers stopped for the first time since they'd begun talking. "My help? Case, you've been a fine boss, but—"

"Look, all I need is for you to keep everyone out of the saloon for the next hour. I had Tuck set a special dinner table for Katlyn and me and I can't have guests or staff interrupting."

"Ah, well, that I can do." He gave Case a wink and a grin. "Anything in the cause of romance. Good luck."

"Thanks," Case said as he turned toward the saloon. "I have a feeling I'll need it."

* * *

Katlyn dabbed a little more color on each cheek, adjusted a hairpin and shoved away from her dressing mirror. She hardly looked her best, though she'd tried for the past hour to mask the sadness in her face and eyes.

She'd chosen Case's favorite dress, the blue one that went with the necklace he'd given her, to wear for her final performance. She'd hoped the sapphires and silver roses would brighten her eyes as they had the night he'd given her the necklace. But tonight, even sparkling jewels couldn't lighten the shadows in her eyes.

She stood, doused her lamp, smoothed her gown the way she'd done countless nights before, then headed downstairs to pretend one more time to be Case's St. Louis Songbird.

Half smiling to herself, she remembered her first night's preparation for her debut performance. What once seemed completely strange and alien to her now felt as natural as if she *had* always been a singer.

She looked around as she stepped downstairs, feeling a sense of pride and belonging at the changes she'd helped to bring to the hotel. The cheery yet elegant wallpaper was her choice, the prints she and Case had painstakingly picked out together, and the sofa in the lobby they'd gone 'round and 'round over until she had finally worn him down and he had given in and bought it. She'd loved gloating to him each time a new guest complimented the beautiful piece of furniture.

Katlyn shook herself free of the remembrances. Case had invited her for one last dinner together, another little tradition she'd come to look forward to at the St. Martin. Only with this dinner, the tradition would end. This place that had become her home, her only real home, after tonight, would be no more than another memory itself.

Looking through the slats of the door to the now magnificently renovated saloon, she spied Case pacing in front of the bar. The sight of his handsome chiseled face, his tall, broad-shouldered frame elegantly clad in a black dinner jacket and tailored slacks, took her breath away. As though he felt her watching him, he paused and turned toward the door. She stepped inside and made her way to the table Tuck had set for just the two of them.

Case met her and took her slender hand in his, lightly brushing his fingers across the back of it. "You look beautiful," he murmured. "Thank you for wearing the necklace."

"Thank you for giving me the chance to wear something so beautiful and for this lovely dinner. You and Tuck must have been plotting all day."

Case pulled out her chair for her. "Tuck and I have learned a lot about the value of presentation, thanks to you. But I wanted tonight to be special."

Katlyn reached across the table for his hand. He met her halfway, engulfing her hand in his. "Oh, Case, I don't know what to say. If you keep saying such sweet things I'm going to cry again and ruin all Becky's hard work on my makeup."

"No, love, no more tears." Case squeezed her hand, then slowly released it. "Tonight we're going to celebrate." He pulled a bottle of expensive-looking French champagne from the cooler and poured them each a glass. "With our first dinner here, we're christening the new saloon."

First and last, Katlyn thought, but didn't let the words escape her lips. Instead she lifted her glass and forced a smile. "To the new saloon!"

Case clinked his glass to hers. "And to us."

Katlyn started to contradict him, stopped, and made a pretense of sipping at the champagne.

Case smiled as her nose scrunched a little over the taste, the familiar gesture endearing.

"Katlyn."

She looked up and he moved to her side, bent on one knee in front of her and drew a small box from his vest pocket.

Katlyn felt the force of her love for him war against a sick foreboding. He was going to ask her to—

"Marry me, Katlyn. I love you and I want you to be at my side the rest of my days."

Pain ripped at her heart. She opened her mouth to speak, but nothing would come.

Why did he have to make her leaving so much more difficult? She yearned to throw her arms around his neck and cry, *Yes! Yes! You're everything to me. Life means nothing without you at my side.*

Instead she sat paralyzed by conflicted emotions that felt like torment.

At last she forced out the words. "I can't," she

said brokenly. "No matter how much I want to, I can't marry you."

"Don't say no. We can work this out, I promise. We'll find a way. Katlyn, don't give away your chance for happiness."

"Case, it's impossible. You can't leave the St. Martin. And I don't know how long we'll be in Las Vegas. Even if we don't stay there, I know we won't be coming back here."

Case stood, still holding the box that held the symbol of his love for her. "I can wait. I'll come to Las Vegas as soon as I can find someone to manage things here. And of course you'll come back here. This is where you belong, we both know that."

Frustrated, anguished beyond words, Katlyn paced the floor in front of him, clenching and unclenching her hands. "We won't. I know her, you don't. Case, please, you have to understand. I don't belong here. I can't marry you."

Her words hit him with the force of a bullet, knocking his determination off balance. She meant it. Once again, he'd trusted a woman's promise of love and found out it was a lie.

Acknowledging that truth should have made it easy to let her go. Instead, it felt like giving up a vital part of himself.

Anger, frustration, pain, all passed through his eyes to be replaced by a coldness Katlyn hadn't seen since her first days at the St. Martin. She half raised a hand to him, unable to bear that look. "Case, please, you have to believe me, I—"

"Don't." He stepped back from her, his face hard. "Don't lie to try and make it easier. It's finished. You made your choice. And it's not us."

Katlyn stood in the shadows by the foyer windows, her hands clenched by her sides. *Hold on to yourself, for only a few more hours.* Except she didn't have anything left inside to hold on to. She could only cling to the promise she had made to Penelope, knowing it didn't let her choose.

She had spent the past few hours packing her few belongings and getting ready for her final performance at the St. Martin. Bucky had taken her bags to the boardinghouse so she would have no excuse to linger after she was finished singing.

It had been hard to say goodbye to all the staff, seeing their confusion and feeling their unspoken censure at her desertion. But it had been less difficult than telling Case.

"Katlyn?"

A small voice tugged Katlyn around in a hurry. Emily stood at the edge of the room. Already in her nightgown, she hugged her rag doll to her chest and looked at Katlyn with wide, hurt eyes.

Katlyn went to her and knelt beside her. "Are you looking for someone to tuck you in, honey?"

"Are you really leaving?"

"Oh, Emily." Katlyn took a shaky breath. "Yes, I am. Someone I care about very much is sick and I have to take care of her."

"I thought you cared about Daddy and me. You said you loved us."

"Honey, I do love you and your daddy, with all my heart. My leaving has nothing to do with either of you. I made a promise to take care of someone and now I have to keep it."

Emily stared at her and her eyes filled with tears. "Are you ever coming back?"

Tempted to soothe the little girl with a reassuring lie, Katlyn shook her head. "I don't know. I don't know how long it will take before my friend is better again."

"But I want you to stay, Katlyn! I want you to stay and be my mama!"

Katlyn couldn't have answered even if she had the words to do so. She put her arms around Emily and hugged her close, feeling Emily's tears wet her shoulder.

Emily clutched her fiercely as Katlyn stroked her back, her cheek against Emily's hair. Then abruptly Emily jerked back from her and turned and ran up the staircase. A few moments later Katlyn heard a door slam—Emily retreating to the sanctuary of her room.

Katlyn stayed in the foyer, her empty arms falling back to her side. She could go to Emily. But what could she say to her, except goodbye?

Getting to her feet, she turned her face to the shadows again and tried to dab at her eyes with her sleeve. There was nothing left for her here save a few final songs.

"Here, try this," a voice said from behind her, and then Jack put a handkerchief into her hand.

Sniffling a little, Katlyn wiped her eyes before offering it back to him. He waved it away.

"You need it more than I do."

"Thank you. I suppose it's time for us to be on the stage."

"In a few minutes. Are you sure this is what you want to do?"

Katlyn frowned a little. "Of course. Everyone is expecting a performance tonight. I can't just—"

"I didn't mean the singing," Jack said softly. He eyed her a moment. "Look, Kate, it's none of my business, but why don't you tell him who you are?"

Katlyn couldn't have been more stunned if he'd slapped her. "How—?"

"Honey, I've been in every saloon from St. Louis to San Francisco. I saw your mother sing once. You look a lot like her, but you're a mite young to be Penelope Rose."

"But—you never said a word. All this time. Why?"

Jack shrugged. "I figured you had your reasons." He flashed her a grin. "Besides, I've done my share of bending the truth in my time when I was in a tight spot."

"That, I can believe," Katlyn said, shaking her head.

Sobering, Jack touched her hand. "You're giving up everything, Kate. Just be sure. Once you walk away, it'll be damned hard to come back."

His gravity made Katlyn smile a little. It was so unlike Jack to take anything seriously. She reached up and kissed him on the cheek, forcing a lightness she didn't feel. "I'm not going to ask you how you know that. Only don't go and ruin my image of you by becoming all earnest now. You're already in danger of being too nice."

He didn't press her. "Can't have that. Well, sweetheart, since this is our last time together, let's make it magic."

Grateful for his understanding, Katlyn took his arm and let Jack lead her into the saloon. She pasted a smile on her face and kept her head high, but she deliberately kept her eyes on the audience, not daring to seek out Case.

He was there, she could feel his presence without seeing him. One look between them, though, and she couldn't trust herself to contain the love and longing so precariously held in her heart.

Somehow, by sheer will, she managed to get through her performance. Close to the end, feeling exhausted in both body and soul, she glanced to the back of the saloon and immediately locked gazes with Case.

It had been inevitable, she supposed, and yet she was unprepared for how much it hurt.

Taking refuge in the only sanctuary she had now, Katlyn began the song that she'd thought of as his from almost the first time she'd sung it for him, here in the saloon, just the two of them.

" 'I wander lonely, lost,
searching for what's true
afraid I'll never know it,
and then I look, and there is you
beckoning me home.
But when I reach out,
there's only longing,
and truth I cannot doubt,
for I am left alone again
with only the dream of my heart.' "

Case stood stiffly in his corner by the bar, not daring to make any move. If he did, he didn't know if he could stop himself from striding up to the stage, sweeping her up into his arms, and carrying her off to his room to make love to her until she gave up any idea of leaving.

As she poured out the bittersweet, haunting notes of the song, he had no doubt she was putting her heart into every word, giving it to him. Realizing that made it worse because he could never convince himself, no matter what he said, that her loving him was a lie.

A thunderous applause rewarded Katlyn when she finished the song, but she seemed to barely acknowledge it. She took her eyes from his to give a brief thanks to the audience before hurrying from the stage and out of the saloon.

Not bothering to consider how wise his action was, Case followed her, catching up with her just as she reached the front door.

"Please," she said, the tears she could no longer stop running down her cheeks. "Don't ask me again. *Please.*"

Case raised a hand, let it drop. "I don't know what's left to ask."

They stared at each other, the air between them vibrating with unspoken desires, unanswered need. Then, with a little cry, Katlyn flung herself into his arms just as Case reached for her.

He kissed her hard and deeply; she met him equally, wanting his possession.

As suddenly as she had come to him, Katlyn tore herself away. "I can't. I—can't. Goodbye, Case."

She whirled from him and jerked open the door, running out into the night.

Case started after her then stopped. He didn't know how to let her go. But after everything, he didn't know any way to make her stay.

Morning sunlight edged its way through the curtains, disturbing the shadows in the foyer, but Case didn't bother to let in more of the light. He sat at the front desk, staring blindly at the book in front of him, trying to pretend he cared what the numbers meant.

Finally he slammed the ledger shut and shoved it aside. He lit up another cheroot and sat back in his chair, closing his eyes. He felt like hell and knew it had nothing to do with the fact that he hadn't slept and had spent a good part of the night with a bottle of whiskey.

Drinking hadn't made him forget, so he had given

it up just before dawn and instead sat alone in his hotel, thinking how dead it was without Katlyn.

He supposed he should be making plans to hire a new singer. But the idea of anyone taking Katlyn's place roused a mix of anger and pain in him. Maybe when he'd gotten used to the idea of her leaving.

Maybe in about a thousand years.

"Mr. Durham?"

At the tentative voice, Case jerked up, finding himself facing Bucky. The boy took a step backward, his expression saying clearly he didn't know what to expect from Case this morning.

Case stubbed out his cheroot and ran a hand through his hair. He cleared his throat twice. "What is it, Bucky?"

"I—um, I brought the mail. I thought you might want it." Bucky stepped up quickly to the desk and pushed the pile of letters at Case. "I got to get back to the stables now," he said, and practically ran from the room.

Absently flipping through the letters, Case thought he'd better attempt to clean himself up before he ran into any guests this morning. He was about to toss the mail aside and go upstairs when familiar handwriting caught his eye.

After all these weeks…he'd nearly forgotten writing the letter to St. Louis. Now, he held the reply in his hand.

And possibly the answers to the mystery of Katlyn McLain.

Chapter Eighteen

Case stared at the letter, not sure he wanted to open it. He should never have written his to begin with and what could he find out now that would change things?

His hand poised to throw it aside. Before he completed the motion he ripped open the envelope, yanked out the two sheets of paper and quickly read them over.

There was little he didn't already know about Penelope Rose. Except the image of the woman painted by the words wasn't Katlyn. It was the woman he'd expected when she first walked into his hotel in her yellow satin and face paint. Katlyn McLain had turned out to be someone completely different.

Becoming impatient, he made to follow through on his first impulse to throw the letter away when one phrase leaped out at him.

I don't know whatever happened to her husband, if she ever had one, but her daughter is lovely, the image of Penelope.

Her daughter… At first Case's mind refused to accept the words. He'd made love to her and he'd been certain she was an innocent. He'd assumed she was experienced and she had never told him otherwise. But with every detail of their night together branded on his memory, he clearly remembered the moment he realized he was her first lover. Surely a man couldn't make a mistake where a woman's virtue was concerned.

Could the companion she secreted away at the boardinghouse have been a child? Her child? Case rejected the idea before it had time to completely form.

He sat staring at nothing for several minutes. Then suddenly it made sense. And he understood now that Katlyn had been deceiving him from the beginning.

Case looked down in the letter crushed in his fist. Tossing it aside, he shoved back his chair and strode to the staircase, calling for Becky as he went.

She came running, eyeing him with obvious uneasiness. "Yes, Mr. Durham?"

"Find everyone and tell them I want to see them all in the dining room in fifteen minutes. We have a lot of work to do."

He was already halfway up the stairs, taking them two at time, when Becky called up to him, "But the stage isn't coming for two more days and there's no dinner show tonight since… Are the guests coming from around here?"

"No guests," Case said over his shoulder. "I want to get everything in order before I leave."

"You're leaving, too?" Becky wailed.

Case turned and smiled at her. "As soon as I can. I'm going to Las Vegas."

Katlyn looked out at the raindrops drizzling over the busy street and shivered. She'd been in Las Vegas for three weeks now and it had never seemed colder. Growing up in St. Louis, she was used to winter, but here, though it was certainly warmer, somehow even the slightest chill seemed to seep through to her bones. Sunshine failed to warm her and the days held no luster; the nights dragged by, long and cold and black.

She admitted it was probably her mood rather than the weather that was bleak. Since she'd arrived, she'd felt listless, unable to focus on anything for long. She'd forced herself to do what she had to do and was grateful when she could sleep for a few hours and forget.

Penelope, at least, had settled into the hospital and her new doctor appeared competent enough. He hadn't said much about Penelope's condition, however, but he'd spent a great deal of time talking with Penelope, examining her, and giving Katlyn reassurances that didn't mean anything.

Maybe working again would help. She had found a job singing at a small hotel, earning the position without making use of her mother's name this time. It paid little, but enough to provide her room and board.

Soon she would have to face the cost of her

mother's ongoing medical care. She'd saved enough to provide for Penelope through the winter. After that, she would have more decisions to make.

But not now. Glancing at the clock, she saw she had time to visit her mother before she started work.

She found Penelope sitting in a chair by the window, humming to herself. Her mother turned, smiling when she recognized Katlyn. "I hope you brought some sunshine, Katie. Maybe it's my eyes, but I don't think I've seen it grayer than today."

Katlyn kissed her mother's cheek, surprised to hear Penelope actually talk about her eyesight without breaking down. Katlyn sat beside her. "How are you feeling, Mama?"

"Well, I'm out of that bed, so I must be better," Penelope said. "You know, Katie, I've been sitting here thinking. It's not something I've done much of before, I'll admit, but that nice young doctor from out East has helped me to realize a few things."

"Like what?" Katlyn asked, smiling a little at her mother's rueful expression.

"Ah, well, I had a long talk with him this morning. A charming man, I must say. So much more tactful than Frank Garrett ever was." Penelope paused.

She glanced at her pale hands and Katlyn had the impression her mother was groping with unfamiliar words. At last, Penelope looked up at her, tears in her eyes.

"I'm not going back to singing, Katie. I know that now." She held up her hand when Katlyn would have interrupted. "No, don't say it's not so. All these weeks, I've been pretending it would be all right. But I've known for a long time it wasn't all right. I just…I just couldn't face losing that life, everything I've worked for, the applause, the attention. I didn't want to let go of everything. I just—couldn't.''

"I know, Mama," Katlyn said softly. She took her mother's hands in hers. "I understand. And I'm sorry. I wanted to believe it, too.''

"No, I'm sorry. I was wrong, Katie," Penelope said, squeezing Katlyn's hands between hers. "And I was wrong to ask you to pretend, too.'' She sighed. "I just don't know what I will do now. I've never done anything but sing. Now…''

"Don't worry about that now. The doctor says you need to be here awhile longer. We have all the time we need to decide what we want to do. We'll talk it over and when you're feeling better, we'll decide.''

Penelope nodded and Katlyn hugged her tightly before reluctantly moving away. "I have to leave for work. But I'll be back to see you later.''

"A new job? So where is the St. Louis Songbird singing tonight?''

"Not the St. Louis Songbird," Katlyn said, settling her shawl around her shoulders. "Just plain Katlyn McLain.''

"You've never been plain, darling." Penelope reached out and took Katlyn's hand. "I'm proud of you, Katie, for everything you've done. I should have told you so a long time ago.''

Katlyn left the hospital holding her mother's words close to her heart. At least, after everything, she had done something for her mother, and the thought made the future seem a little less bleak.

"It's going to be a full house, Miss McLain. Should be a fine night for you."

Katlyn smiled at the hotel manager before he bustled off to greet a group of new arrivals. She supposed it would be a fine night for the hotel, but for her, singing was now just a way to support herself and Penelope.

Still, she put on a good face as she walked onto the stage and started her performance with a lively tune that had always been a favorite with the audiences at the St. Martin. After a few numbers, the audience warmed to her and she complied with several requests for favorite songs.

It was nearly two hours later when she prepared to take a break after one final song that a voice from the back of the room stopped her cold.

"I was hoping, Miss McLain, you would sing 'Love's a Wandering Stranger' for me."

Katlyn felt the blood rush from her face, leaving her momentarily light-headed. He couldn't be here— and yet when she looked in the direction of the voice of her dreams, Case stood there, looking back at her.

Her heart pounding, Katlyn managed to walk to the piano and after a word with the piano player, took his place at the keyboard. Her fingers trembled as she placed them on the keys but the melody came easily because she had memorized it with her heart.

For the first time that evening, her voice resonated

with true emotion as she poured all of her longing and need into their song.

When she finished, Katlyn ignored the enthusiastic applause and the attempt by the manager to catch her attention. She quickly left the stage at the same time Case strode toward the door.

They stood just outside the saloon, oblivious to the noise and people milling around them. It had been nearly a month, and Katlyn wasn't sure what to say to him. But he didn't bother with any preliminary greetings.

"I need to talk to you."

"Not here," she said, glancing to the side. "I have a room close by. We can be alone there."

Quickly, half-afraid he would vanish as easily as he had appeared, Katlyn made an excuse to the manager, tossed her shawl over her shoulders and beckoned Case to follow her the few blocks to the boardinghouse.

When he closed the door to her room behind them and turned to look at her, Katlyn curled her nails into her palms to resist the urge to throw herself into his arms and beg him to stay.

She wished she could read something in his expression that would give her a clue for his sudden visit. But his face gave away nothing. He might have been interviewing a prospective employee for all the emotion he showed.

"I—I didn't expect to ever see you here," she said at last. "Why…is something wrong?"

"Yes, something is wrong." Case moved closer to

her until she only had to raise her hand to touch him. "You're here and I want to know why. I want the truth this time. I know you're not Penelope Rose. You never have been."

"No." She paused, then met his eyes squarely. "Penelope is my mother."

Case said nothing. He had guessed as much, but he wanted to hear her tell him why. It was so tempting, seeing her again, within a touch of being in his arms, to ignore everything between them and pull her to him where she belonged. But he had to resolve this, once and for all. Love without trust would ultimately destroy them.

Despite the fear trembling inside her, Katlyn refused the temptation to walk away from him, put a more comfortable distance between them.

"I lied to you because my mother is ill and I needed the work to pay for her care. She suggested I take her place and I did because I could make more money singing than I could doing anything else." Waiting in vain for any response from him at all, Katlyn plunged ahead.

"Only just today she released me from a promise she insisted I make when we first arrived in Cimarron, that I wouldn't tell anyone she was sick. I don't know if I can make you understand, but all she's ever had is her reputation as the St. Louis Songbird. She's survived because of her singing and she was terrified of losing that. She was alone except when she performed. And that supported both of us from the time

I was born. I couldn't take it from her. I just couldn't. I owed her that much.''

''And now?''

''Now...'' Katlyn shook her head. ''Now, she'll never sing again. She's finally beginning to accept that. Maybe when she does, she can find something else to fill her life.''

Case simply looked at her a moment. Then he released a long breath and stretched out his hand to lightly brush an errant curl from her cheek. ''And what about you?''

''Me? I—I don't know.''

''Are you going to spend the rest of your life pretending this is where you belong?''

Katlyn shook her head. ''I don't belong anywhere now.''

''You do,'' Case said softly. ''You belong at the St. Martin, with me.''

''How can you say that, after all the lies? How can you believe that?''

''Did you lie when you said you loved me?''

Tears welled in her eyes. ''You know I didn't.''

''Then none of the rest matters now.'' Case gave up the fight to keep his distance and took her in his arms. ''I've always known who you are, Katlyn. You only lied about being Penelope Rose. You're still my songbird. You always will be.''

Gathering her close to him, he kissed her, gently at first, then with increasing fervor as desires too long denied surged between them.

Katlyn ached to lose herself in Case's lovemaking.

But no matter how much she wanted to, she couldn't ignore the hard truth still separating them. Easing away from him, she took a few steps toward the window.

"What is it?" he asked, trying to keep the impatience and frustration out of his voice.

"Nothing has changed. I can't leave my mother right now. She needs to be in the hospital here, and you—" She faced him again. "You need to be at the St. Martin. You shouldn't have left it. I know how much making it a success means to you."

"Katlyn..." He came to her and took her face between his hands. "Being with you means more. It's everything. I love you. I want you to be my wife. Trust me, we'll find a way to resolve this, I promise you."

"Oh, Case, how I want to believe—"

The press of his lips to hers silenced her plea. The simple touch ignited the fire that had been smoldering in him since the night she'd left. He pulled her closer, crushing her to him, his need a force that quickly enveloped them both.

Katlyn gave way, willingly, matching his passion with the realization of every night's dream, every waking thought she'd had of being in his arms again. Nothing mattered but Case. The world ceased to turn around them and they came together in a heated exchange of pent-up longings.

Case deftly unfastened each button of her gown, baring her neck, her arms, her breasts, to caress the delights of all that had possessed his every thought.

She moaned softly, arching back as he stripped away her undergarments one by one, relishing the taste and touch of each newly exposed bit of her skin.

"I love you, Case. I love you so much."

"And I love you. That's all that matters now."

"Yes, that's all that matters," Katlyn echoed, refusing to let nagging doubts steal into this precious time.

She gave herself up to him and eagerly met each new advance, her need for him building with the wonder of his explorations. Impatient with the barrier of his clothing, she pushed his coat aside and as he shrugged it off, she stroked her hands over his shoulders and arms, savoring the hard feel of him beneath her fingertips. How many times had she ached to lean against his chest, needed the reassurance of his masculine strength?

As the jacket fell to the floor, Case bent and swept her to him, carrying her to the bed. He laid her down as though on a bed of new lilies, with such tenderness in his touch, in his eyes, she feared her heart would burst.

"You're so beautiful, I haven't told you often enough."

She touched her fingers to his cheek. "But you have, in a thousand ways. You make me believe it. You make me believe anything is possible."

"It is. Let me show you."

Moments later they lay entwined, skin to skin, need to need, releasing all the harbored love empty days and lonely nights had given rise to. His lips sought her tender places and her hands roved his muscular body as each memorized the taste and feel of the other. They lost themselves in the moment, and time ceased to be.

Together they abandoned themselves, delighting in each other, melding into one perfect union of hearts and bodies, until at last, the waves of pleasure crested and broke into the satisfied lulling tides of release.

And they slept, sated, complete at last, in each other's arms.

The next morning Katlyn awoke and turned to watch Case sleeping peacefully next to her. It felt so right, as though they had always belonged in this bed, his arm draped around her shoulder.

At last, when the light grew strong enough to draw golden bars around the edges of the closed curtains, she realized she had to rouse him. Hating to have to disturb him, but knowing she had to be at the hospital this morning, she woke him with a gentle kiss.

"Mmm, thank God it wasn't a dream," Case murmured, eyes still closed.

"No, my love, last night was very real," she whispered, kissing his mouth. "And unfortunately, this morning is, too. I didn't want to wake you, but I have to go to the hospital. There's no reason for you to get up, though, you can stay and sleep here."

Immediately, Case shook himself awake. "Not a chance, sweetheart. The last time I did that, you disappeared. This time I'm not letting you out of my sight."

* * *

Within the hour, Case and Katlyn stood outside Penelope's room talking with her doctor. Katlyn wanted to believe Case's arrival was real and their reunion was an omen her mother's situation might somehow change, too.

But the doctor had nothing to tell her she hadn't already known for weeks.

"She might seem to improve at times," he was saying, "but overall she'll only get worse. The pattern tends to be a slow loss of sight and muscular strength. We have some medications that will help when there's pain, but I'm afraid that's all we can do. I'm sorry, Miss McLain."

Katlyn's brave front faltered a little and Case took her hand firmly in his, squeezing it when he felt her tremble. "What can we do for her?"

"She'll require a comfortable place with enough privacy for her to rest as often as she needs to. But she should have distractions, too, people, things to keep her mind occupied when she's feeling up to it, or I'm afraid a woman of your mother's disposition will simply lose the will to live."

Katlyn nodded. "You know her well."

"When can she leave?" Case asked.

"Case—" Katlyn quickly turned to him, confusion clear on her face. "I don't think—"

"She should be well enough to travel in a week or so, as long as the trip isn't too long," the doctor said.

"Good," Case said firmly. "Because we have just the place for her."

* * *

The stagecoach pulled into the snow-covered station in Cimarron to a rousing welcome. Katlyn glanced out the frosted window at the same ragtag band of musicians playing the same tune they'd attempted when she'd first arrived at the St. Martin. Only this time, freezing temperatures worsened their attempt.

Even so, she smiled. It was good to be home.

She immediately recognized all the familiar faces she'd missed so much during her stay in Las Vegas. So much had happened, but looking at the people she cared so much for, she felt a sense of deep satisfaction. Case had been right all along. This was where she belonged.

As the stage jolted to a stop, Bat and Jack helped the passengers out, while Becky and Bucky stood nearby holding a big red-lettered Welcome Home sign. Sally, Emily squirming in her arms, let the little girl wriggle free.

Emily ran headlong into Case's arms, hugging him fiercely. "Daddy! Katlyn! I missed you!"

"We missed you, too, sweetheart," Case said, kissing her forehead. He smiled as Emily twisted to reach for Katlyn and she returned Emily's hug with love shining in her eyes.

Case then turned to lift Penelope out of the stage and to the seat of the buggy he'd asked Bucky to bring to the station.

"I'd like you all to meet the newest resident of the St. Martin," he said, when Penelope was settled and smiling at the people gathered 'round. "She's going to be living in the upstairs suite. Everyone, this is Miss Penelope Rose."

Every person in the welcoming party stared as if they hadn't heard him correctly and exchanged confused glances. Everyone except for Jack, who caught Katlyn's eye, grinned, and gave her a wink.

"But, Mr. Durham," Tuck said at last. "We all thought Miss Katlyn was the St. Louis Songbird."

"No." Case drew Katlyn and Emily to him, all his family together at last. "This is *my* songbird, Kate Durham."

Epilogue

Katlyn pushed backward into the kitchen at the St. Martin, her arms laden with freshly picked silver roses. "Tuck, Mr. and Mrs. Erickson will be staying tonight. Could you please add their favorite pea soup to the menu? It's another full house, so we'll need plenty."

"Sure thing, Mrs. Durham." Tuck eyed her up and down. "Are you sure you oughta be out there in that sun bendin' over and cuttin' flowers? I thought Mr. Durham said you weren't supposed to be workin' no more."

"Oh, he fusses too much. I'm fine," Katlyn said, laying the fragrant bundle on the worktable.

"Is that so?" Case's deep voice resonated into the room. He came up behind her and put his hands on the swell of her belly beneath the loose green dress.

Katlyn twisted to look at him over her shoulder and smiled mischievously. "As a matter of fact, it is."

"You've always been a hardheaded woman," Case murmured, pressing a kiss to her temple.

"Did you think you were going to change me?"

"Not a chance. But if you can tear yourself away from your flowers, there's something you might want to see."

"How can I resist such an interesting invitation?" Settling the flower stems into a warm bath, she put her hand in Case's and let him lead her to the saloon.

At the piano, Emily perched next to Penelope. "I have a surprise for you, Mama," Emily said, beaming.

She turned to Penelope and the two exchanged a secret smile. Penelope nodded to Emily. "You may begin."

With that, Emily began plunking out the notes of the princess song that had always been her favorite for Katlyn to sing.

"Oh, Emily," Katlyn whispered, smiling through sudden tears.

When Emily finished, Case and Katlyn applauded enthusiastically, and Penelope patted the little girl's shoulder and nodded her approval.

"But when, how?" Katlyn asked.

"We've been working a little each day," Penelope said. "When you lie down for your afternoon nap, Case has been bringing me down here to work with Emily."

Katlyn felt a warm rush of love for her mother and her daughter. Of all the people at the St. Martin, it had been Emily who had first and firmly wormed her way into Penelope's heart and given Penelope a new interest in life.

"That's the song you used to sing to me," Katlyn said to her mother, and for a moment their gazes met, each reflecting their mutual joy at finding this belonging at last.

"And now it's the song you sing to me, Mama."

Katlyn walked over and hugged Emily. "And since Grandma is teaching it to you, someday it'll be the song you sing to your daughter."

"I'm looking forward to that," Case said. Moving close, he put an arm around his wife and daughter. "We have a tradition to uphold around here, one your mama started."

Looking up at him, Katlyn laughed. "A tradition?"

"Of course." Case grinned at her, sharing in the happiness they'd created together. "What would the St. Martin be without a songbird?"

* * * * *

*Harlequin truly does
make any time special....
This year we are celebrating
weddings in style!*

A
Walk
Down
the Aisle

WEDDING CELEBRATION

To help us celebrate, we want you to tell us how wearing the Harlequin wedding gown will make your wedding day special. As the grand prize, Harlequin will offer one lucky bride the chance to **"Walk Down the Aisle"** in the Harlequin wedding gown!

There's more...

For her honeymoon, she and her groom will spend five nights at the **Hyatt Regency Maui.** As part of this five-night honeymoon at the hotel renowned for its romantic attractions, the couple will enjoy a candlelit dinner for two in Swan Court, a sunset sail on the hotel's catamaran, and duet spa treatments.

Maui • Molokai • Lanai

To enter, please write, in, 250 words or less, how wearing the Harlequin wedding gown will make your wedding day special. The entry will be judged based on its emotionally compelling nature, its originality and creativity, and its sincerity. This contest is open to Canadian and U.S. residents only and to those who are 18 years of age and older. There is no purchase necessary to enter. Void where prohibited. See further contest rules attached. Please send your entry to:

Walk Down the Aisle Contest

In Canada	In U.S.A.
P.O. Box 637	P.O. Box 9076
Fort Erie, Ontario	3010 Walden Ave.
L2A 5X3	Buffalo, NY 14269-9076

You can also enter by visiting www.eHarlequin.com
Win the Harlequin wedding gown and the vacation of a lifetime!
The deadline for entries is October 1, 2001.

Makes any time special ®

PHWDACONT1

INDULGE IN A QUIET MOMENT
WITH HARLEQUIN

Get a FREE
Quiet Moments Bath Spa

with just two proofs of purchase from
any of our four special collector's editions in May.

Harlequin® is sure to make your time special this Mother's Day
with four special collector's editions featuring a short story
PLUS a complete novel packaged together in one volume!

Collection #1 Intrigue abounds in a collection featuring *New York Times* bestselling author Barbara Delinsky and Kelsey Roberts.

Collection #2 Relationships? Weddings? Children? = *New York Times* bestselling author Debbie Macomber and Tara Taylor Quinn at their best!

Collection #3 Escape to the past with *New York Times* bestselling author Heather Graham and Gayle Wilson.

Collection #4 Go West! With *New York Times* bestselling author Joan Johnston and Vicki Lewis Thompson!

Plus Special Consumer Campaign!
Each of these four collector's editions will feature a
"FREE QUIET MOMENTS BATH SPA" offer.
See inside book in May for details.

Only from

HARLEQUIN®
Makes any time special ®

Don't miss out! Look for this exciting promotion on sale in May 2001,
at your favorite retail outlet.

Visit us at www.eHarlequin.com   PHNCP01

MONTANA MAVERICKS

Bestselling author

SUSAN MALLERY

WILD WEST WIFE

THE ORIGINAL MONTANA MAVERICKS HISTORICAL NOVEL

Jesse Kincaid had sworn off love forever.
But when the handsome rancher kidnaps
his enemy's mail-order bride to get revenge,
he ends up falling for his innocent captive!

RETURN TO WHITEHORN, MONTANA, WITH

WILD WEST WIFE

Available July 2001

And be sure to pick up
MONTANA MAVERICKS: BIG SKY GROOMS,
three brand-new historical stories about Montana's
most popular family, coming in August 2001.

HARLEQUIN®
Makes any time special®

Visit us at www.eHarlequin.com

PHWWW

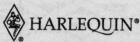